Bolan ducked down as the grenade detonated

He flattened himself to the ground, knowing that the vehicle he was using for cover would take one hell of a beating.

He opened his mouth to equalize the pressure, almost able to taste the explosive that went up with the grenade, the launcher and the missile it carried. Heat swept across him. He couldn't hear the shrapnel hit the side of the vehicle, and couldn't feel it in the shock wave generated by the blast.

He was the first man on his feet; he had to be. Years of training and combat experience honed him to this. The sight that greeted him was one that both elated and worried him. The entire crew of pirates had been eradicated in one swoop, but the blast had also taken out some of the tents and shacks.

Had he inadvertently made casualties of the hostages he had been sent to retrieve?

**Other titles available
in this series:**

Breached

Retaliation

Pressure Point

Silent Running

Stolen Arrows

Zero Option

Predator Paradise

Circle of Deception

Devil's Bargain

False Front

Lethal Tribute

Season of Slaughter

Point of Betrayal

Ballistic Force

Renegade

Survival Reflex

Path to War

Blood Dynasty

Ultimate Stakes

State of Evil

Force Lines

Contagion Option

Hellfire Code

War Drums

Ripple Effect

Devil's Playground

The Killing Rule

Patriot Play

Appointment in Baghdad

Havana Five

The Judas Project

Plains of Fire

Colony of Evil

Hard Passage

Interception

Cold War Reprise

Mission: Apocalypse

Altered State

Killing Game

Diplomacy Directive

Betrayed

Sabotage

Conflict Zone

Blood Play

Desert Fallout

Extraordinary Rendition

Devil's Mark

Savage Rule

Infiltration

Resurgence

Kill Shot

Stealth Sweep

Grave Mercy

Treason Play

Assassin's Code

Shadow Strike

Decision Point

Road of Bones

Radical Edge

Fireburst

Oblivion Pact

Enemy Arsenal

State of War

Ballistic

Escalation Tactic

Crisis Diplomacy

Apocalypse Ark

Lethal Stakes

Illicit Supply

Explosive Demand

Don Pendleton's Mack Bolan®

Ground Zero

A GOLD EAGLE BOOK FROM

W☉RLDWIDE®

TORONTO • NEW YORK • LONDON
AMSTERDAM • PARIS • SYDNEY • HAMBURG
STOCKHOLM • ATHENS • TOKYO • MILAN
MADRID • WARSAW • BUDAPEST • AUCKLAND

Recycling programs
for this product may
not exist in your area.

First edition December 2013

ISBN-13: 978-0-373-61565-0

Special thanks and acknowledgment to
Andy Boot for his contribution to this work.

GROUND ZERO

Copyright © 2013 by Worldwide Library

Printed in U.S.A.

Fighting terrorism is like being a goalkeeper. You can make a hundred brilliant saves but the only shot people remember is the one that gets past you.

—Paul Wilkinson,
London *Daily Telegraph,*
September 1, 1992

If one gets past me, lives will be lost. It's my duty to track the threat and take it out. We cannot let them win. Do not be afraid. Live your lives, go about your business and terrorism will fail.

—Mack Bolan

CHAPTER ONE

The sun began to sink over the cloudless, hot, still and silent waters. The ocean looked like glass, which was the most clichéd observation Marina Foster had ever come up with. She sipped her drink and listened to the laughter of her husband, Frank, and George and Carla Usborne, the couple accompanying them on this trip.

It was beautiful out here, but she was bored out of her mind. George was an old fraternity buddy of Frank's, while Carla was one face-lift short of a lobotomy. This was a beautiful spot, but she would rather have had better company. Or, preferably, her husband to herself. But Frank had been going through a lot of stress at work, and he needed not just a vacation, but also one in which he could completely cut loose. George represented the world before it got complicated for Frank, and if that was what he needed…

Marina was a dutiful wife. She just thanked God and her pharmacist for Valium.

"Baby, you just hear what George said about the fishermen around here?" Frank hailed her. She turned, faking that she had been listening.

"Yes, he's one funny guy," she agreed. She hadn't the faintest idea what George had said, but there was something nagging at the back of her brain that his idiocy had distracted her from…. Something that she'd read just before they left. Something that made her a little uneasy.

WHEN NIGHT ARRIVED across African waters, it came swiftly and with no warning. One moment it was still golden and red as the sun hit the water, the next it was almost pitch-black, the stars pinpoints in the dark sky. It was cold, too; the temperature dropped rapidly. Surely that was the only reason Marina shivered as Frank and George busied themselves at the barbecue they had set up under the canopy aft. They had some fish that they had caught—they were feeling pleased with themselves— and these were gutted and laid on the coals. The smell was appalling to her.

"Are you sure that's okay to eat?" Marina questioned.

"Why wouldn't it be?" Carla asked.

Marina shook her head. "Something about the water around here," she muttered. "I was reading up on this region before we came out here—"

George laughed. It was a stupid, coarse sound. Fitting really, Marina thought.

"That's what you get for living with an intelligence guy for so long, babe," he said. "You get the bug and can't stop finding out shit. You need to marry a banker, then all you do is add up credit card bills, like my Carla." He pealed off another wave of laughter, ignoring the caustic stare shot at him by his wife.

Frank shrugged at Marina, catching the look in her eye. The shrug said all kinds of things: sorry this idiot was his friend, sorry that he needed this kind of mindlessness to relax, sorry that she wasn't enough on her own.

The last was maybe her own suspicion more than her husband's intent, but it still preoccupied her. Not enough, though, that she couldn't hear the sounds of engines across the water. The distant buzz grew louder as she exclaimed, with sudden recall, "Poisoned fish— that was it. Frank, throw that shit overboard, it stinks so much because it's laden with chemicals. There's a lot of dumping in this region that has made it real hard to fish without poisoning half the fisher's village."

Frank huffed as he lifted the charred fish off the grill with skewers. He held it at arm's length to dump it over the side. "Shit, baby, I wish you'd remembered that earlier."

George guffawed. "So much for intelligence gathering, Frankie boy. Good thing there's a stocked freezer and a microwave on this boat."

"That's what you get for borrowing the boss's yacht," Frank replied mechanically as he dropped the stinking carcasses into the depths. His attention was distracted by the sight of two small boats—the source of the noise that had caught his wife's ear—cutting across the water's still surface. Even in the darkness, he could see that both vessels, which now panned out to form a pincer that took port and starboard side, were manned by skinny men who hung casually from the sides.

"Baby, you remember reading anything else about these waters?" he asked, trying to keep his voice level.

"Yes… But it's too late to worry about that now, right?"

Her voice was quiet. He looked around, startled to find her at his elbow. Behind them, George and Carla were arguing, drunk and oblivious.

"I've remembered something, too. Something I really should have been more aware of," he said softly. "I'm sorry."

She clutched his arm with fingers that bit into him. "Those aren't fishing rods they're carrying, right?"

LANDON McCABE LOOKED UP at the ceiling, breathed deeply three times and clapped his hands on the desk. He chewed ruminatively on his lip before rising and moving with determination into the corridor and toward the Oval Office. Some idiot would have to pay for this. How the hell had Foster been allowed out there at all, let alone without any security on hand? The big man wasn't going to like this. He probably wasn't going to like the guy who had to tell him, either. Why did it have to be on his watch?

As he approached, the Secret Service agents straightened. He dismissed them with a gesture. The door to the room opened and he strode in. The President was seated at his desk, feet up, reading a file and frowning. The frown creased his brow when he looked up, and seeing the way McCabe fixed him with a stare did nothing to change that.

"Bad news?" he asked, putting down the file and sitting up so that he was leaning over the desk. McCabe nodded.

The Man pursed his lips. "Is there any other kind?" he asked rhetorically. "Let me have it."

McCabe told him. The President hit the desk hard with the flat of his hand and cursed loudly. "How did that happen?" he yelled. "How, for God's sake?"

McCabe shook his head. "Good question. I'll get you an answer, and the ass of the moron who screwed up. But right now—"

The President nodded. "There are more important things. What are our options?"

McCabe tensed. This was the bit he hadn't been looking forward to.

"Limited, sir. Very limited."

CARLA HAD STOPPED crying. She was leaning over George, who was still unconscious. His instinctive jock sensibilities had made him try to protect his wife when the men had come aboard. Marina had stayed Frank from any such action with a hand on his arm. One look had told her that he was intending to be sensible. Marina had been glad of this when the drunken George had been bludgeoned by a Somali wielding an AK-47. Two blows had put him on his knees and then onto the deck. It was only the clicking tongue of the skipper that had prevented further damage.

Frank and Marina knew why. They had known from the moment that the boats had pulled alongside that the thing to do was be calm, be subservient and go along with what the pirates wanted. For that was what they were, without a doubt; the reports that both had read had come back to them too late. They knew that a couple called the Chandlers had been taken from their yacht a couple of years prior and had been held on the mainland for over eighteen months until a settlement had been reached. The pirates were fishermen who had started to supplement their dwindling catch by taking cargo and goods from merchant vessels. There had been naval moves to put an end to that, so they had widened their range to include people and to include not just the seas. Pirating had taken place in resorts, and rich vacationers had been taken for ransom and killed if they hadn't cooperated.

Frank and Marina had no intention of ending up that way. They weren't that wealthy; certainly they didn't have the resources or family to pay a big ransom. George could, if the idiot could stay alive long enough. Frank knew the bravado would have been knocked out of him by that rifle stock.

"You come with us now," the skipper said softly. There was the slightest click in his pronunciation of English; otherwise it was perfect.

"We'll come," Frank responded. "You're the boss."

The skipper nodded. "Sooner we get back to land, the better." He indicated that they move and gestured to his men to pick up George and drag Carla after him.

"Shouldn't I get some covering for my friend and myself?" Marina asked. "I know you would like us to cover up."

The skipper eyed her up and down, but it was not in the lascivious manner that might have been expected. Finally he said, "You are a clever woman. We will have clothing for you. Do not use our faith to take a chance to leave a message or take a weapon."

"We're on vacation—we don't have weapons," Frank

said mildly. "And our only radio is up there," he added, indicating the wheel deck.

"I know. I have sent men below while your friend is recovering from his stupidity. They may find something of value."

"We are on vacation," Frank said again. "We're carrying nothing of any value to you."

The skipper grinned. "That depends on what you call value," he said slyly.

"COMBINED TASK FORCE 150 and 151 are there for that purpose," the President said, running his hands over his face. "We even sent them some Coast Guard to help bolster it up. We could comb the area easily."

"We could," McCabe agreed. "But why would we press for that just for four civilians?"

"Why not? They're U.S. citizens, after all."

"Ordinary citizens, sir. As far as anyone knows, of course…and we need to keep it that way. The pirates may not realize what they've got. I hope not, anyway."

The President nodded. "You're right. What a mess. We can't negotiate. No government would. And if we start using the task force… Could we send a covert Coast Guard force after them?"

McCabe exhaled sharply, deep in thought. "It might look like a big area of water on the map, sir—come to that, it is one hell of a stretch—but the truth is that it's a pretty tight area if you start using military force. The Indian navy has gone after pirates who've been hitting their nation's traders and everyone got to hear about that and censured it. The Chinese have done the same. And then there are the Russians."

"Ah, yeah... I get your point." The President nodded, recalling the Russian naval vessel that had retaken one of their merchant ships that had been overrun with pirates. There had been no official casualties, but every single one of the pirates had met with an accidental demise while trying to make their escape.

"You've got to love those Russians," the President mused.

"For the benefit of history, I'm going to assume you are being ironic, Mr. President," McCabe said uneasily. "The fact is that we can't send in any kind of force without either alerting the pirates to the importance of who they have or arousing a similar suspicion in any of our allies."

"So what the hell do you suggest we do, Landon?" the President said slowly. "You are my duty security adviser, after all."

McCabe smiled. "As stupid as it may seem, sir, we do nothing immediately. We don't panic. We wait for the pirates to establish contact. Then we'll know if they know what they have. That may determine how quickly we have to act. But either way, as soon as we have a channel of communication, we have a trail. And as soon as we have a trail, I think you need to make a phone call. We need covert, and if rumors are correct, you can reach out."

The President cracked a smile. "You're cheering me up, Mr. McCabe."

BY THE TIME morning broke, the four Americans had been transported to shore and across land. They were kept as couples, but the couples were kept apart. George and Carla had been bundled onto one boat, the man still dazed and confused, his wife hysterical; Frank and Marina had been loaded onto the other. Their skipper was the man who had spoken to them onboard the yacht. They remained silent and subservient but visibly tense. Shooting quick, nervous glances between themselves, neither was sure if they came across as nervous—like the abductees they should be—or nervous with a secret, which is what they actually were. The attitude of the skipper did little to alleviate any fears on that score. He piloted his craft but kept coming back to look at where they were berthed, saying nothing but casting an appraising eye over them and then speaking softly to the men who stood guard.

They anchored just off a sandy, rocky cove that was littered with enough vegetation and flora to give just enough cover to any activity that needed to remain covert. The boats stood in the water about two hundred yards apart, and the captives were ushered into the water without ceremony. Frank and Marina looked at the sea beneath them, trying to guess the depth before they were pushed in. The waters were clear, but the light was predawn and made it impossible to judge. Both feared immersion and the risk of drowning as their hands were bound. Both figured that their captors wouldn't want to risk losing their meal ticket.

It was a correct assumption. They jumped feetfirst into the water and touched bottom. The water lapped around their chests. The soft sand yielded and sucked at their feet, and Marina slipped under the water, then came up coughing and choking. Frank looked at her, alarmed and angry at being unable to assist her. He bit down hard on that anger, not wanting to give their captors any excuse to lash out at either of them; the pain of keeping it in made his chest constrict. He heard Carla cry out as she slipped like his own wife; he heard George bellow incoherently, still not clear-headed enough to fully realize what was happening, and he heard Carla cry again. Differently this time, as George took another blow from a pirate with no time or patience to waste.

As they moved toward the shore, there was more drag on them as the buoyant water receded, but it was easier to keep upright. Once they were on the sand, weariness and shock made them stumble, and they found it hard to keep up with the pace their captors set.

Two guards per couple, with the skipper who had led the expedition out front, they were led into the trees, where a narrow path had been hacked and then disguised. Twisting upward from the beach, it led to a track where a battered Ford flatbed awaited them. A driver waited patiently at the wheel, with a guard who had an RPG-7 casually propped against his thigh. The skipper said something. His voice, as before, was soft, but there was something in the tone and the manner in which the guard jumped to that confirmed the Fosters' view of him as head of the group.

"Back of the truck," he said simply as he turned to the captives, gesturing to the flatbed. The guards prodded them with rifles as they clambered awkwardly upward. It crossed Marina's mind that professionals—

like the ones she had known since marrying Frank—
wouldn't get that close; then again, the pirates were
dealing with tired, hurt and cowed people. They knew
it, too.

"Not far now. Then you rest. We give you something
to cover. Then it begins," the skipper said to them before
turning to sit next to the driver.

He looked back when Marina said, "Why are you
bothering to tell us?"

He shrugged and actually smiled, and she didn't
know if she should take that as an insult about their
condition and lack of threat. "You play the game, figure the rules," he said. "Make it easy for me. Makes you
okay, long as you remember that."

There was an implied threat that neither of the Fosters
wished to consider. George and Carla were too dazed
and scared to take that in.

The drive was long and uncomfortable. The sun rose
above them, hot from the moment it cracked the sky, and
it reminded Marina how long it had been since the last
opportunity to drink something. The road they took was
nothing more than a dirt track, a hardened and flattened
strip across the bare scrub ground. Finally the truck
reached a small village and jolted to a halt. The skipper
and the driver jumped out and ran around to the rear of
the flatbed, gesturing to the guards to bring the prison-
ers down as others from the village slowly filtered from
their shacks, drawn by the noise.

The skipper spoke in a few terse sentences, and rags
were brought out and placed in front of the two women.

"Now you can cover up," the skipper said.

Carla, who had by now started to recover some of her composure, looked uncertainly at Marina as they both stepped forward and took the rags, tying them around themselves as shifts. Following Marina's lead, Carla covered her hair.

"Why didn't they just let us take some of our own clothes?" she asked, genuinely confused.

"Because they didn't want any unnecessary evidence left behind looking out of place," Marina replied calmly, her gaze fixed on the skipper.

He grinned at her. "I don't think it comes to that. Not with your husband."

HAL BROGNOLA HAD had a bitch of a day. They came in batches. What was that old poem? "April is the cruelest month…" Yeah, and May and June and maybe even July. The whole goddamn year could be like that, he knew. Everyone always had problems, and it seemed like the whole world, including his wife, Helen, came to his door for him to sort them out. Wasn't he allowed to have problems? Actually, all things considered, he didn't really have any; that thought made him feel a little better. To be fair, there were days—maybe even a week at a time—when there wasn't that much landing on his desk and he could relax and draw breath. It was just this thing that the work never seemed to be evenly spaced out over the years. It just seemed to either be drought or downpour.

His cell phone rang and interrupted his train of thought. As very few people had his number, that could only mean one thing. He stopped where he was, halfway down the Mall with the crisp night air making his breath frost.

"Sir…Uh-huh…Absolutely. I understand…No, I'm not far at all, sir. I can be with you in less than ten…No, not at all." A polite laugh that he didn't really feel, but it wasn't like it was the big man's fault this had happened. "You haven't put a crimp in any plans."

Like he could ever afford to make any plans, he thought as he disconnected and turned back toward his office. First stop there, and then the Oval Office.

Wonder what Striker's doing right now? he mused silently as he picked up the pace.

"THIS HAPPENED LESS than twenty-four hours ago, sir?" Hal Brognola asked.

"No more than that. Frank Foster was last in contact that recently. At the least, it's been—" the President looked at his watch "—four hours since the report of the deserted yacht was received in this office."

"How did that come in?" Brognola asked.

"Usual channels. The vessel encountering the situation was an Indian boat attached to Task Force 150. Called it in like a usual abduction."

Brognola snorted. "It isn't good when we call this 'usual,' is it? But I take your point."

"So you see why it would not be advisable to use the task force or to try to depute a Coast Guard vessel. Not given the delicacy and balance of the situation," the President said, leaning over his desk and fixing Brognola with an intense stare.

"Oh, yeah, I see it, sir. Need to know as restricted as

possible, with location and extraction—with prejudice if necessary—an immediate priority."

"Can you put Striker on this?" the President murmured.

"As a matter of fact, yeah, I can."

CHAPTER TWO

Two days had passed. Marina knew that because she
had been able to see outside the shack when their food
had been brought to them. They were in a building that
was little more than one room made out of corrugated
iron sheeting, with a bowl and half a plastic fuel barrel
chopped across the middle as a latrine. There was no
light inside, and the only ventilation was supplied by the
corrosion holes in the sheeting. The roof was made of
the same sheeting as the walls, and in the middle of the
day the heat was intense, stifling and bearing down on
them like a lead weight. A molten lead weight.

The water and food they had been given was more
than adequate, but was not enough to compensate for
the discomfort and nausea engendered by the heat and
dark. They were rank with sweat and dirt. Although
there was nothing for them to be tethered to, the pirates
had taken the precaution of shackling them by the wrists
and ankles, with a chain running between the wrist and
ankle shackles to further hobble them. George's wounds
had been crudely dressed when they were first shut up,
but in the heat and dirt the dressing had quickly become
grubby, and the conditions had not helped him return
to full awareness. Carla whimpered and sniveled, even
after all the time that had passed. Marina had forced

herself to concentrate, to keep count. Frank could not see the doorway from where he half sat, half lay, and Marina was determined that at least one of them should keep track.

Was it really just the two days? Time didn't so much pass as drag as if it had a weight as leaden as the heat attached to it. Carla had gone to pieces already, and George's condition seemed to be deteriorating at a rapid pace. She and Frank had said very little to each other. Partly that was about conserving their energies, but she was aware that they could give nothing away about who he was. They were currently just rich tourists who had fallen prey to the region. If the truth were known...

Her reverie was broken by the door to the shack screeching open on rusty hinges.

"Time to move. This place stinks. You go somewhere better, more air and more light. Maybe look at stupid man's head again, patch him up some more. Get up."

Marina and Frank struggled to their feet. Carla and George weren't doing so well, and the skipper clicked an order, gesturing urgently. Two men came in, helped them roughly to their feet and dragged them out. Frank and Marina followed in their wake, emerging blinking into the daylight. The Ford flatbed was waiting for them.

"Where are we going?" Marina asked. Her voice was cracked and harsh; she hardly recognized it. The skipper gave her a ladle of water.

"Don't matter to you—you not know where it is anyway. Point is, farther away and closer to our warlord. You worth a lot of cash, you know that?"

"All Americans or Europeans are, aren't they?" Marina croaked.

The skipper smiled. There was something in his eyes that made her stomach turn. "'Course they are. Some more than others. Why you so stupid as to take vacation in Gulf of Aden?" he asked, changing tack suddenly.

"I don't think we'd realized that we'd come that far down," she said. Even so, a flicker of doubt crossed her mind and she glanced nervously at her husband—quickly, but enough for the skipper to notice. Frank seemed oblivious, and although she was reassured that she hadn't been taken for a patsy by her own husband, she could have kicked herself for arousing the skipper's suspicions.

"You know, we used to fish the waters here, then the Malawi and the Kenyan come and screw us over. Lot of fish, but we don't get near them. So we get guns and we blow the bastards out of the water. Then we realize we can do the same to those who carry cargo. Cargo worth more than fish, mostly. But people…they the best cargo of all. And like all cargo, some bits make more money than others."

It was the longest speech they'd heard the skipper make, and it was the longest they'd get. With a smile that didn't reach his eyes, he issued orders to his men that saw them loaded up into the back of the flatbed. More rapid orders, and a woman came forward—Marina hadn't noticed her before—and tended to the dressing on George's head before stepping off the flatbed and moving out of sight.

The skipper barked a few orders and banged his hand on the side of the truck to signal its departure.

"Good luck, lady," he yelled over the noise of the engine as the truck jerked and began to move off. There was something about the way he left his voice dangling that suggested "you'll need it" was an unspoken coda to his farewell.

"STRIKER, I NEED you. The country needs you. Hell, the President needs you."

Bolan took the cell away from his ear and looked at it, a bemused and sardonic smile on his face. He shook his head and put it back to his ear.

"Hal, it's not like you to be so melodramatic. You don't have to present a hard sell to me."

"No hard sell. I'm not kidding you—this comes directly from the Oval Office. He had me in there himself."

"It's going to be one of those, is it?" Bolan queried.

"It might be. Meet me in an hour and I'll fill you in. And give Jack a shout to put him on standby, would you? I'll fill you in when I see you."

By the time an hour had elapsed, Mack Bolan was waiting in the crisp morning air, watching for the big Fed to approach. As usual, he waited until Brognola passed him and then fell in beside him. Here in the heart of Wonderland it was unlikely that either of them would be followed, but caution was never wasted.

"So tell me about it," Bolan began without preamble.

"Downtime getting to you, Striker? I wouldn't have thought you'd be too pleased at having time off curtailed."

"If the Man calls you personally, then it's important."

"Not at first glance. You know all about the piracy that's been going on off the coast of Somalia." Brognola knew that the Executioner had undertaken several missions in the area.

"That's an understatement. Been there, done that. It's been going on for about a decade, and it started with a fishing war. There's more money in cargo ships than fish, though, and the fishermen who'd armed themselves realized that quick enough. We've got Coast Guard and naval personnel in the two task forces—150 and 151— and although the UN has a line on it, the Chinese, the Indians and the Russians have gone beyond that and hit back. So the pirates have started to look at people. Kenyan resorts and cruisers in smaller yachts have been the preferred targets. Official government policies have been hard-line—don't kowtow and don't pay and don't negotiate. But most of the captured get freed somehow. There's a lot of ransom changing hands and a lot of coldhearted bastards who are making a killing as middlemen."

"That just about sums it up. We have a situation. Four people—two couples—were taken from a yacht twenty-four to thirty-six hours ago. Civilians, tourists…word came in, and the Man called me."

"For four ordinary people? What's the catch?"

"One of the couples is Frank and Marina Foster, from D.C. Frank works for the State Department as an analyst. His specialty is economic forecasting for the movement of arms across emergent economies. To do this he has a lot of intel pass through his hands that could make him a valuable commodity."

"What's his security clearance?" Bolan queried, puzzled that a snatch could be effected so simply given the nature of Foster's position.

"Too high for him to be allowed out there, for a start." Brognola sighed. "Even closer to home or in a safer region he should have had cover. Someone's ass will be in a sling over this."

"So it should," the soldier agreed. "But that doesn't affect the current circumstance or help Foster and his wife."

"Exactly. Which is where you come in."

"A quick, clean extraction. Jack will like this. Do we have a location? Have we even heard from the captors?"

"Negative on both. We're still on hold. Problem is that until we do, we don't know who's got them, what they want and if they're aware of what they've got. Because that's a real game changer."

"Where were they taken and what are the trends for piracy in that region?"

"I'll get Bear to put it together and download ASAP," Brognola replied. "I'll also get him to break down the groups in the region. Best bets are that they're from the Hobyo region. The Galmudug regime in the area is against the Islamist insurgents, and we're hoping that this means that our boys are just opportunists. Most of them are used by the Galmudug just to keep the Islamist warlords at bay."

"If the warlords are making any kind of headway, then they'll either convert their enemies, or else the pirates will pay obeisance so they can fleece the warlords.

Now, that's a hell of a dangerous game for them, but if the captives get caught in the middle…"

"That's why we need to move quickly. You'll travel troop transport routes on the first flight out. Your cover is that you're part of a new Coast Guard detail that's already out there with 151, and you were delayed by recuperation. That should answer any awkward questions. Jack can get out there separately. By the time you're there, Bear should have the intel you need to find a trail…if we haven't heard from the pirates by then." "Bear" was Aaron Kurtzman, head of Stony Man Farm's cyber team.

"It'll be a bonus if you have, but since when have I liked it easy?"

MARINA FOSTER WAS certain that she had passed out for at least some of the journey. The oppressive sun that bore down from overhead seemed to jump in the sky between the moments she blinked. She was dimly aware of the others. Frank was silent, and she was sure that, like her, he was trying to conserve energy and maybe get some rest before they reached their destination and whatever lay ahead. She could hear George moaning softly. It was regular, and she was certain that his head wound would begin to fester unless they stopped soon. It was a good bet that he had a concussion, too, and the longer that went untreated the more concern it would cause. Carla was whimpering, quietly and almost nonstop. Marina was torn between wanting to comfort her and wanting to slap her and make her shut up. The journey and the lack of water were starting to get under her skin.

Hours later, the truck approached a small gathering of tents and ramshackle huts, surrounded by jeeps and trucks. Half a dozen men appeared atop the rocks that were littered around the oasis; three more emerged from behind the dwellings to cover the truck as it entered the enclave formed by the vehicles and tents. All the men carried either AK-47s or RPG-7s, the pirate's weapon of choice as they were easily obtainable from Yemen or Mogadishu. It was a simple task for a *hawala* dealer to pay the deposit and then have the weapons driven to an arranged point, where the pirates would pay the balance.

The flatbed drew up, and the men relaxed as they recognized the driver and guards on the back of the flatbed. They had been expected, as was obvious from the way in which they were greeted. The captives were unloaded and carried—at this moment all four were incapable of walking unaided until food, rest and water had been given—into one of the tents.

Their arrival caused an air of celebration to filter through the camp. While a few were deputed to stand guard on the new arrivals, most of the men in the camp ate and drank, laughing and joking as the day grew into night and fires were lit against the bitter desert cold. The majority of the men in camp were Muslim, but the cold and hard lives had caused them to turn a blind eye to the use of spirits to warm the blood.

Marina and Frank could hear their captors from the tent in which they were now confined. They—like George and Carla—had been unshackled for a short period to enable them to bathe and change into clothes that were provided for them. They were given water and food, and although they were then shackled again, it was noticeable that they were being afforded a level of care that had not been theirs just a few hours before.

Hours? How much time had passed since they had been taken? It was impossible to tell as the delirium of heat and dehydration had overtaken them.

A medic—or at least, a pirate with some kind of medical knowledge and a rudimentary medical kit—had come and seen to George, dressing the wound, disinfecting it crudely and making him scream. The medic looked into his eyes.

"Concussion," Marina said clearly and carefully. The guard nearest her jabbed her with the stock of his AK-47, making her wince, but it had the desired effect, as the medic turned to her.

"Him— He…?" the medic asked, miming a vomiting action. Marina shook her head, and the medic nodded slowly as he turned and looked into George's unfocused eyes once more. "No, not bad. He be all right," he said definitively.

When the medic and the women who had assisted them with bathing, changing and eating had gone, they sat alone in the tent. There were guards outside, but since they were shackled, their captors had seen no reason to stay on top of them.

It gave Marina the chance she had been waiting for to speak to Frank. She shuffled across the sandy floor so that she could lean toward him and keep her voice as low as possible.

"What's coming next?"

Frank pondered that for a moment before replying.

"If it runs to type, they'll contact the U.S. Embassy and say they have us. They've got our ID from the yacht, and they'll supply evidence. Our families will be informed and told that the government can liaise but not take any part in negotiations. Then it'll be up to the families—George's dad will want to pay straightaway. They'll ask for a high sum to begin, and I'll bet he'll pay that—"

"That's not what I mean," Marina said levelly. "There will be interested parties in government. What will they do?"

Frank's jaw tensed. "Careful what you say. They won't do anything unless it's obvious they have to. Keep it a regular situation and it's fine. If it's not, then they'll see what is known before they make a decision."

Marina looked away. She didn't want to see her husband's face when she spoke again.

"What if certain things are known and that makes it worth more to someone other than the government? What happens to us then?"

The silence told her all she wanted to know. For the first time since they had been taken, she began to feel that the situation seemed hopeless, and tears burned and in her eyes.

"Don't—" Frank was cut off by the sound of someone approaching from outside. The tent flap was thrust aside by one of the guards, and a tall, thin man with a goatee and a hard cast to his eyes entered, his gaze sweeping over them.

"So this is what they bring me," he said softly.

"What do you plan to do with us?" Frank asked, hoping to cut to the chase. Perhaps he seemed too keen, too quick. It caused the Somali to look at him with an amused detachment.

"What would any so-called pirate do with a Westerner?" he asked mockingly, rolling his tongue around the words. "We will ask for money for you. That's what we want, after all, isn't it? You are a piece of meat that we can sell at market to make some of the money that your kind have made so necessary in the first place. You take our freedom, you make us live by your economy, you starve us of the resources and take others without comeback, and then wonder why we have to strike back in whatever way we can?"

"But we're not at war with you—" Frank began.

"We are at war with the world. It is all we can do to survive. In order to do that and see that our people do not starve as they have for generations, we must use whatever means are made available to us. So we take from boats that are stupid enough not to be well defended and we take money from fools who want to see their families again. They would not do as much for us. And then, every once in a while, something a little better falls into our hands. There are people who appear to be tourists and yet may be so much more."

Marina looked at Frank. He was white with the effort not to vomit. He knew what the Somali meant. Marina felt faint. She could see that George was still oblivious to what was going on, and Carla looked somewhere between terrified and confused. Not Marina. She realized that the pirates knew about Frank's value to the U.S. government, and that could only mean death for three of them, as they were surplus to requirements.

What made her feel worse—what had made Frank go white with fear—was that she knew that although she would most likely die, there was a worse fate in store for her husband.

The Somali stepped forward and cupped Frank's chin in his hand—surprisingly small for someone his size— and said, "A man with your brain is worth much to many. We shall see what they have to say. It is a pity we can't just cut it out and sell what you know without having to worry about anything else. But perhaps there are ways of doing this…."

Marina's vision swam as she thought of what they would do to her husband. Frank stayed silent, but she noticed that a wet patch had spread across his groin, and she knew the fear that he was trying to hide.

She knew at that moment that there was no hope.

CHAPTER THREE

It took Bolan long hours in uncomfortable troop transports to get as far as Yemen. His cover story wouldn't stand up to too much scrutiny, so he swerved any questions by spending most of his time sleeping. He'd slept in far worse conditions, and if he was right in his assumptions, then he wouldn't have much opportunity to rest once he reached his destination.

During the time that he was awake, he occupied himself by scrolling through his secure smartphone and absorbing the intel he had been sent. He was soon up to speed on the current state of play in the seas and the land along the coast. The complex situation in Somalia, where Puntland and Galmudug seemed to have contrary policies, would not make it easy to negotiate the territory. Puntland had set up its own maritime police force to work alongside the two multinational task forces, but even so it had its hands tied when the pirates went inland and crossed over provincial lines. The authorities had a hard job, and he didn't envy them. Under any other circumstances he would have sought their aid, but the way things lay at present, he needed to stay so far under the radar that he was subterranean.

Under the radar in the sense that no one could know where he came from and who he represented; with a wry grin to himself, he doubted that having Grimaldi and *Dragonslayer* around would be keeping "under the radar" in any other sense whatsoever.

After landing at Camp Lemonnier at Djibouti, the former French colony across the Gulf of Aden from Yemen that was currently the U.S. headquarters for anti–al Qaeda activity, he went through the military clearance procedures as usual and, on pretense of leaving the base to meet up with the rest of his unit for a long-awaited reunion, drove out of U.S. territory and into the Arab land beyond. He needed to pick up some hardware for his trip, and he needed to contact Grimaldi and arrange a rendezvous.

As he drove, he pondered the situation facing him. Currently he had no indication of where his target resided. If his enemies did not show their hand in some way, then he had to figure out a way of tracking them. It would have been nice and easy if he could have just slipped across the Gulf and into Yemen immediately. Arms were plentiful there, and his war chest would have been welcomed. Intel would also have been easier to obtain, since from Yemen it was a straight line to Somalia and the Islamist group al-Shabaab, who were known to have affiliated themselves with al Qaeda.

Geographically, Djibouti was closer to Somalia; politically, it was a different story. Pirates who just wanted to cash in were easily handled. Those with a political agenda were harder to slap down.

As things stood, the Executioner was in a position where he had a task to perform and at present little idea of where the enemy was located.

No worries. He'd take it one step at a time. The soldier's network of contacts across the globe, who knew him under many names over the years of his War Everlasting, extended to Djibouti, and he had somewhere in mind to purchase his armament. He intended to keep munitions to a minimum for ease of movement. Grimaldi and his aircraft's souped-up gun ports would be good backup.

After a half-hour drive, Bolan pulled into the courtyard of a stucco house that indicated a man of some wealth was resident. It stuck out in the district, which was generally run-down and poor. Bolan was greeted as a friend, even though he had never met the man. A call during which he had been able to drop names and details that ensured his credentials had been enough. A perusal of the merchandise the man had to offer and a selected purchase that was expedited by the cash from his war chest that he had been able to bring with him, and soon he was on his way again.

Step one complete. After making sure that he had not been followed, he drove to a secluded spot and punched in a speed dial number.

"Jack? Where are you?"

"Close enough, Sarge. I've been here for six hours, waiting for you. What took you so long?"

"You're a funny man, Jack. Anyone ever tell you that? I had a few essentials to purchase, but I'm ready to go. We need to rendezvous. Can you get clearance for the base here?"

"If Bear can get Hal to pull a few strings. You know the stupid thing, Sarge? I'm in Somalia now, just to your southeast. How come it's easier for me to find a back door into here than it is to get into somewhere we've actually got forces?"

"Because Somalia is still bandit country in places. You land here and it could cause an international incident. You land there and someone will just make you an offer for *Dragonslayer*. Or try to kill you and steal her."

"Funny you should say that… I said no, but maybe in stronger terms. Can't you make it down here?"

"I could, but if we get a line on where our targets are, then it'll be quicker to hit and run."

"Good point. Get me that clearance and see what intel has come in."

"And what are you going to be doing while I'm doing all the work?" Bolan asked wryly.

"Me? Sarge, I'm going to be heading to Djibouti— that's the kind of faith I have in you."

McCABE PUT DOWN the phone and looked at the sheet of paper on which he had just scribbled the results of his conversation. He could have read an email directly and just printed it, but he preferred to do things the old-fashioned way. It gave him someone to shout at on the end of the phone if he wasn't happy with what he heard. And, frankly, he was far from happy.

After passing the Secret Service agents who nodded him through, McCabe gave a perfunctory knock and entered. Four men were seated in a semicircle with the President, who looked up at McCabe.

"Gentlemen, this may be news of the matter I was referring to," the President murmured.

"Sir, we have news from Somalia regarding Foster and his traveling companions. It's not good from a security point of view, sir."

"Tell me the worst," the Man ordered.

"The worst is that they know who Foster is and that what he knows could be of potential worth to them. I don't know how they know, sir," he added, forestalling the question. "But the fact is that there are a number of ways they could have ascertained who Foster is, including torture. If it comes to it, then someone will pay this end—"

"Okay, but for now we just need to get him back. What are they asking?"

"Ten million dollars for all four hostages. The good news is that the other three are still alive. The bad is that they're probably considered little more than deadweights in the deal, and if we don't settle over Foster—"

"They won't be coming home," the President finished. "Ten million is a lot for piracy. More than the British have had to pay for any of their people. Unofficially, of course. But I guess they figure Foster's knowledge makes him worth that to us…or to anyone else who values the intelligence he carries. Do we know if they have made any other bidders aware of who they have?"

McCabe shook his head. "Not for sure, but the problem they may have is that if they go public too soon, then they could attract too much attention. Puntland is working hard to wipe these guys off the face of the earth, so most of them are in Galmudug. That has a heavy Islamist presence, and those guys would kill— literally—for Foster."

"So why not go directly to them? Why ask us first?"

McCabe sniffed. "We're more likely to have ten million than al-Shabaab, who would be likely to want our boys to hand Foster over for nothing more than the greater glory of Islam. That's fine when you're dead, but it doesn't feed villages or families and doesn't buy you guns."

"So the last thing they want is for the local warlords or rival pirates to know too much too soon. That buys us a little time, I guess. How long have they given us, and have we made any kind of track on them?"

"Twelve hours. They contacted us via email, which was sent from a smartphone. I'm figuring that it was a stolen and ripped one that they thought was untraceable through Lord knows how many hands. But I tell you, sir, you've got to love these Scandinavian phone manufacturers. They leave a back door that means most GPS can't be totally knocked out, and we've got these mothers pinned down. They've taken the hostages inland about sixty-five klicks. I'm guessing—though it's not relevant—that they landed at a fishing village about twenty klicks from where the yacht was located, as there's very little else around there that would give them the opportunity. Of course, when our operative has completed his mission…"

"Point taken, but let's concentrate on getting our people back first," the President stated. "You know I've given Hal Brognola the authority to coordinate this. Have you told him yet? What about our operative?"

"You're the first person I've told, sir. Brognola informed me our operative is in Djibouti awaiting further intel and is ready to move."

For the first time in several hours the ghost of a smile flickered across the President's face.

"Then what are you waiting for, Mr. McCabe?"

BROGNOLA TOOK THE call in his office. Within moments of speaking to McCabe, he'd relayed the intel to Aaron Kurtzman at Stony Man Farm, the nation's most covert antiterrorist installation, so that he could add it to his data for analysis and relay. Then he called Bolan.

"Hal, I was about to call. I need to speak to you," the soldier greeted him.

"Striker, not as much as I need to speak to you," Brognola began before detailing what he had just been told and the action he had taken. Bolan listened intently before filling the big Fed in on his own progress and the contact he had made with Grimaldi, leading to the pilot's request.

"You know, normally I'd be moaning at you and Jack for that, as it's not going to be easy, but under the circumstances I'm pretty sure a word from the President in the right ear will ensure top-level secrecy and no one outside the immediate landing field being told."

"That's good, Hal. I'll call Bear and get him to provide me with any satellite images and maps of the target area. Soon as Jack can get here, we'll hit the sky. You make your call. I'll make mine."

"MOVE, YOU MOVE now—get up!" The guard seemed panicked in his haste, prodding all four of them in turn

with the end of his weapon and yelling, falling into his
native tongue as his words got more hysterical.

Marina was still fuzzy from sleep—the first she'd really had for some days—and was slow to react. For a second she couldn't remember where she was; then it came
back to her, and the feeling of dread descended again.

"What—" She felt the sharp jab of the rifle again and
yelped in pain and surprise. The guard yelled something
in her face. "It's okay, no real panic…" She heard her
husband's voice, surprisingly calm in the sudden flurry
of activity. As she righted herself on the camp bed, she
saw he was already sitting up. Once she, too, was upright, the guard devoted himself to yelling at George
and Carla, who were inevitably slower. Looking at him
again, Marina could see that the guard was no more than
twelve or thirteen. Intoxicated with power and a gun;
scared that he would anger his chief and be stripped of
the rank he had attained.

"Frank, what the fuck is happening?" she asked. Her
words were angry, but her tone was weary and resigned.

"Nothing to worry about." He allowed himself a bark
of an ironic laugh. "It's just a precaution. They're moving us on to another location."

"Why would they do that already? We've only been
here a day or two." She was aware of the whine in her
voice. Their clothes were clean, they had been well fed
and the beds were if not soft, then tolerable. They were
still shackled, but she would expect that. Frank's voice
had an edge that he tried to hide, unsuccessfully. "They
must have made contact with the government and issued their demands, whatever they are. That's why we're

being moved. They probably think that they're untraceable, but they're not so stupid as to take that for granted."

Marina felt a sinking sensation inside her. It continued, like a stone in her gut, as they were led out by a phalanx of armed man and loaded into yet another flatbed truck. Around them, the camp was being packed, ready to move on. Most of the people would come with them, only a few remaining in what had once been their village. They knew they may face the wrath of an incoming force, but they feared the local pirate chiefs more. It was not a situation to foster hope.

BOLAN DROVE BACK to the base. He would have to run security at the entry point with two bags of illegal weapons and contraband explosives stowed in the rear. He hoped that the guys on the gate would be slack for once and not conduct a full search.

It was an interesting dichotomy that he was hoping for exactly the kind of lapse he would otherwise condemn. If they did let him through, he'd be grateful and then make sure that the lapse was reported so no other U.S. soldier or airman would be at risk.

His smartphone went off as he approached. Cursing, he slowed a fraction to give himself time to answer before he reached the gate.

"Striker, not an inopportune moment, I hope."

"Could be better, Bear. Unless it can wait, it'll need to be quick."

Kurtzman chuckled. "I've downloaded all you asked for, and if Jack could be bothered to make his own calls and not use me as some kind of message service, then

I wouldn't detain you. He's on his way and has an ETA of twenty-three minutes and counting. Apparently he has clearance to land, though I'd take that with a pinch of salt."

"I'll be sure to tell him to make his own calls in the future," Bolan replied before disconnecting. He was now approaching the gates, and he slowed for the barriers.

Two guards approached. One kept his distance while the other directly approached the window. They had been on duty when he'd left and obviously recognized him.

"You're back quick, Cooper," the guard said good-humoredly, using the alias that Bolan currently used. "Not much to see around here really, is there?"

"Sure isn't," Bolan replied.

"Got your papers? Just a formality." The guard held out his hand, and Bolan handed over the documents that covered his arrival, exit and entry and departure from the base. The guard gave them a perfunctory scan.

"When are you shipping out to join your detachment?" the guard asked.

"A flight's been laid on. That's why I'm back so soon. It would help if this could be as quick as possible," Bolan said in as noncommittal a tone as he could muster.

The guard grinned. "Can't wait, eh? Man, you haven't been on a tour for a while, have you?" He stepped back and ushered Bolan through; the barrier opened at his gesture.

Bolan drove though with mixed emotions. It had been the passage he had wanted, but by the same token there could have been anyone or anything concealed in the vehicle. He would have to get Hal Brognola to follow up on this. But for now, there were other matters to attend to.

He parked and headed for his barracks. His kit bag was there, stowed in a locker, and he would need it along with the two that he now had on his shoulder. The last thing he wanted was to be stopped and the contents examined, but he didn't have the time to do anything other than carry them with him.

He entered the barracks and headed for the lockers, exchanging brief greetings with a couple of the men who had been on the transport and were in a similar situation to him—except they were genuinely awaiting dispatch to their units. One of them made a feeble joke about him cleaning out the town of tourist gifts, made allegedly funnier by the base being located off the beaten tourist track. Bolan responded but still hurried as he took out his kit bag.

Bolan's face was set hard as he made his way across the airfield. Checking his watch, he saw that Grimaldi's ETA was now eight minutes. He expected to hear *Dragonslayer*'s approach shortly. Hell, it was hard enough to miss. He would need to be in place, and they would need to move immediately to forestall too many questions.

He approached the control tower, which looked archaic and showed the age of the base the United States had leased. It would be an easy target in this day and age, but with no real foothold in the region, what other option had there been? It was also easy to approach on foot, although the way in which he was greeted when he'd showed his ID to the guard there suggested that Brognola had dropped words into the right ears, and he was expected. Maybe he had misjudged the guys on the gate, too.

The Executioner ascended to the main room, where he was greeted by the officer in charge.

"Cooper, I don't know who you are, but when the commander in chief says jump, I'm already in the air. I know you can't tell me your mission, but if you have a flight path, then we can sure as hell do our best to keep it clear and clean for you."

"Appreciate it," Bolan acknowledged. "My pilot will be able to tell you that. He should be here in—" a quick check of the watch "—three minutes now. In fact, that's him you can hear."

They looked out of the conning tower and saw the sleek chopper approach. On the ground, Bolan could see personnel look up and wonder at the craft that came in to land. It was recognizable as U.S. military issue, but only just. Grimaldi had customized the chopper so that it was suited for heavy-duty warfare as well as swift movement, and the 30 mm mounted ordnance was far beyond that carried by most comparable birds.

"That, my friend, is not standard issue," the officer in charge murmured with a low whistle. "You could do some damage with that."

"That's what we're hoping," Bolan answered softly.

Grimaldi's voice crackled over the comms, requesting permission to land. It was granted, and he was given space away from the main cluster of buildings. The officer in charge obtained Grimaldi's flight plan and guaranteed a clear path and eyes on any outsiders. Then he turned to Bolan.

"You don't want prying eyes, and I'll get you a jeep to take you out there quickly, soldier." After a barked order into the comms, he indicated that one would be waiting. Bolan acknowledged that and hurried down to the base of the tower, where a vehicle and driver were waiting. He was amused as the guard, not quite knowing what to do, saluted him as he threw his bags into the jeep.

The driver took off for where the chopper waited, its rotors still moving. Bolan liked the way that the driver concentrated on the job at hand, saying nothing and asking no questions. When he did speak, as Bolan alighted, all he said was, "Good luck, sir, whatever it is," before throwing the vehicle into Drive and heading back to the tower.

"What kept you, Sarge?" Grimaldi quipped as Bolan settled next to him.

"Yeah, funny, Jack. Let's just get airborne. We've got a location but we need to get on it before the trail goes cold."

Grimaldi nodded, his face grim as he remembered the hostages. He took the chopper into the air, circled the field and headed out over the Gulf of Aden toward the coast of Somalia.

"Relax, Sarge, we've got a couple of hours before I reach the map reference Bear gave me. I bet he's given you some homework, too."

Bolan grinned as he settled in to study the intel downloaded to his smartphone. One thing for sure: there would be no time for this once they landed. He needed to be fully prepped as soon as he hit the ground.

CHAPTER FOUR

The back of the truck was pulled down, and the guards poked the captives into life with the muzzles of their weapons. George and Carla were slow to respond. The woman got the butt of a rifle in her stomach for her tardiness and was unceremoniously shoved into a heap on the desert floor as she tumbled from the flatbed. Marina glanced at Frank. He knew she wanted to protest, but he signaled her to stay quiet. She would only be punished herself, and it would change nothing. George was treated less harshly. He was grabbed by the arms and hauled out, but there was some deference shown for his injured state.

Once down, Frank Foster took the opportunity to scope out their new camp. It looked much like the last one: tents, shacks built of corrugated metal sheeting, with jeeps and flatbeds scattered about. Again, there were few women, and those that were resident were covered in the traditional Muslim manner. Unlike the last camp, however, there was less variation in the way the men dressed. Those he could see were more traditionally Islamic in their dress.

A group of five men were gathered by the largest tent. They were deep in discussion, shooting glances at the new arrivals. With a nod, one of the men detached himself from the group and approached them. He cast an appraising eye over them as though they were cattle. He was over six feet tall, heavily built and didn't look pure-bred Somali; there was something more Arabic about his mien. His full beard was flecked with gray, and one eye was milky and blind.

"So this is what they bring us, eh?" he began. "Worthless and pointless, except for one thing. You, Foster—" he pointed a gnarled finger accusingly "—you work for the government that would seek to oppress us and impose your will upon us, denying us the right to live as a spiritual people…"

Frank's gut twisted with anger and a desire to bite back; the hypocrisy was making his gorge rise. There was some grain of truth in his words when applied to some places in the world, maybe, but that was small compared to the holy war declared by 9/11. He wanted to say that but knew it would probably sign all their death warrants immediately. Better to stay alive as long as possible.

"But they do not reckon on landing us with a perfect weapon. You have information to add to our store of knowledge. We can also sell you back to them and get money to buy more weapons, possibly from the very places that you can tell us about." He threw back his head and gave a throaty laugh. "That would be good. That would be just. But first we must find out what you know." His face split in a vulpine and predatory grin. "That will be enjoyable."

"LOOKS EMPTY TO me down there, Sarge," Grimaldi commented as they approached the location given them by the GPS readings downloaded from Stony Man.

"Jack, the whole country looks empty," Bolan said as he surveyed the land from horizon to horizon. Stony, sandy semidesert with a little scrub and some small oases of water scattered across the landscape. Most of the land was low-level, split here and there by long, desolate plateaus. It was hard to see how anyone could live off the land. It had been the same from Djibouti and over the unmarked border between the two countries.

Below them was the encampment where the GPS reading had come from. In a land like this, it would be impossible for them to approach with any kind of stealth. The only way was to go in hard and direct. They would be seen in the late-afternoon sky, which was cloudless, with the sun beginning to fade. Even that wouldn't provide them with much cover. The Stony Man pilot maneuvered so that he would be coming into target with the sun at his back.

Bolan went back and suited up: concussion and flash grenades hung from the web harness on the blacksuit, with extra ordnance for the guns he would use. The chopper was unmarked; his blacksuit was not identifiable in the same way the weapons he used were untraceable in case it became an issue. He'd chosen to buy a couple of BXP10 SMGs. They were simple and serviceable weapons, knockoffs of MAC-10s. He also carried a Chilean SAF machine pistol. It was a good weapon in close quarters, and a compromise between carrying a handgun that might just be deadweight and another SMG that may be too clumsy.

"Want me to lay down some cover?" Grimaldi asked over the comm system as Bolan prepared to fast-rope to the ground.

"Too risky with your ordnance," Bolan answered. "We don't know where they are down there, and we can't risk taking them out."

"Okay, Sarge, but you're making it hard for yourself."

"I can live with that, Jack. Just take her in and hover, and then pull up when I tell you," Bolan replied as he adjusted his headset.

Grimaldi looked down at the settlement as he approached at speed. The key was to get in position quickly, before anyone could fire at him. There was no sign of any heavy ordnance down there, but no way of being certain. Below, he could see that his approach had been spotted and men were running around, raising the alarm.

Grimaldi leveled the helicopter and hovered about eight yards above the surface of the desert floor. The backwash of air from *Dragonslayer* raised clouds of dust that obscured the vision of the men now spilling into view. It was the best he could do in providing cover, and it wouldn't last long, so…

"Go, Sarge!" he yelled into his comm unit.

Bolan, waiting for the word, adjusted the goggles he had chosen almost entirely for protection and opened the hatch, dropping the rope down so that it hung straight in the eye of the dust storm.

With a BXP10 cradled in one arm, he wrapped himself around the rope and pushed out, descending rapidly and hitting the ground in a running crouch. He signaled for Grimaldi to pull away, and, as the chopper rose, the soldier was able to see through the settling dust more clearly than the enemy, whose eyes were still gritted by the choking clouds.

He sprayed an arc and took out six men with one burst, reducing the odds immediately.

In a running crouch, Bolan headed for the largest group of tents and shacks. The sand at his feet was chopped up by AK-47 fire from behind him. He dived into a shoulder roll, dropping the BXP10 in his grasp as his wrist rapped against a rock, and came up in the shelter of a flatbed truck. Cursing to himself and ignoring the pain in his wrist, he pulled the second BXP10 machine pistol from its nestling place and returned the fire. He saw another man go down.

Four women came running and screaming from one of the tents. They were unarmed, and he held fire, wondering if this was just panic or something else. His question was answered when a grenade sailed over them, landing just in front and detonating with a crump. The soldier ducked behind the vehicle and felt the impact of the shrapnel on the other side of the truck; window glass shattered above and over him.

After pulling a concussion grenade from his web harness, he armed the bomb and lobbed it over the top of the truck toward the tent, rising cautiously to check the action. His injured wrist was his right, and a spasm of agony made him grind his teeth as the grenade soared straight and true, landing at the tent flap.

The concussion grenade detonated. Bolan counted to five and moved out of cover. He kept the BXP10 in his grip, scanning the camp for any signs of movement, unable to rely on his hearing until the effects of the detonation had worn off.

There was no sign of any life. It appeared that the inhabitants of the camp were dead, unconscious or playing possum. The last was a possibility he kept in mind as he scoured the tents and shacks.

Empty. All of them. Anyone inside had come out, and there was no sign of the hostages.

Bolan cursed softly to himself and reconned the rest of the camp. It was light on manpower for the amount of tents, and it was obvious that when the hostages had been moved, there had been a heavy guard on them. The question was: Where did they go?

There was very little paperwork in any of the tents, especially the most luxurious, which he could safely assume was the camp leader's. *Luxurious* was a relative term: the camp was poor. The only thing he could find, under bedding and blankets in this tent, was a smartphone. It was incongruous to find one on its own in this place.

"Jack, can you read me?" Bolan snapped into his headset.

"Sarge, do you want a pickup?"

"Yeah, you can do that. The target's gone, but we might be able to trace them. I've got a phone, and I'll lay you odds it's the GPS we were given."

"Then how do we follow them?"

"You come in and land, Jack. We might have to use some more old-fashioned methods."

"IT'S VERY SIMPLE, Foster. You tell us all you know, and we don't hurt you."

"It wouldn't be worth your effort," Frank replied with a nonchalance he really didn't feel. In truth, his best efforts still betrayed a quaver in his voice.

"It would," the bearded man said simply. "We would reward you with life. You have nothing to look forward to in death except oblivion. There are no martyrs beyond the true faith."

"I've read your book. I work with people who have your faith. You're talking crap. It says that life is sacred and only in cases of defense should any force be used. I'm not scared of oblivion, but you should be for betraying the words of the Prophet."

The bearded man's face twisted into a smile. "Very clever. You seek to undermine me by using the words of my own faith against me. I can see why you are such an asset to your people. But your words are empty, for this is a war of defense. Defense of the holy word against the nonbeliever. You seek to oppress us, and so we will fight back. It is that simple."

"Nothing's that simple," Foster said with resignation. He knew that any amount of stalling for time, trying to reason or anything that would delay the inevitable was doomed to failure.

"It is if you wish it. Life is a simple thing, and it is we foolish people who seek to complicate it. But I have no time for philosophical conversation. It is pointless.

There is much to do," he added with a dismissive wave of his hand.

Frank Foster was tied to a cane chair. The seat had no padding, and he was naked. He felt uncomfortable, and despite his better judgment tried to shift his weight. The discomfort changed to pain as his body weight bore down on his scrotum, pushing it into and through the cane fretwork. He winced and bit back on the cry that rose in his throat.

The bearded man smiled.

"You understand what will happen? Eventually, you will emasculate yourself. It will be extremely slow and painful. You will beg for us to untie you and tell us anything we wish. Of course, you can forestall this…."

He left the rest unsaid, but unwittingly he had steeled Foster's resolve. The longer he could hold out, the greater chance… Did he really believe that the cavalry would be on the way? Was he fooling himself? The doubts must have played across his face, for the bearded man laughed shortly.

"You have the makings of a strong man for someone who has been bred in such a weak land. You seek to last as long as possible. I wonder if I have the time to waste on you? Perhaps we should expedite matters in some way."

He gestured to one of the men who had been standing by the tent flap. There were four other men in the room. One had a digital audio recorder, waiting for Frank to talk. Another stood at his rear, cradling an AK-47. Two were at the tent flaps. Such a guard was hardly necessary for a naked, trussed man. They were there to add intimidation, and Frank knew that. By not looking at them, he sought to nullify the effect, but he couldn't help but wonder where the guard was headed as he pulled back the flap, allowing in a glaring burst of late daylight. This question had to have shown in his face.

"It is sometimes necessary to use methods that we would condemn in others. For the greater glory there is occasionally a need to plumb depths."

Foster's gut flipped. He knew what the bearded man meant.

"You bastard. What has she got to do with this? If you harm her—"

"That's up to you, Foster. It matters not to me. Your people always speak of freedom of choice. Well, now is your chance to exercise that freedom."

It was only a matter of a minute or two, but it seemed like an eternity until Marina was dragged into the tent. She was silent, her eyes full of fear. They widened as she saw her husband, and she stifled a cry.

"You have strength, too, woman. Let us see how much…."

"ARE YOU SURE he's the right guy?" Grimaldi asked as he watched Bolan drag the unconscious man across the sand by the back of his neck.

"He was in front of the tent where I found the phone, and he used those helpless women as a shield," the soldier replied, indicating the corpses fanned out between the tent and the flatbed truck pitted by shrapnel.

"Nice guy," Grimaldi commented. "Can I kick the bastard yet, Sarge?"

"What's the point? He's out cold and won't feel a thing. But you could give me a hand here."

Grimaldi grinned and jumped down from *Dragonslayer,* then helped Bolan lift the unconscious man into the chopper. He had brought the helicopter in and landed on Bolan's request, and was now wondering just what the next move would be.

"How much juice have you got in this thing?" the soldier asked, banging the fuselage.

"Depending on how I push her, maybe five, six hours. What's the plan, Sarge?"

"They can't have gone that far in the time frame we've given them," Bolan explained. "The question is where, and in which direction. We're looking for another camp, or maybe even a convoy or one flatbed or jeep on the trail. I want to narrow that down by asking our friend here a few questions. That's if I don't get what I need from this," he added, holding up the smartphone. "If I do, then we can lose our passenger."

"You'll want me to put down again."

"Maybe." Bolan grinned mirthlessly. "I'm not sure he deserves to be treated with such humanity." He looked out the hatch at the camp. It was still quiet; survivors were reluctant to reveal their presence.

"Let's get her up and out of here, Jack. The less time we waste, the better."

With his unwilling and unconscious passenger and the hatch secured, Bolan began to scroll through the intel on the smartphone as Grimaldi took the chopper into the air.

"I'll take her high and circle, see if I can pick out anything while you check the phone," the pilot said over the comm link. "The whole country looks empty, though. I can't even spot any wildlife."

"It's not an easy place to live," Bolan murmured as he continued his search. "Most of the people hug the coast. And there's not much for any wildlife to survive on."

The smartphone held some photographs of a personal nature, no voice mail, no texts and no stored numbers: the directory and call log had been wiped. There was an email address that had been left signed in, and from that Bolan could see that there were messages in Arabic and French. His French was good. His ability to read Arabic as rusty and basic but functional, so he was able to read the messages without asking Stony Man for translation. What he read made his blood cool: information about the hostages had been exchanged, and it seemed that Foster was considered valuable by one of the warlords who dealt with some pirate groups. One with links to al-Shabaab, a chain that linked Foster directly to al Qaeda.

It was not just the lives of Foster and his fellow hostages that were now at stake. The knowledge he carried, if taken from him, could contribute to the deaths of countless others.

To learn this much was one thing. Frustratingly, there was nothing else on the phone that gave a clue as to where the hostages had been taken.

"Jack, can you see anything?" Bolan said over the comm link.

"Negative, Sarge. I take it there's nothing on the phone that's of any use?"

"Second that negative. Keep her up but use as little juice as possible. I think it's time to wake up our friend and ask him a few questions."

The pirate was still unconscious, laying on the deck on the chopper. Bolan stood up, took a bottle of water from the supplies and cracked it open. He emptied its contents over the face of the supine prisoner. The steady flow caused him to splutter, choke and return to consciousness. He cursed in Arabic and tried to move, struggling against his bonds.

"What's your English like?" Bolan asked, standing astride him. The man looked at him and feigned incomprehension, but his eyes betrayed him.

"Okay, if you want to play it that way, we'll play it," he continued, switching to Arabic and noting the fear creeping into the pirate's face. "There's no escaping by pretending you don't understand me, because I know you do. I'm going to ask you a question and you're going to answer me. The four people you had in your camp. The Americans. Where have they been taken?"

The pirate shook his head and said nothing. Bolan sighed. "If you want to make this hard, then that's your call. It doesn't have to be that way. You see that rope around your ankles?" He indicated the rappelling cord, which he had secured around the pirate's ankles when he had tied him earlier. "Now watch…"

Bolan opened the hatch, steadying himself for the change in pressure and the rush of air. He strode back to where the pirate lay.

"This rope is all that keeps you from falling. Remember that."

He pushed the prone man toward the hatch, rolling him over. The pirate voiced his fear with imprecations and pleas. When the man was near the edge, Bolan leaned over him and yelled, "Your choice. Tell me now or you go out."

The pirate shook his head. Bolan sighed and took a knife from where it had been sheathed in his blacksuit. He showed the man the blade before wrapping the cord around his other arm. Bracing himself, he began to push the pirate's head and shoulders out of the open hatch, so that the rushing air whipped at his face. The man began to scream.

Bolan hoped this would work quickly. From the man's previous behavior, he had him marked as a coward. There was no way that he could play the man out slowly without risking himself. He would have to throw him out and hope that his own weight wouldn't rip his feet off at the cord. No one would win that way. But the psychodrama with the knife and the cord might just work.

Still screaming, the pirate was pulled back from the edge.

"I can be merciful," Bolan yelled above the roar of the chopper and the rushing air. "Tell me now."

Sobbing, the pirate gave him the name of a wadi, swearing that it was marked on any map. He even blurted half a map reference, swearing that he could not remember the rest. Bolan slammed the hatch, glad for the relief from the noise and air pressure. He relayed the name of the wadi and the half reference to Grimaldi.

"No worries, Sarge, I can find it from that." Grimaldi's voice crackled over the comm link.

Bolan's attention was distracted by the pirate speaking nonstop to him, words flowing and rushing over each other in such a way that it was hard for him to keep up. He barked at the pirate to slow down, and as the man repeated himself, Bolan realized what it was he was trying to say.

He fixed the man with an iron-hard stare. "You're going back with us to face trial for what you've done. You're lucky that I'm not the coldhearted bastard you are." He pushed the prone man so that he rolled over and fell against the side of the fuselage. He untied the cord because he would need it. The pirate made a feeble attempt to fight but was soon dissuaded when the soldier rapped his temple with the butt of his pistol. Prisoner suitably subdued, Bolan left him there while he spoke to Grimaldi.

"Jack, listen up. We've got no time to waste, and we're going to have to go in with guns blazing."

FOSTER BLINKED AS the tears rolled down his face. He felt as though his throat was constricted, and even if he wanted to talk he would find it hard to spit out the words. Come to that, he wanted to tell them everything so that they would stop. But he knew they wouldn't. The U.S. government couldn't kowtow to a ransom demand, and the security services would realize that he would be tortured for information. Even now there were factions that were probably acting to seal any leaks or cracks that would come from the information he could give, rendering it almost worthless. Meantime, these bastards would realize some of that and just amuse themselves as they extracted information.

The whole thing was a nightmare from which he couldn't wake. The throbbing pain in his groin, pulsing with his heartbeat, meant nothing to him. The greater pain came from his heart as he watched the bearded man take delight in torturing Marina. Whether the scum took pleasure from harming the woman or from the mental damage he knew it was inflicting on the man was a moot point. The simple fact was that as he extracted each painted toenail with pliers, he grinned at the agony of having the nail ripped from its bed. It was such a small thing to do, yet the nerve endings exposed and ripped screamed with a pain that was out of all proportion to the size of the damaged area.

Marina had stopped screaming after the third nail, her voice reduced to a croak and sob. Only a low moan escaped from her throat.

"Just stop. I'll give you anything you want if you just stop," Foster choked out.

The man with the digital audio recorder stepped forward. "Speak first, then stop," he barked.

Foster opened his mouth, but there was no chance for him to utter a syllable.

Because that was when the door to hell opened....

CHAPTER FIVE

Bolan reloaded the two BXP10s, having checked the recovered weapon for damage and replenished the ammunition and grenades. He would go with the same hardware as before.

He made his way to the cockpit, ignoring the sullen glare of his captive.

"Jack, progress report?" he queried.

"Locked onto the map ref, Sarge. Dead easy. Not a lot of ground for us to cover, though a lot with a flatbed on that terrain. With luck, given the time, they've arrived but they haven't been there long enough for any collateral damage."

"I hope so. It'd be shame to come all this way for nothing. Well, nothing except to wipe out a few thugs and cut the chances of it happening again."

"Something's better than nothing, but I figure we can do better than that. See that, dead ahead?"

Closing fast was an encampment not unlike the one they had recently left. A quick head count as they closed revealed that there were three more dwellings and six vehicles. Estimate up to twice as many enemy between them and their target.

"Want me to set down some covering before I drop you, Sarge?"

"Affirmative. More than that, Jack, once I'm down I want you to pull up and keep up a barrage. I can't take them out and search for the hostages at the same time. I'm going to need you to try to knock out as many as possible for me. But do me a favor. Steer clear of the tents, okay?"

"You don't need to tell me. I'll take out the vehicles. The smoke and fire from them should give you some ground cover. Get going, Sarge—twenty seconds and we're on them."

Bolan moved back and prepared himself as the chopper banked into the sun to make its approach. He opened the hatch and prepared to pay out the rappelling cord. The wind whipped against him, and he felt the powerful 30 mm ordnance of the chopper pump out a covering fire. Under the roar of the rotors he could just about hear the dull *whump* of gasoline explosions as some of the heavy chopper fire hit the vehicles. He felt the chopper level out and start to drop and he paid out the rope, cradling one of the BXP10s as he prepared to drop.

The sight that greeted him as he descended was one of chaos. Three of the vehicles were ablaze, and some of the men were torn between trying to put out the fires or engaging in a firefight. The confusion suggested that whoever was in charge of this team was either an idiot or absent.

Bolan hoped that it was the former, as the latter would suggest that Frank Foster was being interrogated. Maybe it was already too late.

Maybe for him, but not for the other three; there were four lives at stake here. Bolan hit the ground and swept an arc of fire as he moved toward the first piece of cover he could find—one of the vehicles that Grimaldi hadn't successfully strafed. There were two men close by, but they were blinded both by the smoke that drifted across them and by fear. Easy to take two taps and eliminate their threat.

Racing to cover, the soldier took stock of the situation. His presence had been noted, but there was no concerted attempt to attack his position. Grimaldi had taken *Dragonslayer* up and was now circling, firing bursts at the remaining vehicles and tearing up the sandy soil between them. He was staying conspicuously clear of the tents and shacks, and Bolan wondered if the pirates would realize that. Best to give them no opportunity. He tried a quick head count, but it was difficult to establish enemy numbers. All he could tell for sure was there were more of them here than at the previous camp.

They were giving themselves away. Forming up into something approaching a unit, a group had been detached to cover one of the shacks, while another was moving toward a tent that already had two armed guards outside, both of whom were uselessly firing at *Dragonslayer* rather than concentrating on the man on the ground.

Obviously the two dwellings were where the hostages were kept, separated in some way and for whatever reason. The question was: Which to take first?

There was, however, a more immediate problem. Two of the pirates appeared from the direction of one of the tents carrying a two-man version of what looked like an SA2 Russian surface-to-air missile launcher. They dropped down into a space between the fire zone and the tents, preparing to sight and fire on the helicopter.

With a grim smile, Bolan saw that they were close enough to the remaining group of pirates—who had not as yet fanned out to approach him—to put them in his firing line. Their idea was obviously to take out the aerial threat and then attack him with impunity.

It was a terrible decision for them. Not so for Bolan. He took a shrapnel grenade and primed it, sending it in an arc toward the two men with the missile launcher. They were distracted by their task, and although some of the men behind them tried to shoot the grenade out of the air, that was a foolish and desperate measure that could only end one way.

The grenade landed softly in the sand at the feet of the man shouldering the launcher. The cries of his compatriots were drowned out in the fury of combat, and he looked down with an expression of surprise. Bolan ducked as the grenade detonated. He flattened against the ground, knowing that the vehicle he used for cover would take one hell of a beating.

He opened his mouth to equalize pressure, almost able to taste the explosive that went up with the grenade, the launcher and the missile it carried. A wave of heat swept across him. He couldn't hear the shrapnel hit the side panels and couldn't feel it in the rocking of the vehicle that the blast wave generated.

He was the first man on his feet, and the sight that greeted him was one that caused him both content and worry. The entire group of pirates had been eradicated in one swoop, but the blast had also taken out some of the tents and shacks, while others were damaged.

Had he inadvertently made casualties of the hostages he had been sent to rescue?

GEORGE AND CARLA were huddled together in their shack. Her husband had regained consciousness, and when the sound of heavy gunfire began outside, he had gathered her to him protectively. They had no weapons, nothing other than their bedding, and were alone. Even so, he felt the need to put his body between his wife and any harm that may befall them. They could hear yelling outside, over the sound of combat, but as they couldn't comprehend Arabic they had no notion of what was happening.

They were defenseless, and as the wave of heat hit them, the heavy fabric of the tent splitting with the explosion beyond, George gathered Carla closer to him, so that she almost lay beneath him and he could shield her from the sand, rocks and God alone knew what else showered in on them.

They may be about to die, but he would still do whatever he could, no matter how little, to protect her.

WHEN THE EXPLOSION hit, Frank and Marina were thrown sideways as the sides of the tent were ripped asunder. A terrible tearing pain ripped through Frank as he was thrown off the chair and skin tore from the cane work that trapped it. He felt bile in his throat as nausea washed over him; he coughed and choked as it spilled from his mouth. His wife was almost unconscious from the torture she had received, yet the first wave of gunfire had stopped it, and being bowled over by the shock wave of the explosion had the paradoxical effect of waking her up.

She could see her husband on his side, vomit dribbling from his mouth and his groin covered with blood. She was sure that they were about to die. The one consolation she had was that before the attack had started there had been no time for Frank to speak. He had not given anything away, and there was no record left behind even if the bastards in this tent with them were all to die—as she hoped they would.

At least she and her husband could die with honor.

IN THE RELATIVE silence that followed the detonation, George was aware of the distant and rhythmic thumping of chopper blades and the chatter of gunfire. There were screams of men dying and shouts of men panicking and trying to avoid their own demise. The gunfire grew more sporadic, and the sound of one regular and controlled burst became prevalent. And then it stopped.

He heard rapid footfalls enter the tent through the gaping hole in the side. He still did not dare look up, just huddled over his weeping wife and prayed that they would be taken quickly. It never occurred to him that it might be a rescue mission, and so he had no idea how or what he should feel when he heard a voice that held compassion but was still commanding say to him, "Stay where you are. Do not move until I return. This is a rescue mission. Do as I say and you'll be safe."

George could find no voice for response. He couldn't

even look up until he heard footfalls retreat, and then he saw the back of a man dressed head to toe in black heading for the next tent.

BOLAN MOVED ACROSS the space between the two tents, aware of the fact that most of the enemy had now been eliminated. Nonetheless, a feeling in his gut told him to stay frosty and keep his eyes open. There had been two hostages in the tent he had just secured; there should be two where he was headed. He knew that he had taken out a number of the pirates who had been clustered around this tent. Had that been all of them?

He slowed as he approached. Over the sound of the hovering helicopter, he couldn't hear anything, but at the same time he couldn't believe that these men would give up their bounty so easily.

Something—a sense, maybe a sound or the flickering of shadow at the periphery of his sight—made him veer off from a direct approach so that he would come at the gaping maw in the tent from an angle.

"CLEVER, BUT NOT as much as he thinks."

The blood of both Frank and Marina Foster ran cold when they heard the voice. He was behind them, as he must have been all along. When the others had rushed to attack the incoming enemy, he had stayed behind. Someone had to tidy up, after all.

The bearded man stepped over their prone bodies so that he was now in front of them.

"I will die a martyr. That does not bother me. We all live or die at the command of God. But you will not live to see another day. This action will be in vain, and your people will not triumph. It is just a pity that I could not get anything of use from you in the time I had."

He raised his gun to fire at them. Frank was semi-conscious and unable to focus, but Marina could see the man with an awful clarity.

And then, just when she had steeled herself for the end, there was a flicker of shadow behind him, and his leer changed to an expression of slack-jawed bemuse-ment before the light faded from his eyes. He crumpled, revealing a man in a blacksuit standing behind him, a knife slick with blood in his grip.

"Rescue mission. You'll be safe now. Your friends are also safe. We just need to get you out of here."

Shock, perhaps, or relief: whatever it was, Marina felt her vision swim as she blacked out.

BOLAN RECONNED THE camp quickly. All dead, with the exception of the hostages, a clean sweep. The air stank with cordite, explosives and death.

Dragonslayer landed, and Grimaldi left his aircraft to help Bolan get the hostages ready for transport. George and Carla were strong enough to walk, and the two men helped them into the aircraft first. Blankets, coffee, med-ication: all were administered quickly before they took stretchers to the tent where Frank and Marina Foster had been held.

Carefully they untied Frank and placed him on a stretcher before carrying him back to the chopper. He was groaning in pain with each movement, but a swift painkilling jab made him more comfortable while they returned for Marina. She was still unconscious, so it was easier to load her.

"Tend to them, Jack. I need to go and sweep up any intel I can find," Bolan instructed. "We need to sweep this as clean as possible."

Quickly Bolan checked out the tents and shacks. There was nothing but corpses and bedding until he returned to the tent where he had found the Fosters. There was a radio set and some smartphones. He took these and a laptop, as well as the digital audio recorder, before trashing the radio set.

"Okay, Jack, take her up and let's get moving. I'll tend to our passengers," he said as he climbed back aboard.

While Grimaldi took the chopper into the air and set a course for Djibouti, monitoring for any aircraft that may cross their flight path, Bolan dressed wounds, administered medication and gave Marina coffee when she came around. Having assured his charges that they were now safe and would soon be returning home, he took himself away so that he could make a preliminary examination of the equipment he had found.

The digital audio recorder was empty. The smartphones were as empty as the one he had taken from the first camp. But the laptop was another matter. What he saw on there made him glad that he had been sent on this mission. There would be another to come, and soon.

After making sure that his passengers were comfortable and that his prisoner was still secured, he went to the cockpit. The first thing he did was call Brognola, report success and request a transport plane to pick up their cargo from Djibouti and an ambulance to ferry the passengers from chopper to plane.

"I'll arrange it with the base commander so that you're kept in isolation until it arrives. What about the prisoner?"

"We're going to need him back on American soil, too. I'd be surprised if he knows much, but he might know more than he thinks he does. He's a small fish, but the man he was answerable to was much, much bigger than that."

"It's a pity you couldn't have taken him alive, too."

"Hal, if I'd done that I'd be short two passengers."

"Point taken. You said there was something else?"

"Oh, yeah…I'll give you bullet points, but you'll love this," Bolan said before telling the big Fed what he had found on the captured laptop.

"Guess you'll be taking the first plane back, too," Grimaldi commented when call had ended. He had been party to the conversation so he would know landing plans.

"Jack, fate is a bastard, but not always an unkind one," Bolan replied.

THE HELICOPTER LANDED in Djibouti a few hours later, at the outfield from where the mission had begun. As the chopper settled, two ambulances and a jeep raced across the field. Bolan stepped in front of the hatch so that no one could enter uninvited.

The same officer in charge who had seen them set out on the mission was in the jeep, and he signaled his men to stay put as he alighted and walked toward the Executioner.

"Good to see you back in one piece and with your objective attained," he said wryly. "Transporter is three hours away and will have a two-hour turnaround time. We can take whoever you've got to our sick bay if you wish—"

Bolan stopped him. "I appreciate that, and your discretion up to now. This has to be locked down, so it would be best if only the ambulance crew deals with the cargo and that the cargo stays in the vehicles or the chopper until the transporter is ready. You'll have to isolate your men until debriefing can be arranged."

The officer in charge nodded. "If you think that's best. You were placed here because it's about as isolated as you can get, and I'll get meals sent over from the canteen for you and your pilot as well as for— Well, I'll just get provisions sent over," he finished. "Security is as tight as it can get here. I take it this means you'll be sending someone in for debrief?"

Bolan grinned. "I'm not that important. But the man who sent me here will see to that. And your help won't go unrecognized."

LANDON MCCABE ENTERED the Oval Office. It was the middle of the night, and the President looked like a man still dragging himself from sleep.

"This had better be worth it," the Man growled.

"I think you'll find it is, sir," McCabe replied before relaying the report he had received from Brognola. The President looked relieved when he heard that the hostages were safe, more so when he heard that Foster had maintained silence. It was only when he heard the final part of the report—concerning what Bolan had found on the laptop—that his expression changed.

"What are we going to do about this, Landon? It's all a little too close to home."

"It is, sir," McCabe agreed. "But I think it's in the right hands now. I suggest that we inform the NSA but let our operative handle it."

"If he does it like he's handled this one, then it won't be us who are uneasy in our beds," the Man stated.

"No, sir. You can be sure of that," McCabe agreed.

CHAPTER SIX

Washington, D.C., was never Bolan's favorite place. The United States and the constitution were one thing—sacrosanct and something to believe in—but the successive governments and their own agendas were another matter. The way in which they interpreted that constitution was a matter of opinion. Bolan had his own views, which didn't always match those of the powers that be. Yet when he did visit the capital and took a walk down the Mall, he was reminded of the people who had shaped the land and made it something that he could believe in, something that would endure beyond the caprice of any political agenda.

The people made a country. It was the people who were at risk if the information found on the laptop was correct. He saw no reason to doubt that.

It had to be assumed that the information was correct and they should act on it accordingly, which was why he was now walking toward Hal Brognola, who stood waiting for him. As Bolan approached, the big Fed fell into step with him.

"Good work," he began without preamble. "The Man wants you to follow up on this personally."

"I was hoping that would be the case, though it's a

shame that the security services weren't more on the ball with this."

Brognola shrugged. "You can't really blame them. It's the nature of al Qaeda and its offshoots that it happens this way."

"I know how al Qaeda works," Bolan stated. "Most of the time we find a group, we locate the leadership and we eliminate them. Gangs—criminal or political—are just like pack animals. The leader dies, and unless there's someone there to take his place—which we take care of by eliminating the central body as a whole—then the pack disperses and is rarely more than an irritation. An itch that can be scratched."

"But al Qaeda—"

"I know, Hal. It's not like that. That was my point. Al Qaeda by its nature is a series of separate cells that have little if any connection. You want to be part of it? All you have to do is say you are and buy into the ethos, and what do you know? Before too long others saying it, too, will notice you and get in touch. It's more like the way a religion or cult springs up around a figurehead. Bin Laden didn't actually have to be hands-on after 9/11. The fact that he existed was enough."

"Which is why the security agencies didn't know about these cells you found on the laptop," Brognola said. "They're new—they've done nothing to come out from under the radar as yet. Their contact with al-Shabaab is fresh. Even al-Shabaab has only just been confirmed as connected to al Qaeda."

Bolan sighed. "This one connects to that one and now they're a known threat. These guys have been stockpiling weapons. They've been getting explosives. And they've been doing it under the radar. They all do it under the radar so that it escapes notice. You have to wonder why Homeland doesn't keep track of illegal arms dealers."

Brognola sighed. "You're not wrong, and maybe I don't exactly disagree with you, but whatever our opinions, the facts remain the same. The various security agencies hadn't noticed that these boys existed."

Bolan's face darkened. "We need to find these cells before they can carry out any of their missions. Otherwise there's going to be a lot of red faces and guys having to explain to the Man just why D.C. got hit and they knew nothing about it."

RODNEY FRASER CLOSED the door of his apartment and let out a deep sigh. Outside, the noise of police sirens, shouting people, loud music beats and the playing of children screaming to be heard above the racket was still going strong. It permeated the thin walls of the project apartment building where he had been living for the past eighteen months. Inside, it was sparsely furnished, with a small and barely used TV the only visible sign of any kind of modern technology. The smartphone, tablet and laptop that he owned and only used for business were kept hidden under the floor beneath his futon.

Maybe it was the clean, sparse decor that gave the room an aura of peace and silence. Perhaps it was the prayer mat that he took from a cupboard before facing the east and praying. When he got to his feet, he felt calmer inside. He put the prayer mat away, poured himself a glass of water and sat on a dining chair to consider his evening's work.

Rodney had been his given name, but since his last term of imprisonment he had been Mummar al-Jaheeb. Inside the joint, there were several ways to go—gangs of one kind or another were rife, and those that united men by religion were those that gave you the best advantage. Maybe because the faith required—if it was genuine—gave you the strength of conviction and spirit that would take you that one step further. For Rodney—Mummar—this was the case. He had grown up learning about Malcolm X, and it had meant little to him. He hated the stupid little ties and hats and the suits. If you wore those around these parts, you'd end up beaten on pretty damned quick, that was for sure. But the Black Panthers were better; they had street style. That made more sense.

In both cases it was a bad call. It was only when he was inside prison that he came to realize that the uniform didn't matter. It was what you thought and believed and how you acted that mattered. Those guys had been that way because of the time and place they lived. Now was different; now required a whole other way of looking at it.

This was why, even though he hated it and felt unclean, he came out of prison without telling anyone of his conversion and why he used his birth name even though it meant nothing to him. He got a job working in an auto shop—the one useful skill he had learned during his term—and went to work every day in jeans and a T-shirt or sweatpants. The traditional dress that symbolized the new Mummar—which he wanted to wear to show this—was something that he could not keep in his apartment. If he appreciated irony, he would have figured that now that he understood the power of uniform, the knowledge was of no use to him. But neither did he have any use for irony, not when there was serious work to be done.

Every day he rose as Mummar, dressed and left home as Rodney, acted his old self all day and came home exhausted by that artifice before he could be Mummar again. The only thing that kept him going through it all was the knowledge that he had important work to do that would dignify the life he had to live in the eyes of his creator.

He made a simple meal, blocking out the world around him as he prepared couscous with beans and pulses. More water to purify his system. Now he was Mummar.

Being Rodney was hard; exhausting, even. He was glad he didn't have to do it more than once a day. He had an imaginary girlfriend living upstate that kept suspicions at bay. Eunice—the name of his baby mama from the days before his conversion—was also good cover for those weekends spent at training camps.

His meal finished, Mummar washed his dishes and made ready for his evening's work. He looked out the windows of the small apartment at the streets outside. He could see gangs gathering, old people weaving among them trying to pretend they weren't there and dealers on the street corner peddling the latest crack and smack. Everyone out there was wrapped up in his or her own world, oblivious of what was going on just a few hundred yards from them, which was exactly the way it had to be. They were his people by birth, but they were also part of a corrupt and godless system that needed a wake-up call that the jihad was coming home.

He pulled down the blinds in every room so that his apartment was in semidarkness. The locks on the door and windows were checked. Only when he was sure that he was secure, and that the noises coming through the walls proved that his neighbors did not even realize or care he was home, did he move the futon, take up the rug beneath and pry open the loose floorboard.

There was a gap between his floorboards and the ceiling of the apartment below. Wiring and piping ran through it, and across the joists between there was a case wrapped in chamois leather. He pulled it out and unwrapped it. It had a combination lock, and he keyed it in. As he opened the lid of the case, he carefully moved the wire that connected the lock to the small charge that was placed within. Try to open the case without the combination and the charge would not only take off your hand, but it would also destroy the contents, rendering the memory and SIM of the tablet, laptop and phone useless.

He took out the three items, all of which had been stolen and retooled before being put back into circulation, and powered up the laptop. He had an internet connection via a dongle, a pay-as-you-go unregistered device, so that he was about as untraceable as he could get. To the outside world and good old Ma Bell, Rodney Fraser was a man with no interest in phones or the internet. Mummar al-Jaheeb was another matter.

He connected to the email account that had been registered from another state and checked his messages. The account was empty except for the three unread messages that had arrived overnight, all of which were immediately deleted on being read, as were the answers. Nothing stayed in the boxes for more than twenty-four hours maximum. The networks in which the mailboxes were set up were as secure as anyone could be certain.

Mummar read the messages, which were coded, considered what they said, then replied briefly—also in code. He then deleted all messages from his in-box and sent box before closing his account.

There was work to be done. He smiled. At last, it would begin.

SECURITY WAS SUPPOSED to be tight at Ronald Reagan Washington National Airport, more so than Dulles, according to the publicity handed out by the airport itself. There was certainly a presence within the main terminal, and those heading for departures would find themselves subject to some strict searches.

Despite that, Mack Bolan couldn't help but look at the overt show and wonder if it was a good thing. A little more discretion may lull potential threats into a false sense of security. It may also make them more inclined to take risks. As it was, you cut out one source of traffic but only by diverting it to another route. A little discretion and craft, and maybe a potential threat could be nullified.

It was just a thought the soldier had as he sipped his coffee and waited for the latest arrivals. A quick consultation with Aaron Kurtzman and his crack cyber team had given the soldier a number of leads to illegal arms dealers in the Washington area. Given the lockdown on security that had occurred post-9/11 and continued to the present, it was unlikely that an attempt would be made to bring in a large cache of weapons or explosives. It was much more likely that any enemy would attempt to use local dealers and local knowledge to piece together a cache from within the immediate area.

So far, even with the best cipher skills of Akira Tokaido on hand to help, Kurtzman had found it difficult to crack the codes that were used in some of the material found on the laptop and tablets that Bolan had retrieved in Somalia. It was a stroke of luck, therefore, that the pirates allied to al-Shabaab were careless and lazy when communicating with one another. It had been frustrating, like reading fragments of a document that had almost been burned to ashes, trying to piece together the whole and fill in the gaps. It had also made his blood run cold.

An attack on the Capitol building, striking symbolically at the National Mall and also the Smithsonian, would mean an assault on both patriotic pride and American culture, with it being the precursor to an attack on the White House.

The most alarming part of the situation was that the NSA had no indication of any such impending attack. There were two cells mentioned in the Arabic sections, both of which were located in the greater D.C. area. No names had been used, but from references that were translatable, it appeared that one cell was composed of four men, the other of five.

So his task was to track down nine men, none of whose identities were known, in a population of just over six hundred thousand within the metropolitan area. Still he scanned the arrivals as this played through his mind. A steady stream of people, few of whom were paid much attention by security, flowed past. Most of the recent arrivals had been from internal flights, which made security less inclined to expend much time on them. There was an assumption that they were not carrying anything dangerous, as stringent procedures were carried out at point of departure. It was also assumed that any persons of a dubious or suspicious nature would have been cherry-picked similarly.

That was all well and fine. It did, however, depend on whether they were known to the authorities in some way. The fact that both cells had sprung up under the radar made that unlikely.

The third arrival in line was from New York City. That was the one he had been waiting for. Bolan had a list of known arms and explosive dealers in the D.C. area—from the smallest crackhead dealer with a spare gun to those who dealt in larger items—but to work through them methodically would take time he didn't have. So take a quantum leap of logic...

Undetected men would not have been resident in the D.C. area very long. They may have radical and fundamentalist links, but this would make them more traceable. They may be ordinary guys. But suppose that they had been recently converted, and that they had only been in the area for a short while.

One source to examine were the criminal records of men who had been inside prison in recent times and had links to gangs and factions within the prison system that were known to be radical Muslim. Narrow that down to those whose affiliations were not just with Muslim gangs, but with those who had affiliations with al Qaeda sympathizers.

It was an almost daunting search through the database, but Aaron Kurtzman's cyber team would be up for the challenge. It was amazing how swiftly the Farm came up with a dozen names, one of which was the man Bolan was waiting for right now.

Bolan pulled up the information on his smartphone. Edward James Heider. Looked like a true blue-eyed, blond Aryan. Any other time Bolan would have had him marked down as a natural for the far right. Sometimes assumptions just didn't cut it. Heider had been a radical on the left all his life, and had been jailed for his part in a raid on a liquor store that was intended to "fund" his group's activities. He believed in freedom and equality—except, apparently, for the Indian liquor store clerk who had been too slow to hand over the cash and had been blown away by one of Heider's associates. Heider had been the driver, which was the only reason his sentence had been lighter than the two men with him when he was picked up. Closed-circuit TV revealed that he hadn't been in the store when the clerk was killed.

Still, at his trial he had been fingered as the brains behind the "fund-raising" schemes that the group pulled off. Once incarcerated, his resentment at what he saw as his political imprisonment had radicalized him even further, causing him to convert to Islam as he wanted to demonstratively turn his back on the Western world and its ways.

He came out of prison as Shakur Abu Dalir. Was he really a radical now, planning to bring his previous criminal experience to his new zealotry? Kurtzman's research suggested he was. Heider had been to New York City for a week and was resident in D.C. He lived in Columbia Heights, which, despite the gentrification and attempts to rid it of its old image, was still a dangerous place if you wandered onto the wrong block. While he was in New York, he had been untraceable. Prior to that, he had held down a job in a print shop but spent a lot of his time either mixing with his new community or going back to those he had associated with as a leftist lawbreaker. His very presence gave a concrete link between the two communities. Local knowledge could not tie him to any known fundamentalist or extreme groups in the area, so he had not been considered a threat.

Heider walked through arrivals without drawing a second glance. Dressed in a sober windbreaker and jeans, he didn't look like a radical terrorist. He made straight for the link to the Metrorail station that would take him from Arlington into the heart of the city. Bolan drained his coffee and waited a beat or two before rising and following.

There were enough people in the terminal making their way toward the Metrorail to make following Heider without being spotted a relatively easy task. There was no outward sign that Heider was anything other than a man returning from a trip and going about his everyday business.

Maybe that's all he really was. Bolan hoped not. Time was too short for that.

Once they were on the Metrorail into D.C., the soldier kept some distance from his target. Heider showed no signs of awareness that he was being followed. He sat down and pulled a book from his pocket, becoming engrossed in it to the exclusion of all else.

The man alighted in the Mount Pleasant district. To come straight from a flight from New York, without even hand baggage, and go directly somewhere before his Columbia Heights home was not suspicious in itself. To come here did, however, make sense if Bolan's suspicions had been correct. Mount Pleasant was one of the districts of D.C. that had a high percentage of ethnic populations, mostly South American, particularly Salvadorian. The latter group contained some of the ordnance dealers on his list. That was one hit.

The clincher was that Mount Pleasant also housed the small percentage of D.C.'s population that was of Somalian origin. Now, that would be a major coincidence under the circumstances.

Bolan followed Heider for two blocks before the blond, bearded man stopped in front of a grocery store, where he was greeted by two African Americans and one Somali, all with beards. Their clothes were Western, but were oddly plain and devoid of logos. It was a leap of deduction, perhaps, but it did seem that any fundamentalist avoiding traditional dress in order to stay in cover would still find it uncomfortable to wear commercial logos and symbols of the society they despised. Trained agents would force themselves to do that; these men were not trained agents. They may be zealots, but they had found their own way, for the most part.

The four men went into the grocery store after making a show of picking over the fruit and vegetables on display outside. That gave Bolan a chance to catch them all on his smartphone before messaging the video and screen grabs to Stony Man along with a request for any identification and known associates.

The soldier noted the address of the store, running through the addresses in his head of arms dealers who were known and listed.

It tallied with one man: Samir Younis, a Somali who had been resident in the United States for fifteen years and had served time for minor offenses before keeping his nose clean for the past decade. Officially he was also a federal informant and dealer in arms to a couple of the local gangs, information about which had kept the heat off his back.

Bolan figured that had been shortsighted. Younis was either moving in bigger and nastier circles than his handler realized or he had genuinely gotten in over his head. Either way, Bolan made note to deal with him personally before too long.

It had started to rain heavily, and the crowds thinned out as people sought to escape the deluge. It was harder for the soldier to be as inconspicuous in front of the store, so he made the decision to go around the back to investigate.

Crossing the road and avoiding traffic, he walked along the storefronts until he came to an alley that ran between the two blocks. At this time of day there were no deliveries or pickups under way, no garbage collections. The only risk was from workers coming out the rear of any of the stores. He kept an eye out for that and was able to make swift progress to the rear of the grocery store. A small yard was walled in, with a gate for entry that was locked. He scanned the windows that stared blankly out at the buildings opposite. There was no sign of life here.

The wall was only three yards high, and he used a garbage bin to scale and mount it with ease. He paused for a moment at the top of the wall, then dropped into the yard. It was strewn with rotting fruit and vegetables, some spilled from boxes, others in pallets that were piled a few feet high. The yard was slippery underfoot from the filth and was devoid of any visible security devices. There were no cameras, no trips of any kind. In the pocket of his raincoat Bolan had a monocular night-vision headset that carried infrared and heat functions. He palmed the device and slipped it on briefly to take a quick recon to see if there was anything going on that he should know about.

Nothing. Younis was either careless with security or kept his stock at a separate location. The soldier tried the rear entrance to the building, knowing that it would be locked but hoping maybe he would get lucky. Not this day. There was a fire escape hanging down, but he didn't want to chance the ladder being rusty and noisy. Better to use the drainpipe that ran the length of the building. He risked being seen, but it was a chance he was willing to take.

He scaled the pipe quickly and with ease, sure-footed on the slick metal. A couple of the bolts on the brackets that kept it to the wall had seen better days, but thankfully they held.

On the second floor, he could hear voices muffled through a closed window. He had a small listening device in his pocket, and he fished it out. A dexterous move of the fingers and he had an earpiece inserted while the unit amplified the voices once the sound pad was directed correctly. The voices were overlapping and hard to distinguish, but the gist was clear enough.

"…five hundred pounds of GPU each. Claymore mines, man, they shoot shit like ball bearings or shrapnel. That can do a lot of damage, man, and to anyone fool enough to get in the way…"

"Yeah, and how are you gonna get a five-hundred-pound bomb close enough, eh? You'd need to put that in a car, and no way are you gonna get a car that close—"

"Who needs a car? We're doing this for greater glory, man. We carry it on us."

"You asshole, what are you, Samoan? How are you gonna carry that weight? Even if you could, how's that not gonna look suspicious? You're gonna look like some kinda clown in a fat suit, man—"

"Stop arguing about it, and keep your damn voices down. You can talk about GPU all you want. You aren't getting it off me 'cause I don't have it, and I can't get it without arousing more suspicion than I'd want. You want that, then you're going to have to find someone else. Semtex and fragmentation grenades I can sell you. You could put together something lightweight and nasty enough with a combination of those."

"Okay, if it has to be that—" this last voice had authority, and Bolan had little doubt it was Heider, the man with experience in jobs like this "—then we'll need to arrange delivery and payment."

"How soon?"

"Twenty-four hours."

Bolan stopped listening. So that was how long he had. Younis could wait until that night. The other men in the room could be traced and identified via Stony Man. The first thing he should do was take out Heider without the others being aware of it.

With luck, he had at least one cell identified here. If he was really lucky, there were representatives of both present.

Bolan descended quickly, reaching the back wall and scaling it without being seen before making his way back to the front of the block, so that he could watch the front of the store.

It was still raining hard, and in spite of his raincoat he was soaked through as he entered a café opposite the grocery store. He ordered a coffee and waited.

He didn't have to wait too long until the four men began to emerge from the grocery store. They left individually, each clutching a grocery bag as though they had simply been shopping. Heider was third to leave, and Bolan got up and followed.

Heider made his way back to the Metrorail and traveled to Columbus Heights. It was less crowded on the trains as the early evening rush of commuters had not yet begun, yet it seemed that Heider had little interest in whether he was being followed. Bolan couldn't make up his mind if this was amateur hour or arrogance. Certainly, it was no bluff as Heider kept his head buried in his book and alighted at his stop without paying any attention to whoever left the train at the same time.

Bolan kept a few hundred yards behind him. He knew where Heider was headed because his address was listed. Sure enough, within a few minutes' walk in the now-dry evening, they were at the run-down apartment building where Heider called home. The soldier watched him go in from the other side of the street. His apartment had a front-facing window, and Bolan saw a light go on.

The soldier felt conspicuous; his raincoat and black pants made him stand out in a street where older people were dressed poorly and younger people were almost entirely in brands. He also knew the reputation of this part of Columbus Heights. It hadn't been tamed like some other sections, and the last thing he wanted was for his appearance to provoke some kind of action that he would have to answer in kind. He would come out on top, no doubt, but at the expense of becoming more visible than he would like.

Bolan made his way across the street and entered the building. He used the stairs to get to the floor where Heider had his apartment. The stairs reeked of urine and cheap disinfectant, and they were littered with garbage and drug paraphernalia. The noise from the thin-walled apartments seeped into the stairwell. He was glad when he reached the right floor.

The hallway was empty. He could try to break in, but that might alert Heider and might be difficult if the door had a number of locks. The direct approach might just be disarming enough. He rang the bell and waited.

He could feel Heider looking at him through the peephole. He heard a muffled "What is it?" and held up an ID card quickly.

"I've come about your telephone."

"I don't have one," he heard through the door.

"I know. That's what you ordered and why I'm here," Bolan replied. He might have to get violent on the door if Heider suspected anything. But if he wanted to keep a low profile, then he might just open the door.

There was a click of locks and slide of bolts, and the door opened a crack. Two heavy chains kept it in place, and Heider's face was visible in the crack.

"I haven't ordered anything. I don't have a phone and I don't want one. Are you sure you have the right address?"

Bolan reeled off an address from the next block, and looked suitably surprised when Heider corrected him. "Ah, so I have the wrong address. But you are Mr. Heider, right?"

The bearded man was momentarily caught off-guard by that, which was all the opening that the soldier needed. His Tekna knife was spring-loaded on his forearm, and a flex of the muscle brought it to his hand. As the weapon slid into his palm, his arm was already following through. The blade slipped into Heider's abdomen, under the ribs, and tore across as Bolan jerked it savagely.

Heider's mouth dropped open in shock, and the momentum of Bolan's thrust tilted him backward. He fell to the floor, blood spilling around him, allowing the soldier the space he needed to reach around the door and slip the chains from their mounts. He slipped inside and closed the door behind him, pausing to look back through the peephole and see that the hallway was still clear.

He bent over Heider; the man was dead. Bolan extracted the knife. One down. He'd search the apartment, then confront the arms dealer, Younis.

CHAPTER SEVEN

Mummar was becoming Rodney again. It was like being an actor. The idiots in Hollywood thought they were so great pretending to be someone else—they should try doing it when their very freedom and lives depended on it. They had no idea, though Rodney guessed that he had the drop on them because he was acting himself. Or his previous self, at least. It felt like Rodney Fraser was some dude he had read about in history. His previous life was far removed from where he was now.

And where he was now was something pretty spectacular. The more he thought about it, the more his stomach flipped. The plans he had been formulating had been intense, but these new instructions for the cell were a real switch on what they had been working on. His boys he could contact easily enough, but Heider's cell was another matter. Security dictated that they keep apart, with Mummar and Heider as the only link between them. That was why he had helped the fool get an apartment here.

Rodney did not like Heider. He didn't trust him. Not because he doubted that the man was anything less than sincere, but because he was a fool. He had a background in radical politics, and he'd developed what Mummar saw as a liking for sticking his head above the sand and making a big noise to show how important he was. That was the last thing they wanted. What they did want, however, was the knowledge of armament, the group strategy and the working relationships with local arms dealers that none of the others in these cells had. Heider's boys would have been introduced as a matter of course. Mummar and his men were still in the dark. So even though he had the lurking fear that Heider's ego would expose them, he was in no position to do anything other than go along with the fool.

Thinking of Heider reminded him that the man would have returned from his trip by now. He would probably be home soon. His instructions on departure had been to report progress to Mummar immediately on his return. The knowledge that he had recently picked up only made him all the keener to see Heider and pool information.

Mummar looked at his watch, then out the window onto the street and saw a man in a black raincoat leaving. The way the man walked was not like anyone around here. There was something about the way he carried himself that made Rodney uneasy.

If he hadn't heard from Heider in an hour, he would have to go and see if the fool had returned and forgotten the arrangements. He hoped that was all the problem was.

BOLAN RETURNED TO Mount Pleasant by Metrorail. The search of Heider's apartment had yielded nothing. If he was the holder of communication devices in his cell, he was smart enough to keep them elsewhere. Hopefully, Stony Man would have some answers for him.

Right now, the priority was to take out their arms connection. It was dark, but the streets were still alive with people since the stores stayed open late. Hours were as flexible as the lifestyles of the population wanted them. Now that the rain had ceased, the streets were packed with people, making it harder for Bolan to make his way to the back of the store owned by Samir Younis with the same kind of discretion he had managed earlier.

It was still too early for the arms dealer to have left and gone to where his stock was located. The store that was used as cover was still busy, and as Bolan had passed he had seen his target serving customers.

That was good. It would enable the soldier to gain access at the rear with ease and wait for his target. Bolan was over the wall in the same way as before. He scaled the drainpipe and tested the second-floor window he had listened at earlier in the day for alarms. As he'd thought—it was clean. Opening the simple catch was an equally simple task, and he was inside with the window closed within moments. The room was dark and damp, with incense covering the smell of rotting and stale food. The paint on the walls was peeling, and there was a bare table with four chairs and a hashish pipe. Nothing else suggested habitation or use. Bolan listened at the door, noting that business was winding down in the store below, and settled down to wait.

The hours passed, and soon the clamor from below was reduced to the sound of a few people shutting up shop. Bolan listened to the store staff clean up and the owner cash out before going on to his second, more lucrative business.

Younis saw his staff out the rear of the building, and Bolan watched them go from the side of the window. He heard Younis lock up and climb the stairs. Taking the Desert Eagle from its holster, the soldier opened the door leading to the hall and stepped out in front of Younis as he reached the head of the stairs.

"Try it and you die now," Bolan said softly as the shocked arms dealer automatically reached for his own weapon.

At the soldier's tone, he let his hands drop to his sides. "Now take it out carefully and slide it across the floor," he continued, waiting patiently while Younis complied. "I want to see your stock."

"All my stock is here, mister. And the money I took in. That's all there is," Younis said with a ghostly smile.

"Grocers don't usually carry Glocks," Bolan replied wryly. "You know what I'm talking about. You can die here, or you can show me your stock and maybe we can talk."

Younis snorted. "You're a customer? You've got a strange way of doing business, mister."

"Call me careful. I hear you're the best-equipped dealer around here. I need your stock, but not the kind of pineapples you have in the storefront." Bolan sighed at Younis's baffled expression. "Skip it. It wasn't that funny. Take me to the real storefront now, okay?"

"I don't usually have a buyer and myself with no security."

"You don't normally die from a no sale. Let's go," the soldier snapped, leaving little room for negotiation.

They went down to the rear of the building, with

Bolan bearing in mind what Younis had let slip about "security." The arms dealer was expecting to go to his warehouse and so would be expecting his guard. One man or more than one? As they reached the back door and Younis unlocked it, his body language relaxed. Bolan tensed and stepped back, kicking out as he did so. Taken by surprise, Younis tumbled forward, stumbling from the kick he had received in the back of his thigh. He sprawled onto the filthy stone floor of the yard, yelling as he did so.

Two men appeared, framed by the door. One of them was distracted, his attention drawn to his fallen employer and what had caused his fall. The other was square on to the doorway, a dark shape against the faint illumination of the night. His stance told Bolan he was armed, but there was no clue as to his weapon. He hesitated as he tried to sight in the comparative dark of the store. Bolan had no such problem. The Desert Eagle barked, and the guard grunted as he was thrown backward by the relatively close impact of the .357 round. His chest and upper abdomen were ruptured by the heavy slug, and he was dying as he hit the stone.

Younis yelled again, trying to scrabble away, and tore himself from the guard, who was trying to help him. In so doing, he signed the man's death warrant. Off balance and with his employer getting in his way, the guard was unable to draw, aim and fire in the time available. Another bark from the Desert Eagle and he was thrown backward, scored by a hit to the thorax.

The way Younis froze, and the look on his face, told Bolan that they were now alone in the yard. Not for long, though. Gunfire was not rare in D.C., but it would still bring unwelcome attention. Bolan gestured to Younis to get moving, and the arms dealer complied with a posture that spoke of complete submission.

The soldier didn't bother to hide the gun as they made their way to Younis's car. They would be gone soon enough, and any discretion had been lost by the necessity to unleash firepower.

Sirens could be heard in the distance as they drove out of Mount Pleasant, and in less than twenty minutes they were at a small industrial park, where storage units were available for hire.

"You're kidding me," Bolan said as they pulled up. "You've got it in a normal storage facility?"

"What do you people say?" Younis asked without humor. "Something about hiding stuff in plain sight. What else would you do in storage units but store stuff?"

Bolan shook his head in disbelief and indicated that they should get moving. Keeping close enough to his prey but far enough to avoid any attempts at sudden movement, Bolan followed while Younis tapped in the security code at the entrance to the storage facility.

It was brightly lit but empty inside. A maze of crisscrossing corridors housed small blocks of shuttered units. By day, people ran internet sales businesses from units such as these, and the place would be alive. By night, they were long gone, and it was easy for Younis to come and go with impunity—apart from the security camera, which Bolan noted as he looked up. Younis saw it and shrugged.

"I own the building. You think I earn that money and

put myself at risk that easily? What? You think I'm still some village peasant?"

"I think you're smart. You're playing the law enforcement by feeding them scraps and going deeper than you'd have them believe. Now shut your mouth and open your stockroom."

Under Bolan's watchful eye, Younis unlocked the conventional locks on the front of the storage unit and then pulled—with exaggerated care lest it get him shot—an infrared trigger from his pocket, which he used to switch off the alarm system.

When he rolled up the shutter in the unit, it was all Bolan could do to stop himself whistling. The unit was stacked with boxes and cases, some marked and some unmarked. That didn't matter. Bolan recognized the design of many of them, and could pick out the Heckler & Koch, Glock and Uzi cases, the AK-47s and the grenade carriers and the boxes of ordnance for each weapon. There were also cases that he knew carried Semtex, a small quantity of GPU22 and RDX mines. Younis had not been entirely honest with his customers earlier in the day.

"So, you really interested in buying or you going to stand there with a hard-on? I don't have all night."

"I've got the gun," Bolan reminded him.

"Yeah, and you keep us here too long and we take risks. I don't like risk. I sell—I get out quick. Then I'm not going to get raided by law or bandits.'

Bolan wasn't listening. His plan had been to eliminate the arms dealer and torch the arms dump. Let it go up as a warning to other dealers. He clearly hadn't thought this through. The amount of armament in the unit would not only take out the entire storage facility, but might just cause collateral damage to the neighborhood. True, they were fairly isolated here, but why should innocent people, their livelihoods and maybe even homes be at risk?

"Close it up. I think we need to go for a little ride, see a few people with badges who aren't your friends."

Younis's face hardened. "Who are you, man? You're not a buyer. You're not the Feds. What do you want from me?"

"I want you out of business, and I want you to tell some people I know all that you know about the terrorists you've been supplying."

Younis glared at the soldier. His eyes blazed and his flabby body quivered, but there was nothing he could do in his current situation. Slowly, he turned to the unit and made to trigger the shutter release.

Bolan sighed to himself. Of course the man had a weapon secreted for emergencies. He could tell by the way Younis was holding himself that as he triggered the release he was reaching for a gun that was just out of sight. The shutter started to fall, and the arms dealer turned with a Smith & Wesson snubbie in his fist. It wasn't the most powerful handgun, but it still had the advantage of being small, easily hidden and accurate over short distances.

If a person had the chance to use it. Younis was too close to the still partially open shutter to risk a head or chest shot that might pass through at such close range and into the ordnance to his rear. Bolan lowered the Desert Eagle and put a slug through Younis's thigh, aiming downward so that if it ripped through flesh and exited it would be angled into the concrete floor. As he did, he moved swiftly to his left, dodging into the cover provided by the intersection of two corridors. Younis, screaming in pain and frustration as he fell awkwardly to one side, snapped off a shot that went wide of the mark, ricocheting off the metal shutter of the unit opposite and fracturing a strip of neon, blowing out one tube and setting others off to strobe along the corridor.

Bolan cursed. He didn't want Younis to fire wildly again. A ricochet could easily bounce back by chance into the storage unit. Then it was goodbye Younis, goodbye building, goodbye Bolan....

Not on his watch. He stepped out of cover, sighting the prone arms dealer in the flickering light. The air stank of cordite, and a thin film of smoke drifted on and off in the strobe. Blood was pumping from Younis's thigh, and it was slick across the floor as he tried to crawl back under cover of the still slowly closing shutter. The light from inside, constant as it was, formed a pool into which he moved. With an artery ruptured, he would be dead soon enough. It would have been preferable to get some information from him before this, but fate had other ideas. Although the arms dealer still weakly clutched the snubbie, he seemed more concerned with gaining cover than seeing if his enemy was on his back.

Bolan had a clear head shot, and as the man was already prone, he was saved the trouble of working out a downward angle. Younis bled out before the Executioner could take the shot.

He stepped forward and searched Younis for the infrared locking trigger and for his key fob. He found them and triggered the lock. At least the unit would be secured until Hal Brognola could get men down here.

Leaving Younis behind him, Bolan left the storage facility. He took out his smartphone and placed two calls as he walked to Younis's car. One was to Brognola, informing him of what had just gone down. The other was to Stony Man. Information regarding the four men he had seen with Heider had been obtained and was downloaded to him.

He got in the car and gunned the engine, leaving the storage facility to a cleanup team who could handle the ordnance and dispose of Younis. That was the good thing about working in the States: you didn't always have to clean up your own mess. As time was tight, this was an advantage he would need. He drove back toward Mount Pleasant. It was early morning, and even a district with a twenty-four-hour lifestyle had downtime. This was one of them, and it would be easy to dump the car back near Younis's store and put distance between the vehicle and himself.

He needed sleep. He wouldn't get it.

There was too much to do.

BOLAN SAT IN a coffee shop near the Smithsonian. It was 6:00 a.m. He had taken the Metro back across town and needed to take a half hour out to consider his next move. Espresso followed by two cups of black coffee wasn't the best way to start the day, but he needed the jolt to keep him awake until his task was complete.

The Stony Man team had come through with all four

of the men associated with Heider. Two of them had records, and the other two were known by their associa-
tions, although both had so far been clean.

Richard Sahir, twenty-two, was the child of Somalian
refugees. He had served eighteen months for an assault.
Was known to be useful with weapons but, although he'd
been pulled in several times, nothing had stuck. Lived
in Columbia Heights a few blocks from Heider.

Mohammed Kadir, twenty-four, had no record, but
was known to associate with the gang Sahir had been a
member of. Both men had been born Muslim, but had
no known affiliation with any extreme or fundamentalist groups. Kadir also lived in the same neighborhood.

David Soffitt, thirty, had a similar background to
Heider. The move from one kind of extremism to another was not so unusual. It was something about the
psychology, as though they were of a personality type
that could not exist unless they felt they were oppressed
and under threat. He lived in an apartment building on
Logan Circle.

As did Albert Mohan, the last of the four. He was two
years younger than Soffitt and had met him in prison.
His offense had been assault and possession of firearms,
but he was also known to have been a small-time drug
peddler and have gang connections. Like Soffitt and
Heider, he had been a convert to Islam during his prison
period, but, unlike them, he had not adopted an Islamic
name on release and seemed to have returned to his
previous life, although he had seemingly stayed clean.

Bolan paused in thought. He would be paying all four
of these men a visit in the next few hours, but first he

had a question for Kurtzman. He took out his cell phone and hit a speed dial number.

"Morning, Striker. You've been busy, I hear."

"I don't like being idle, Bear, you know that. I have the intel you've collated, and it's very helpful. But it's got me thinking. The last man on my list—Mohan— came out of prison a convert but didn't make a show of it. The others use their adopted names, but he doesn't. You could have put that down to him not being concerned once he was on the outside, but now we know different."

"And you'll be wondering if there are any others who may just be following a similar pattern?"

"Do we run checks like that?"

"By 'we' I assume you mean the NSA rather than any more specialized unit."

"I guess. Any antiterror units, covert or otherwise."

Kurtzman exhaled loudly. "Now that is a question. By their very nature the most covert would be out of bounds. Like us. Noncovert, on the other hand… I can check, but I don't think they do. I know we don't."

"Anyone covert we're not going to know about and we haven't got time for Hal to go through channels. We'll just assume they don't. How long would it take you to do that for the past six months, Bear?"

"How long have I got?"

"How long have I got?" Bolan returned. "I have four targets. It's just past six. I give myself until midday. There are five men out there we need to find, and unless I get something out of any of these four, we're in the dark and on the clock."

"I'll do it. Don't ask me how, but I'll narrow the parameters somehow and get it done."

"Your country loves you," Bolan cracked.

"Yeah, well, it better give me a commensurate pension when this shit finally fries my synapses," Kurtzman replied.

Bolan disconnected and finished his coffee. The four targets lived in two locations, grouped close together. The time traveling between them would be a minimum factor. What would eat into the minutes available to him would be searching their apartments and rooms for any communications equipment or intel of any kind. That could be vital. The thing that nagged at him was whether any of them would actually carry intel. Cells of this kind worked with one man acting as a portal and the rest of the information carried by word of mouth and memory. Any kind of recording was kept to a bare minimum. Maybe a person could get lucky and find a careless cell member who had to note things down because of his memory. If they had been trained, experienced agents or terrorists, that would be a no-no. As they were young men flushed with fanaticism and a bare amount of camp experience, it was a maybe. But a slim one. He would have to hope that one of the four was the contact man for the cell.

But what if none of them was? There were two cells working together. That was unusual. Keeping them separated was a part of the strategy. It was the size of the mission that tied them together: they needed the manpower.

So what if the communications link was in the other cell? The four-man cell that he had no ID for as yet?

What if these four were taken out of the game but yielded no clues to their compatriots? Where would he stand then, with hours left before the strike?

These unsettling questions were dismissed as he left the Metro and hit Logan Circle.

It was time to concentrate on the business at hand.

CHAPTER EIGHT

Mummar looked at his watch. It was now two o'clock in the morning, and he had been sitting in the silent darkness of his room for the past hour, wondering what his next move should be.

It had to have been the man in the black coat. He had looked so out of place in the neighborhood, and there was something about the way that he carried himself that spoke of military or paramilitary training. Mummar would not have recognized it before he had been to any of the training camps. The fools he had met in D.C. had not been like that. Petty hoods and ex-gang members like himself, they had been looser and less controlled in the way they did things, the way they held themselves. But after the training camps, things were very different. Whether they had been through the mill in an army of whatever country of origin or they had been drilled in such camps by men who were ex-army, they had a different way of holding themselves. It was something that Mummar acknowledged that he did not have. He wanted to have that degree of skill and bearing, even though he would have had to work hard to disguise it when in the field. He did not have it, but he sure recognized it, and when he had seen the man a sense of foreboding had lurked at the edge of his consciousness.

As time crept on and he still had no word from Heider, the foreboding grew stronger. The fool should have been home and should have made contact. Although he tried always to stick to the arrangements, Mummar felt an overwhelming urge to go against the grain and go to Heider's apartment. Protocol would be broken, but that was the last thing on his mind at the moment.

Even so, he gave the fool the benefit of the doubt and strung it out until his nerves were too taut to bear. Was he afraid of what he might find? Perhaps that was it. Eventually, even that thought had become too much to stand without knowing the truth. If Heider was there and had forgotten, then Mummar could berate him for the lapse. Better that than the creeping fear that overtook him.

As the darkness descended, the block became more alive. A lot of the people in the area did their business by night, whether it was illicit or just the kind of low-paid menial night jobs that were available to this socioeconomic grouping. The kind of phrase Rodney wouldn't know, but Mummar did and had to keep hidden. Especially as those groups were his people, and the rage that built in him when he thought of it fueled his fight.

His peephole enabled him to see that his own floor was empty before he left his apartment. He wanted to avoid contact, but in truth it was not here but on Heider's floor that he really wanted to avoid being seen. There should be no link between the two men, even of the most casual sort. To give him credit, Heider had always been strong on that aspect of security. But had he slipped up somewhere else?

Mummar used the stairwell, wrinkling his nose at the stench. Silently he made his way to Heider's door. He didn't realize until he was directly outside that he had been holding his breath. He tried to breathe normally and felt the tension make his gut churn.

The apartment door was closed, and when he tapped softly there was no reply, no sound from within when he put his ear to the door. But it was more than that. The apartment seemed void behind the closed door. Not just vacated but sucked dry. It made no sense logically, but it was an instinct that confirmed Mummar's suspicion and made him do something that he would not normally contemplate.

Checking that the hallway was clear, listening for any signs of approaching life, he nodded shortly to himself and took a small slip of celluloid from his wallet. If this worked, then something was wrong. Heider had locks like he had on his apartment, and if he had not yet arrived, or was inside alone, then they would all be secured. That was their training. If the latch was the only lock on the door, then something was very wrong.

Sweating from the effort of controlling himself so that he did not make enough noise to alert the neighbors, Mummar swore softly under his breath as the lock clicked back and the door yielded.

He opened the door and slipped inside, closing it behind him and scoping the hallway through the peephole to check that it was still clear and that he had not been observed. He was immediately aware of two things.

There was a sickly sweet smell that he knew immediately was spilled blood, and beneath the sole of his shoe the thin rug was slick with something that shouldn't be there.

He looked down and saw the dark stain on the rug, and the ragged trail that led back into the main room of the apartment. He knew what he would find before he was even in the room. Heider was in the center of the floor, his jacket and pockets turned out and an idiot expression on his face. His clothes were stained and soaked with his blood. There was nothing dignified in death. Mummar tried to tell himself that as a martyr for the cause Heider would get his reward in the place he had gone to. Heider was dead. Had there been anything in the apartment that had connected them in any way? Was there anything that could connect Heider to the rest of his cell, or to Mummar's? He steeled himself and looked away from the body, scanning the room around him before beginning to search the remaining rooms. The apartment showed every sign of having been thoroughly turned over with no regard for concealing the fact. The man in the black coat had no need to cover his tracks or else did not have time. Unless, of course, he wanted his presence to be known as a warning. All of these things raced through Mummar's mind as he conducted his search in the wake of the intruder.

The flooring and some of the boards had been torn up in every room. The mattress and chair cushions had been sliced with a razor-sharp knife—the cuts were clean enough to tell him that—and if there had been anything incriminating, it had been removed. Mummar was doubtful. They had been careful to keep these things to a minimum, and only he had any communications equipment.

His vision blurred for a moment. Had he been stupid? Had the man in the coat been keeping surveillance, waiting for someone to make a move? He felt so paranoid that he could barely breathe without feeling as though he was giving himself away.

Mummar needed to think. He needed to get the smell of death out of his nostrils and gather himself. He left Heider on the floor and left the apartment in the same mess that the man in the coat had left it. Let someone else clean up. With the same caution that he had exercised on arriving, he made his way back to his apartment.

Part of the tension and nausea in his gut was due to the fact that this man in black had taken out Heider with ease, and he had been within a few hundred yards of Mummar as he did it. Sitting, breathing deeply to try to calm himself, Mummar became Rodney for a few moments.

If this man knew of him, then he would have come for him at the same time. No doubt. So he was panicking because it was on top of him, but he was safe for now because he was still alive. He was the only link now between the two cells. If he wasn't known to the enemy, then he had to assume that the rest of Heider's cell would be. Maybe they would be okay, and would be waiting for their leader's call. Let them. Mummar was the man with the information, and he knew he could do the job with his own cell of four. There were no other links between the two.

Okay. It was time to get out of town. He had to contact his men and mobilize them. The hell of it was that Heider and his cell had been the men with the contacts and the access to arms and explosives. He would have to get his men to the target location and try to pick up the network there, using them instead. It made things tight, but it could be done.

Mummar went to the bedroom, went back and checked his locks again then returned to where he kept the communications equipment. He could take the smartphone, but he could not risk carrying anything else. He sent a message relaying the situation, requesting contacts in the target area. He then took the tablet and the laptop and destroyed them. The hard drives for each he extracted and slipped into a small plastic bag. He would dispose of them elsewhere. They had been wiped, but it would still be possible to retrieve some information. Dispose of them elsewhere and it became harder. He also wrapped the smartphone in a bag.

He had a war chest hidden behind a vent in his kitchen. He took it out and packed a small duffel bag. He wouldn't need much. Truth was, he would soon be dead. Mummar didn't fear death; as a martyr he had become accustomed to the idea. But death before this, at the hands of an enemy, held the same fear that it had always held. It was a paradox he ignored as he left his apartment for the last time.

His task now was to round up the other three cell members and hire a car that they could use to get to the target area by the allocated time.

Like the other members of Heider's cell, the three in

Mummar's all lived close to each other. There was risk in this, but it did allow them to mingle in a way that did not immediately seem suspicious and in an environment where they did not stand out. After all, Mummar had often thought, a man like himself was just another dude around here. In the areas that were middle class or being cleared for the new Washington, he would have been immediately noticeable.

Hide in plain sight. Except it was no longer time to hide: something that the target area and indeed the world would soon know.

BOLAN STOOD OUTSIDE the old apartment buildings on Logan Circle and checked his phone. He had addresses for Soffitt and Mohan. Which one should he visit first? Which one would have communications equipment? Capturing that would be invaluable. The line to the arms dealer had been eradicated. Hopefully, Stony Man would get him some leads on the other cell. More likely he would get it from any intel he could pick up here.

Mohan was nearer. It was still early. Chances were he would catch Mohan and Soffitt before they went to work. If they had jobs. It would be better for their cover if they did, but the ability to hang around a Mount Pleasant grocery store at an hour when they may have been gainfully employed meant they either worked shifts— which could be tricky—or else they had other sources of income. Their social security records showed little to give any indication other than they weren't drawing welfare.

Mohan lived on the second floor of his town house.

It was pink and stood out. Because of that Bolan felt conspicuous as he entered the building. It was simpler than he could have hoped: a lucky piece of timing, head down, and he was inside past someone coming out before they could even cast a second glance in his direction.

The second floor had several apartments leading off the hallway. Mohan was at the far end, with a view that looked out onto the streets rather than the rear of the building. It was run-down, but in a bohemian way rather than having been crushed by poverty. These were mostly middle-class people enjoying the feeling of slumming it. Mohan had to have been conspicuous here, which would mean anyone visiting would be equally visible.

It was quiet inside, people either already gone or still asleep. Hopefully Mohan was one of them. If he had the same security as Heider, then it would be difficult to effect entry without detection.

Bolan walked up to the door and rang the bell, following that up by hammering on the door with his fist. Looking over his shoulder, he could see that the noise had not brought out any curious bystanders. He heard a man approach on the other side of the door.

"UPS delivery for a Mr. Mohan," he said loudly. He jammed his eye up to the peephole so that he could see a little through to the other side. It was indistinct, but he could see Mohan in blurry outline that became a shadow as the man pushed his eye to the lens.

Bolan slipped his Glock 23 from its armpit sling and fired a rapid burst through the wood door. It was a pine door, flimsier than might have been expected from the security-conscious fundamentalists. It splintered under the onslaught. Above the chatter of the bursts, Bolan could hear Mohan splutter and scream as the slugs bit through the wood and carried on into his chest as he stood unsuspecting on the other side of the door.

The locks stayed in place and anchored one side of the door. Two hard kicks with his combat boot split the frame on the hinged side and hit it wide. Mohan was on the floor, gurgling and drowning in his own blood. He was semiconscious, and there was no way Bolan could get anything from questioning him. Not that he had time anyway. Another tap finished the terrorist with a mercy he shouldn't have shown. Bolan moved through to the main room, holstering the Glock and taking out his knife. He sliced through the furniture, tore up carpets and moved on to the bedroom, slitting open the mattress and pillows. He pulled the bed frame out and tore up the carpet searching for loose boards.

Finding nothing and noting the distant sirens that were growing louder, he moved to the bathroom and kitchen. No false tiles in the former, but a vent in the latter that hid a stash of high-denomination bank notes. The cell's war chest, obviously. He left the money in place and routed the cupboards, scattering kitchenware and foodstuffs as he emptied them with a minimum of effort and delay.

Stepping back, he could hear the sirens were in the near distance. Would Soffitt be curious and see where they were going? Would he be on edge enough to get— in this case justifiably—paranoid?

More to the point, empty-handed, how would Bolan make an exit?

From the kitchen there was a fire escape that led up to the roof along the rear of the building. Taking a quick recon to see if anyone had been curious enough to poke their heads out, and to note if the wailing sirens had cut off the back of the building as of yet, he climbed out and went up toward the roof. Down was pointless. He would walk straight into the approaching black-and-whites.

Soffitt was half a block away. If he could get up on the roof, he could cross three or four houses and come down around the back of the circling cops before they had a chance to realize the route he had taken.

Bolan didn't look back. If they were behind him at some point, he'd soon know about it. He ascended to the floor beneath the roof and clambered onto the rail of the fire escape, reaching up to the coping under the gutter and taking a firm hold. He pulled himself up, kicking at the brick to get purchase and push up. He felt his shoulder and biceps strain as he took his full weight and hauled himself upward, hoping that the old mortar and brick wouldn't give way under him.

Breathing a little harder, he flattened himself to the tiles as he was able to scramble onto the roof itself. He felt some of them slip beneath him, but he didn't falter or hesitate as he propelled himself up the angle of the roof, moving across toward the adjoining building as he did so.

The house next to this had a flat roof and was a three-yard drop down. He made the leap, and was glad to be on a level footing as he ran at a crouch toward the next building, which had a two-yard rise toward another ga-bled roof. He cursed that this could have been easier but took a running jump. His fingers clutched at the incline and his toes found purchase in the brickwork. Protest-ing muscles ached as he hauled himself up again. The roof here was slate once more and had an incline more shallow than the first roof, so it was easier to get across. There was a walled gutter that he dropped down to that afforded a little cover.

When he reached the end, there were two more flat-roofed apartment buildings before the row ended, and he dropped onto the first of these before taking a look back and then down. No one had appeared on the roof or the fire escape yet. Moreover, down below, the police were only just decamping into the street that ran along the back of the row.

Bolan dropped off the roof and onto the fire escape of the end building, descending quickly with one eye on the police vehicles that had pulled up a few town houses away. If he was swift enough, he could get into the main drag and vanish in the crowd. By the time at least one of the locals had looked back, he was headed toward the crowd that was gathering out front. His breathing was now easy. He looked like nothing more than the passer-by he had become.

The soldier crossed to the opposite sidewalk and walked past the crowds and police line, casting the brief-est of glances. No one paid him any attention.

It was less than ten minutes to his next destination, which was another apartment building. This one was four stories, with a flat roof. Soffitt lived on the ground floor, and as Bolan approached he saw Soffitt outside the building, talking animatedly to a man he did not recognize. He took out his smartphone and got some footage of the two men from across the street. It wasn't clear as there was some traffic and crowds of people passing between where he stood and the two men opposite. However, there was enough footage for Stony Man to get some screen grabs and run ID on the man Soffitt was talking to. He looked Somali, and Bolan allowed himself the possibility that this man may just be a lead.

He sure hoped so, as the longer he stood talking to Soffitt, the more it screwed with the soldier's timetable, which was already tight enough.

Patience was a virtue that Bolan had learned to live with over a long career, and it stood him in good stead, for he ignored the way his gut was telling him to get across, hustle them both inside somehow and ask a few questions of the Somali and Soffitt, regardless of the dilemma it gave him in Soffitt's execution. Even though he was itching to get on with his task, he held on and was rewarded when the two men seemed to part on less than harmonious terms. Spitting contemptuously into the gutter, Soffitt went back into the house while the Somali walked away, muttering to himself.

Bolan crossed the road and entered the apartment building, the main door of which had been left ajar by Soffitt. He entered with caution, wondering if this had been done as an enticement: a notion that he was soon disabused of when he went farther into the ground-floor lobby and saw that the door of Soffitt's apartment was also ajar, with a backpack standing against the jamb, keeping it open. He could hear the man banging about inside, making little secret of the fact that he was ready to leave. He sounded panicked.

Did he know that Mohan was dead? If not, then why was he about to run? For this looked more like flight than being ready to move out on a mission. It was too obvious.

Bolan picked up the backpack as he went, dropped it inside the door and slipped the latch carefully and quietly so that he was now inside the apartment with Soffitt, who seemed unaware that he was no longer alone. Bolan slipped his knife from its sheath and held it loosely in the palm of his hand. He waited by the door until Soffitt came out of the interior of the apartment. He was moving with a spasmodic intensity that made him almost oblivious to the soldier until he realized that the door was closed. It was only then that he looked up and saw Bolan standing there; Soffitt's blank stare spoke of his shock.

"Who are you?" he asked quietly.

"Someone who wants to ask you a few questions," Bolan returned.

"Questions about what?"

"I think you know. Heider is dead. So is Mohan."

"And I'm next." It wasn't a question. Bolan stayed silent. "There's nothing I can tell you."

"I don't have time. You tell me all you know and maybe you can live."

"What for? To spend years rotting in an internment camp? I know nothing. Heider knew. We were to learn today. If you didn't learn anything from him, then you screwed up."

"You're remarkably calm for a man facing death," Bolan said mildly.

"I'm already dead, and you know it," Soffitt replied. "I have nothing for you. We die for the greater glory of God."

"Then let me rephrase that—you're remarkably calm for a man who won't be dead for the right reasons and won't be residing in paradise with virgins."

Soffitt's face hardened. He could be philosophical about a death he had already prepared for, but to be mocked was something that upset his worldview, and he lost his cool. He lunged toward Bolan with a silent determination.

The soldier was not about to underestimate his opponent. He had his back to the door and so could be pushed into a hard surface, driving the air from his lungs. His opponent had no weapon, but it was fair to assume that he had been taught unarmed combat and had the determination and drive of a man with nothing to lose.

Bolan braced himself, held the knife away from his body and shifted his weight onto the balls of his feet to alter his balance. The hallway inside the apartment was narrow, with less than the width of two people between the walls. Not much room to maneuver, but perhaps just enough....

Soffitt closed on the soldier, his eyes glinting and unblinking, his teeth gritted. He knew he would have just the one chance. He flung his full body weight against Bolan, trying to slam him back into the angle of the wall and door. He found himself up against something that felt like a wall of unresisting granite. He groped for the wrist that held the Tekna knife and closed his fingers around it, trying to force the soldier's hand down and in toward his own body. He found himself grasping something like steel cord as he felt the tendons tighten in Bolan's wrist, forcing his arm back up.

Soffitt was stronger than he looked, Bolan had to give him that. More, he had determination and desperation. The soldier felt himself tense as he exerted his strength against the onrushing fury.

His enemy had made the mistake of putting all his effort into one action and leaving his body open to attack. Everything was in the upper body; the lower was forgotten. But not by the soldier. He brought up his knee sharply and it hammered into Soffitt's groin.

The excruciating pain made Soffit loosen his grip before he had time to react in any other way. Bolan followed up on this advantage by slamming the cupped palm of his free hand under his opponent's chin as Soffitt bent forward, snapping his neck back. Bolan then hit Soffitt across the head with the hand that grasped the Tekna, using the handle as a club.

Soffitt grunted and slumped to the floor. He was unconscious, and the soldier bent and grabbed him, dragging him back into the main room of the apartment. Killing him in the narrow hall would make his exit more cumbersome than was necessary. Once in the room, he dropped Soffitt in the center of the floor and administered a swift killing blow.

The short fight had been conducted in almost complete silence, so he had no reason to fear interruption as he started to methodically ransack the apartment, using the same techniques that he had used for Heider's and Mohan's apartments. He was quick but unhurried, not wanting to miss anything. But if there was anything, it was so well concealed that it would take dismantling the apartment brick by brick to find it.

Bolan finished his task with a sense of frustration. He had now taken down three of the five-man cell, and so far had found no communications equipment, only the banker. There were still two men to eliminate, and so he would get what he wanted eventually. The sooner he gathered intel, though, the sooner Stony Man would be able to piece together an overall plan.

The apartment tossed, Bolan stood in the center of the living room, looking down at Soffitt's corpse and then around him. If only he had been able to take these men in and let them get interrogated at length. But there was no time; the threat needed to be eliminated immedi...ely.

He looked at his watch. Time was tight, and he needed to get to Columbia Heights. Time waited for no man. He was willing to bet that neither did Richard Sahir or Mohammed Kadir.

WASHINGTON WAS AN unusual city in many ways. Its early immaculate planning had been marred by the almost random building of a railway station in the National Mall. By this time, the first slums had already started to develop as speculators tried to make the most of any cheap housing and building opportunities while neglecting the original grand plan of a city full of open space and parkland. Corruption in city hall led to corruption on the streets. This was why there had been legislation at the start of the twentieth century that had led to the relandscaping of the Mall and the Heights of Buildings Act of 1910, which had led to the city having no buildings that were taller than the width of the adjacent street and an extra twenty feet. Popular legend had it that no buildings were allowed construction that were taller than the Capitol building, and it was this oddly worded piece of legislation that made Washington one of lowest-level cities on the continent.

The effect of this was the original layout of the city had not been corrupted by subsequent development. It was still divided into four quadrants that—though unequal—worked on the grid pattern of the original design. The roads included lettered or numbered abbreviations that indicated their geographical direction, while all houses were still numbered according to their approximate number of blocks distant from the Capitol building. This made it one of the easiest cities in the country to navigate, especially given the standard of the Metro system.

Sahir and Kadir lived within two blocks of each other in Columbia Heights, enough distance from Heider to ensure that they would not be seen in too close proximity unless they engineered it. Close enough for Bolan to be careful in the neighborhood. It was less than twenty-four hours since he had been in the locality. Although there was no official record of his existence should DNA or even security camera footage flag him, there were enough black-ops organizations that would know of him. Right now the last thing he needed was interference of any kind. The area was quiet when he left the Metro, and walked briskly to the block where Sahir resided. He was first on the list by virtue of geography, nothing more. Looking up at the blank windows of Sahir's building, Bolan wondered if there were some other means of access. Using the front was risky, and every time he adopted that approach the chances of his cover being blown increased.

The rear of the building had a fire escape. It was also quieter there. Sounds of daytime TV blared out of some windows; distant beats came from others. But no people were hanging around here or using the open windows.

Bolan pulled down the ladder of the fire escape and ascended until he made his way up and along to where Sahir's apartment was located. Access through the window was simpler than he'd expected. It had a simple catch that he was able to trip from the outside. Surprising. He would have assumed that any of the cell would have had the same level of security on the windows as they had on the front doors.

Unless Sahir had left it that way because he had already vacated the apartment.

As soon as Bolan climbed through the window, he knew that this was not the case. He could hear a man moving around in the bedroom, talking on a cell phone. The soldier paused as he listened to the one-sided conversation.

"I know, honey, I know…No, no, don't do— No, don't do that…Listen, I know what you're saying, babe, but that's just whack. You can't mess like that…Why? 'Cause you'll end up iced, sugar!…Because I'm not even supposed to have this damn cell, let alone be talking to you about it…Well, because you understand. Or I thought you did…You knew it would be like this, and you believed as much as me, and now you want to just screw it all off…No, you stupid bitch, you do that and I'll come and slit your throat before you have a chance to talk…Fuck!"

The call ended abruptly. Sahir's rising anger had either reached a pitch or the woman on the other end of the call had hung up on him. Whatever the case, Bolan heard the cell phone shatter against the wall where Sahir had thrown it in fury.

Bolan slipped the Tekna knife back into its sheath and drew the Desert Eagle from the holster at his back. If Sahir had broken protocol enough to have a cell phone, there was every chance that he kept firearms on the premises, too. It made the odds that he was the man with the communications equipment abysmal, which was a pain. The search would be perfunctory, but first he needed to neutralize the threat.

Bolan moved from the kitchen through the hall that bisected the apartment. On one side, the bathroom was empty. Beyond that lay the entrance to the bedroom and to the main room, almost opposite each other. Sahir could be clearly heard in the bedroom. The room opposite appeared to be empty, but Bolan would have preferred being able to check it out before having to turn his back on it.

There was only one option open to him, though he would have to be quick. He slipped a mask from his pocket and then took a smoke grenade, which he primed and tossed into the doorway of the living room.

He heard Sahir curse as the grenade detonated softly and smoke started to fill the enclosed space, swiftly spreading into the hallway and bedroom.

Sahir appeared in the doorway, coughing, his eyes streaming. He was clutching a Beretta 93R, which he brought up as he sighted the man standing at the end of the hallway. He could hardly see him through the rapidly spreading smoke, and his arm waved wildly as he was racked by coughs. The chances of him hitting the soldier were minimal, but that was still a chance too much.

Bolan lifted the Desert Eagle and loosed a single shot that sounded immense in the confined space. It drilled into Sahir's throat and blew it out. He was dead before his body hit the angle between the floor and the front door.

The smoke and noise would draw the police and fire services within minutes. There was little time to lose.

Bolan stepped over Sahir's legs and combed the bedroom. There was a carryall that was half-packed. Nothing in the man's belongings was of any use to him. The floor was pulled up where the gun and the cell phone had been hidden. Nothing else had been stored there. The cell phone itself was useless, and was not a smartphone. Nonetheless, Bolan took the SIM card and stowed it in his pocket.

Even with the smoke slowing him down, he was able to search swiftly as Sahir had done most of the job for him. Money had been hidden in the living room, and there was still open space where bricks had been moved.

Bolan made a quick search of the kitchen on the way out, but there was nothing obvious, and it was safe to assume that Sahir had revealed all his hiding places as he'd stripped the apartment before either setting out on the mission or taking flight.

As the soldier stepped out of the window and onto the fire escape, with the mask still in place to avoid identification, he wondered if Kadir was acting similarly, and if he could reach him in time.

CHAPTER NINE

Mohammed Kadir sat on the edge of the bed, got up again, paced the room then sat once more before repeating the whole process for the fourth time since he had finished packing. The visit he had received fifteen minutes earlier had agitated him in a manner he hadn't thought possible.

Tunje was a good man. That freak Mummar and the fake Sheik Heider would have shit bricks if they had known that he was in communication with both Sahir and Kadir, but what those jerks didn't know wasn't going to lose them sleep.

What Kadir now knew from Tunje could lose him a lot more than sleep. If the brother was right, then it could cost him his life. Why he was getting so stressed over that was a weird one, considering he was quite happy to make himself a human bomb and blow shit up. Maybe it was because this would be his life wasted if some guy took him out before the mission had been accomplished. What would be the point dying before you made the big gesture you had prepared yourself for?

Kadir had been a waster all his life, drifting into petty crime and gang life, getting wasted and only just evading the Feds by the skin of the teeth that hadn't been punched out. It meant nothing. Al Qaeda gave him a purpose. The jihad meant something, meant that he would be using his life to further a great nation and a great people. To be part of something for once. He didn't want to blow it now, not when it was so close.

Mummar had told Tunje they were moving out and that Heider was dead. Plans had changed and they needed to move. Tunje had a rendezvous for his group, but Heider's were to be cut loose. That was okay for Mummar to say. He didn't know these guys like Tunje. Sahir, Kadir and Tunje had been blood. Mohan and Soffitt were outsiders in that sense, but they were still tight. If Heider had been killed and they were in danger, Tunje wasn't going to leave them hanging out to dry. So he had decided to make the rounds and spread the word before heading off.

Only to find that it looked like shit had already gone down: Soffitt was missing, not at home, and Mohan's apartment building was surrounded by Feds. It looked like someone was taking the cell out one by one. Tunje had been relieved to find Sahir and warn him.

Sahir would be okay. Heider had been really insistent on them keeping clean and not having weapons or phones or anything that was incriminating around the house, no matter how well hidden. Soffitt would have stuck to that, the pussy. Kadir was like Sahir, knowing that a little extra security never went amiss round here.

As soon as Tunje had left, Kadir had packed a few things and pulled out the vent duct where he kept his cell phone, piece and stash. He had two grand, a phone and a SIG Sauer P229 with some spare magazines. The piece was rammed down the back of his waistband, the magazines in the pockets of his combats.

He didn't know what to do. His mind was racing, and he couldn't marshal his thoughts into any kind of order. Should he take off on his own or go with Sahir? What did this all mean, anyway? Had they been fingered as part of a cell or was this more random? No—that didn't make sense. Kadir wanted to at least talk to Sahir, who he had always looked up to as the one with more experience and the ability to think clearly.

And now he wasn't there. His phone kept going through to voice mail. If it was still switched off, that would make sense. But he was about to run, and Kadir knew that Sahir would have his phone out, just as he now did.

A gnawing in his gut told him that there was a simple reason it was switched off. Whoever had gotten Heider, and maybe Soffitt and Mohan, had now gotten Sahir. That meant he knew who they all were. It was only a matter of time before whoever the hell it was came for him.

So why was he sitting here like some fool?

Kadir stood up again, muttering to himself lists of things to do, options he could take in running and where to run. He nodded several times, took up his backpack and checked for the tenth time that everything was inside. He patted down his pockets and reached behind him to check that the gun was still there, even though he could feel the metal in the small of his back.

Kadir was ready to go. He had a cousin upstate who wouldn't be pleased to see him unannounced but wasn't the type to complain. He wondered if Sahir had gotten away and was just being cautious, and if he would go with his woman or alone? He thought of anything to distract from the feeling that Sahir, too, was gone.

Still muttering to himself, he left the apartment without looking back. He was preoccupied with where he was headed and forgot all the security checks that had been hammered into him as he left the building.

BOLAN WAS CLOSE enough to identify the man as he turned the corner and walked toward the apartment building. Maybe Kadir was going to save him a lot of trouble by leading him to the other cell. Certainly, from the way he was walking with purpose, and from the fact that he had a backpack, it would seem that the soldier had caught up with him just in time.

The Executioner fell into step at the rear of the terrorist, keeping people between them. Kadir did not look back and seemed to be walking with a determined stride, the posture of a man with purpose and destination.

Bolan was torn. Should he try to isolate the target now and extract as much intel as possible before executing him, or should he keep the tail and see if the target led him to members of the other cell?

He took out his smartphone to check messages. Stony Man had downloaded intel to him regarding the Somali he had seen talking to Sahir before he had taken him down. This could be the deciding factor. The man was Tunje Banjo, which was assumed to be a false name as it was more common as a Nigerian name rather than Somali. With one eye on his target as the man entered the Metro, Bolan scanned the intel about Banjo that had been forwarded to him.

Banjo had a similar background to Sahir and Kadir in that he had been in the country as a refugee since he was a child and had grown up in Columbia Heights, where he had been known to associate with the same gangs as both men. Like them, he was a relatively recent convert to Islam, and also like them it had been a conversion fueled by a radical preacher rather than the mainstream of the religion.

It was the section on his known associates that really rang alarms, one of them in particular. Rodney Fraser was a small-time hood who had converted while in a prison gang but had reverted to his birth name when outside and seemed to have turned his back on Islam. The fact was, no one turned his back on his gang, no matter his religious calling, unless that gang had reason for leaving the person alone. Fraser had the hallmarks of someone going into deep cover, and chances were he had fallen through the cracks.

His address clinched it. Fraser lived in the same block as Heider. It was a good bet that he was the link between the cells—or one of them, at least. Banjo was obviously another link. These two men were joined on the associate list by three others who were known to have close links as gang members or past activity.

Five men: the size of the other cell he was seeking. If Bolan was having a lucky day, then maybe Kadir was leading him to the others as they set out on their mission. There was one nagging doubt. If so, then why did it appear as though Kadir was headed for the airport when the mission was supposed to be in D.C.?

Unless Bolan's actions had precipitated a split between the two cells or a splintering so that each man was taking flight for a later, arranged meet.

Bolan stayed one car down, people between himself and his target so that the man was unlikely to eyeball him. The soldier kept the target under observation, and what he saw was far from encouraging. Kadir shifted uncomfortably in his seat, trying to avoid eye contact with those around them and glaring at any who did meet his gaze. He kept trying the cell phone he was holding, cursing and looking at it irately when it elicited no response.

This was no man headed toward a purposeful rendezvous. This was a man in flight, and he could be dangerous to innocent bystanders even before he was approached by Bolan, or by any security or law enforcement officers whose attention he would inevitably draw.

The soldier had to find a way to draw him off before they reached the airport, to isolate him so that he could be taken down without risk to others. Logic said that if he was headed for the airport, then he wasn't armed. Logic had nothing to do with the state of mind of this young man. They were two stations from the airport when fortune favored the soldier. While he had been seeking a strategy for isolating the terrorist, the Metrorail itself presented him with an opportunity. By fluke, the car in which Kadir sat had been gradually emptying, while the one in which Bolan stood had remained almost full. Now the last passenger other than the terrorist disembarked, while those embarking avoided the car altogether. This, then, was his chance. As the doors began to close, Bolan seized his opportunity to slip out of the full car and into the one that contained Kadir. As the doors closed and the train moved off from the station, Bolan found himself alone with his target. It was less than ideal, as they could be seen from adjacent carriages, which also carried the risk of collateral damage in the event of the terrorist being a walking bomb. In truth, though, the soldier had little real option but to act immediately.

Kadir did not, at first, notice that there was anyone else in the train car with him. He was still muttering to himself, staring at the cell phone that still refused to respond. It was only when he felt the soldier's eyes boring into him that he looked up. Shocked, and seeing in the face of the man slowly approaching him an expression that betrayed his professionalism, Kadir scrambled to his feet and groped at the small of his back to take hold of the SIG Sauer. He was nowhere near quick enough at the best of times, less so now when he was so anxious and distracted. Before his fingers could close on the butt and trigger guard, Bolan had drawn his Desert Eagle and trained it on the terrorist with a two-handed grip to allow maximum accuracy as the train car rocked on the rails.

"Just bring your hands out where I can see them and I won't blow you away," the soldier said firmly and clearly. He was not happy about having to draw a weapon where he could be plainly seen from the other cars. One way or another, there would be a welcoming party at the next station that he would have to deal with. Kadir, meanwhile, had slowly brought his hands around, holding them palms down away from his body.

"You're the man who's been taking us down? How many you got, Mr. Fed? You get my man Rich?"

"Sahir's dead. He went down fighting, if that means anything to you."

Kadir grinned. "Yeah, that sounds about right. I should blow you and this train all to hell."

"You won't. You haven't got the ordnance."

"You taking quite a chance, Mr. Fed. How do you know I'm not wired up?"

Bolan's lips quirked. "Nice bluff. You didn't get any explosive or grenades from Younis, and he was your contact."

"Smart, Mr. Fed. What if I told you we had a bomb factory?"

"Sure, you might have had training in making explosives. If you were doing that, why did you need Younis for anything other than guns? No, you weren't going to risk being traced by a grocery bill. It's safer and quicker to use Heider's contacts, right? Except he's dead. Younis is dead. They're all dead except you. Now you're headed toward the airport with a piece in your back. Why? You can't get past security like that. So what's the plan? You meeting there because it's one of your targets?"

It was a long shot, didn't tally with anything else he knew, but the soldier needed to force the issue in some way as the Metrorail ate up steel to the next station. His bluff about knowing Kadir was not wired had paid off, so why not this?

"Man, you are so stupid, Mr. Fed. You think I'd be so stupid myself as to lead you to the target area?"

"Maybe…if you were panicking. Unless you were panicked because you'd been cut loose and were running for cover."

A flicker of fear crossed Kadir's face, telling Bolan he had hit a nerve. This was a dead end as far as the second cell was concerned.

"That's it, right? Banjo warned you about me because the other cell knows I'm on your tail, but they don't want me to mess up their plans. And you're heading for the hills like a scared kid because they won't back you up."

Kadir didn't say a word. He didn't have to; his face told Bolan all he needed to know. Just as it told him that the terrorist had faced up to his inevitable demise and was going to go out fighting. Arms flailing, Kadir reached for the gun in the waistband at the small of his back and tried to pull it out and snap off a shot. The sudden movement against the momentum of the train made him stumble and fall as he pulled the weapon free.

He didn't stand a chance. Bolan's steadied firing hand followed the arc of his fall, squeezing the trigger as the terrorist pulled the SIG Sauer free. The Desert Eagle boomed over the rattling of the train and Kadir dropped his weapon as the shot took him in the chest.

The SIG Sauer rattled a rhythm of its own as it skittered across the carriage, far from the terrorist's grasp. Kadir lay on his back as the soldier approached him, training the Desert Eagle on him, ready to snap off a follow-up shot if the first had not completed the task. As Bolan stood over Kadir, he saw the light extinguish in his eyes as the terrorist headed for whatever hereafter was reserved for those who failed their mission.

Satisfied that the threat had been eliminated—and with it the last of the five-man cell taken down—Bolan holstered the Desert Eagle as the train slowed and rolled into the station. He turned toward the doors facing the approaching platform, knowing that he had accomplished half the mission, but that time was ticking down on the second half, and he was still no nearer to pinning them down.

Time: the one thing he was short of, and the one thing that was guaranteed to be denied to him. Passengers with cell phones had done their duty as citizens, and the platform was cleared of all but armed law enforcement as the train came to a halt.

Bolan held up his hands as the doors opened and the first commands were barked at him.

It took less than two hours for Bolan to be freed from the moment he lay facedown on the station platform. He had allowed himself to be searched and his small armory taken from him. He had a wallet but no ID of any kind. He was manhandled into an armored transport and taken to a downtown location. There was something about the attitude of the men who detained and escorted him that suggested they were holding back, were wary of him in some way.

It wasn't really surprising when he considered it. Some of the hardware he was carrying was extremely hard to get on the open market. The lack of ID and his bearing had an effect, even though the men detaining him should not have been swayed by that. And, in truth, the fact that he had taken down an armed man who was Somali perhaps made them wonder who the mystery man really was. It was a dangerous assumption. Still, given the tight schedule fate was putting him on, Bolan was glad of any slack.

He sat in a room with an armed guard for most of the time, stripped to the buff and wearing a whitesuit while his clothes were taken for analysis. They wouldn't even find a laundry mark to identify him by, though there would be enough DNA to link him to four other deaths—unless Kurtzman had had enough time to doctor various internet files. The two men assigned to guard him said nothing, refusing even to make eye contact. He had coffee, which suggested someone had an inkling whose side he was really on.

It was a question of two things: Would this get through to Hal Brognola, and if so how long would it take? The President knew of the mission, but culpability ended way before then.

When the major in charge of the operation entered the room and indicated to the two guards to leave them alone, Bolan knew that Brognola's network had been keeping busy. The major was younger than Bolan, still fresh faced and with glittering hard eyes. A dedicated career man and a good soldier to rise so swiftly. Bolan was glad to be talking to a man whose demeanor told of his capabilities.

As he sat, the major pushed another coffee across the desk and sipped his own.

"My one vice," he said blandly. "I didn't know if you

wanted another, but figured this waiting was frustrating you." He waited until Bolan had thanked him and taken the fresh coffee before continuing. "I don't know exactly who you are, but you've taken out five men in just under twenty-four hours without anyone catching up with you, and you have some very important friends who have their ears close to the ground. Now I don't know, but I'm guessing you're black ops. And it doesn't take a leap of imagination to figure that the men you've eliminated were not so innocent."

Bolan remained silent. The major nodded.

"Fair enough. My orders are to turn you loose. Your clothes are on their way here, and all the hardware and ordnance you were carrying is also en route. My orders don't stretch further than letting you walk out the door, but I figure if you haven't finished yet you might be open to some transport. I could let you get the Metro, but y'know." He finished with a wry smile.

"I appreciate the offer, Major. I don't know where we are right now, but I need to be in the Columbia Heights area as soon as is humanly possible. More so, if you can run to that."

"I can try," the major returned with a quirk of the brow. "It's a—uh—busy area right now, I'd say."

"It is."

The major nodded. "Listen, soldier, as soon as your clothes and ordnance come, I'll get you a car and a driver if you want one. Unmarked."

"Of course. Thank you, Major."

Without another word, the younger man rose and left the room, leaving Bolan alone. The soldier sat and sipped his coffee, seemingly calm but still having to quell the impatience rising within him. Things were in progress; he just had to wait.

It seemed like hours but was only minutes before a young man entered with Bolan's clothes over one arm and a plastic bag with his hardware grasped in the other. He nodded briefly as he dropped them on the table, then left Bolan alone to dress and secrete away his armory. Checking his smartphone, the soldier could see that it was now past noon. He would likely be chasing shadows, but at least if he was quick he may be able to pick up a trail. He could also see that Brognola had left him a brief message: Don't make me have to do this again.

Smiling to himself, Bolan finished his preparation and waited for the major or one of his men to return. He knew that the room had to have cameras and he had been monitored. Sure enough, within seconds the door opened and the major entered.

"I have a car waiting for you. There is a driver if you want one. If you're unfamiliar with D.C., he might save you some time. He can drop you off wherever you want and is under orders not to ask questions or follow."

Bolan nodded. "Thank you. Lead me to him."

Half an hour later, the driver dropped Bolan in Columbia Heights. The soldier watched him go before turning and heading toward where he hoped to pick up the trail.

CHAPTER TEN

Bolan stood inside the vacated apartment and cursed to himself. Rodney Fraser—Mummar al-Jaheeb by any other name—lived in the same apartment building as Heider. He had been one floor away from his prey all the time. If only he had been able to make the connection between Banjo, Fraser and the other cell quicker.

The apartment building was still crawling with CSI teams and detectives who were following up on the death of Heider. Little did they know that the perp stood in the same building as them, completely unconcerned by their presence. Well, to say that he was completely unconcerned by their presence was not entirely true. He suspected that their presence had hastened the departure of the man who had become his target just a fraction too late. The very visible signs of their activity in the building would also deter anyone coming near who may have been able to supply a lead of some kind. Bolan had little doubt that the cell led by Fraser had decamped en masse.

Banjo had been warning the others and had made himself scarce. However, it was certain that there was a community of activists in the political and religious underground of D.C. that was tight-knit, and that Fraser, Heider and company had been a part of that. The spate of deaths for which the soldier had been responsible had no doubt caused ripples, if not waves, of alarm through the underground. If fortune had favored him, there was every chance that Bolan might have been able to run into a small-time activist who knew more than perhaps he thought.

Not now; not with D.C.'s finest trampling through the corridors of the apartment building and attracting crowds of curious onlookers on the street beyond. Anyone with something to hide would turn and walk the other way as soon as he came within a block. The soldier himself had been forced to approach the building from the rear. The front was buzzing with police activity, and as a matter of course anyone entering was questioned as to purpose. Fraser had led an admirably spartan life. The kitchen was stocked with healthy foods and nothing else. The bathroom and the living area had been clean and free of clutter. A few books, mostly on religious philosophy and motor mechanics, were on a shelf. There was a small TV. No music, no pictures on the walls. The chairs and futon were hard and functional. The table was scrubbed clean, which may have been less a desire for cleanliness than a need to scour away any evidence of chemicals used in bomb making, and under the rugs the floorboards had been varnished and polished.

There had been only been the one hiding place in the wall in any of the rooms. Whatever had been behind the vent had not been big enough to be ordnance of any power. Bolan's guess was that it had held cash. It was only when he reached the bedroom that he had found any kind of evidence that there had been concealed incriminating materials. Even then, he could only guess at what they might have been, as there was no physical evidence to clue him in. He doubted that it was ordnance, as the supply chain seemed to point, for both cells, toward Heider. His guess was that Fraser was the contact man with the wider web of al Qaeda cells that spread across the United States. A laptop, a cell or smartphone, perhaps all three: it didn't need much to keep the ether open for contact. Certainly, the space he had found suggested that it was nothing much bigger than one or both of those items that had been concealed. Fraser had taken the items with him, and had no intention of returning as he hadn't even bothered to replace the rug, floorboards and the bed when he had removed these objects for the last time.

The trail seemed to run cold here. There was nothing that could give him a clue. Fraser, Banjo and the other men in their cell had gone. The question was to where. So far, from the intel he had been given, the assumption was that the strike was to be in D.C. The targets had been known.

But what if that was a blind, designed to plant a false trail?

Or what if this had been a genuine target, but there had been another set of targets that had been planned in parallel? A plan that could either be used by another cell at a later date or put into operation if it became necessary to switch from one target to another because of a radical change in circumstance?

Fraser, Banjo and the two men as yet unidentified—what if they were not just running or regrouping to come back and hit D.C.? What if there was another target, and they had simply switched to plan B?

It would make sense. When he had picked up Heider at Reagan National, the target had been returning from New York City. He had seemed to be doing very little there from the intel received. It appeared to be nothing more than a social visit. Maybe it was. But maybe it was more.

What if there was another target, and that was in New York? It was a long shot to make an assumption based on nothing more than a hunch and the fact that his initial target had been coming in from that city. But maybe he could back this up. He had the SIM card that he had taken from Sahir's phone just a few hours earlier. He had almost forgotten it. Bolan reached into his pocket and took out the SIM. It was still in the small plastic bag that the military had stored it in. He walked across the room so that he was by the window and in the best possible light. He could see the street below and the seemingly aimless movements of the police units as they went about their business, seemingly because each of them had a precise function to perform. He followed the line of a man in a whitesuit as he tracked a bag of evidence across to the van in which it would be sealed until it reached the labs. The van was parked under a streetlight, and Bolan noted it was the light at which he had paused the night before, prior to entering the building and eliminating Heider.

If Fraser had been sitting at the table or standing by the window, the soldier would have been in clear sight to him. Considering the state of almost paranoid awareness in which the terrorist undoubtedly lived, Bolan felt almost sure that he would have been tagged. Fraser was a trained soldier, albeit of a different sort. Bolan had little doubt in his mind that his presence had probably alerted Fraser to danger the previous evening.

It was too late for recriminations.

He took the back off his own phone and slipped out the SIM before replacing it with the one he had taken from Sahir.

As a network SIM that had been simply bought over the counter, it could be used in any handset as long as the handset itself was not network locked. Although Bolan's smartphone had any number of security measures put in place by the team at Stony Man, it was not network locked, so that the soldier could switch SIM cards with impunity if circumstance dictated.

The SIM carried little information. It took the soldier very little time to scroll through what it contained. There were some numbers saved to the directory, though most of these were attached to female names. Fraser— as himself or as Mummar—was not on there. Neither was Banjo. In truth, it would have been hoping too much for a schoolboy error like this. There were no saved text messages, though there were some photographs: Sahir with women, with a man who looked like Banjo in an apartment that looked like the one in which Sahir had met his end. One of Banjo in conversation with a gaunt and serious-looking Fraser. He had lost weight and aged since his prison shots, but there was still no mistaking him.

Everyone made an error from time to time, no matter

how careful he or she was. Sahir's was a random mistake. He had assiduously cleared the call directory of every call he had received and every call he had made. But he had forgotten to clear the directory of missed calls. There were seven, three from the same number that was identified as one of the women on the directory. One was an unknown number. Presumably this had been a blocked landline number. No matter—it was not easily traceable.

This left three calls with two numbers that had been stored. The single missed call from one number had been several weeks ago, and Bolan wondered if that would yield a worthy result. The hair on the back of his neck bristled at the other number. It was a cell number, and the call had come twice in the past four days, each time in the early hours of the morning. Banjo was the link between the two cells. Banjo was a friend of Sahir. Was it too much of a leap of faith to hope that this was his cell? To hope that it was Fraser's was a step too far, but this was a distinct possibility.

Bolan slipped the SIM out of his phone and replaced his own. As soon as the phone had rebooted, he hit speed dial for Stony Man.

"Striker, I notice you slipped off the radar for a couple of minutes there. After your interesting meeting with the military, I wondered what escapade you had managed to embroil yourself in this time."

Despite himself, Bolan grinned. "Bear, you have really got to stop trying to read your way through the Bond books. No amount of wishing is going to make your job like Q's or M's."

"Striker, the way Hal talks to us sometimes, I think we're searching for the letter past *Z*," Kurtzman replied with good humor. "But enough banter. You didn't call for idle chitchat."

"There's something I really hope you can do for me."

Briefly the soldier outlined his situation to Kurtzman and reeled off the number that had been on the SIM card. There was a pause while Kurtzman ran it through a database.

"Interesting…" he murmured. "There's been a lot of activity on that number, and mostly during the early hours of the morning in this time zone. It's not registered to anyone by name, as you'd expect, but I've got to say I do love the Scandinavians."

"I'm sure you've said that before, and I've no doubt you're going to tell me why once again," Bolan replied as he watched the D.C. police clean up outside the apartment building. The main teams would be gone soon, which was a tacit reminder of how time was moving on.

"Well, now," Kurtzman said, warming to his theme, "the man who invented GPS was a smart soul. It's a very useful tool, and of course in a democracy there should always be the option for the user of the phone to switch off that GPS so that they can have complete privacy and anonymity if they wish."

"That seems reasonable to me. You're going to tell me that whoever owns the phone with that SIM in it has turned off the GPS."

"Indeed they have."

"And you're going to tell me that it makes no difference at all, aren't you?"

"I've run through this with you before, haven't I?" Kurtzman sighed. "Indeed, they have turned off their phone but, as you're probably well aware, it makes not the slightest bit of difference as the handset itself also carries a tracker so that it can be located by the manufacturer. Cross-referencing the signal from the SIM when it was in use and the handset in which it was placed, I can tell you exactly where the possessor of that number is at this present moment."

"And you can be certain that the SIM is still in the phone you have a trace on?"

"Striker, have I ever struck you as the slapdash type? The correlation between the handset and the SIM is consistent throughout all records of use. The owner of the phone has always used the same handset. And whoever it is, he is now headed toward New York City. He's on Amtrak by the look of this route, so maybe you could get a jump on the person by getting yourself airborne. Only try to avoid Reagan National—the sight of you might make the security guys a little jumpy."

"Funny."

"I would have thought you were more of the comedian of late. The way you've got Hal shouting and cursing over the past couple of days has certainly been making me laugh—when I haven't been ducking for cover. I believe he has some issues with you over your understanding of the terms *covert* and *low-key*," Kurtzman replied with some relish.

Bolan smiled to himself. "Hal shouldn't worry. He's got the President's blessing on this one. Whatever happens in D.C., he's got his back covered. Me, on the other hand… Being pulled in and then released is one thing, but it's getting too close for comfort as to whether or not they'll shoot first and ask second. It might be a good time for me to head out of town."

"Any idea why they're headed for New York?" Kurtzman asked, suddenly serious as he changed the subject.

"It's only a feeling—instinct, I guess—that got me chasing that cell phone. I figure they've got a second set of targets, but what they might be…"

"How can you be sure they're not just running to regroup?"

"It's a possibility, but we've not got too much experience of these kinds of attacks in the U.S., Bear. We've been lucky. They've had more of this in the United Kingdom, and it's always followed the same pattern since the 7/7 attacks in London, even though their security services have managed to avert any real damage. The cells have at least two sets of targets, to be activated at the same time. Maximum confusion and collateral damage are the objectives. Because of the intel we had, we just assumed that there was only one set of targets for the D.C. cells. But if that was the case, why risk putting two cells in contact when the usual MO is to keep them separated and unable to form an evidential chain? I assumed this was correct, and then figured that they had a plan B set of targets. But what if that was wrong, too, and all the time there had been a set of D.C. targets and a set of New York City targets?"

"Then why no intel for the New York targets? How could we pick up on one and not the other?"

"That's just it. The only reason we had one set of

targets and any intel at all was because of something I came across entirely by chance. What if the Somalis only had so much information that they were storing and passing on? The way al Qaeda works is reliant on keeping information piecemeal. Why should this have been any different?"

"You've sold me. Bet you'll sell Hal and the Man, too. The problem that leaves us with is how can we get the jump on the cell. We can send out a team and either pick them up or eradicate them. We have the GPS from the phone handset."

"That's assuming they're all traveling together. It would be a fair assumption, but if we're wrong, that still leaves one or more terrorists running around New York City with a target in mind that we have no knowledge of."

"I can keep them—some of them, at least—tracked. The next thing—"

"Is to get me a flight to New York double-time," Bolan finished. "I want to be there when they get there. If there are four of them, they get taken down. If there's less, then I use those who are there to find the missing."

"And then?"

"And then I take them down, too."

MUMMAR WAS PLEASED with his progress. Not so pleased with Banjo, who sat opposite him. The younger man was squirming in his seat, looking out the window or at a newspaper. Anything, in fact, to avoid meeting Mummar's eye.

"It was stupid. Really stupid," Mummar said softly,

so that his words would only carry across the narrow table between them and not be heard any farther beyond the rattle of the tracks.

"C'mon, man, you can't give me shit for that," Banjo complained, shifting to avoid eye contact. "We're solid, man. I just couldn't leave it like that. If the Feds were on to them, I had to give them a chance to get their asses out the firing line."

Mummar's eyes were cold as they fixed on Banjo. "You stupid kid, you just don't get it, do you? This isn't some stupid game. We don't have 'friends' anymore—we only have comrades. We look out for each other's backs in battle, but we have no time for sentiment. Each man should know that he is expendable and that he should lay down his life for his comrades and—this is the important bit, shithead, so listen well—the cause. That is what we live and die for. The greater glory of God and the furtherance of his will."

"Shit, Mummar—"

Mummar made to bring his fist down hard on the table, then stopped himself, aware of the attention the noise would draw to them. He was quivering with rage.

"You jackshit mother," he whispered through clenched teeth. "I am Rodney Fraser while we are on this train and when we reach our destination. I am only my true self when we are behind closed doors. How difficult is that for you to understand?"

"Well, I'm sorry, Mr. Rodney Almighty Fraser, but maybe I'm a bit stressed because some bastard Fed is going around wasting my friends. They want to die, that's one thing. They get killed before they can do the right thing, then that's some other piece of shit altogether."

"As long as you're not going chickenshit on me and trying to back out, Tunje. Because if you are, I swear to you that I will off you myself before we reach New York, and no one will be any the wiser."

"I would have run like my man when I had the chance if that was the case. I believe, and don't you ever doubt me," Banjo said softly but with a brittle hardness to his voice that brooked no argument.

Mummar studied him hard, his gaze raking his face and searching for any sign of weakness. He had to be fair. He asked the important question, and Banjo had answered with a determination and steel that he had started to doubt. He held the younger man's stare for some moments before nodding briefly.

"That's good. All I need to know. But your action— no matter how good the intention—has made things difficult for us. We've set in motion something that we can't stop now. It's not going off as I wanted. We should have traveled by van, all four of us, so that we could keep together and arrive at the rendezvous in one unit. That was why I hired the van. But you screwed that up, Tunje. I couldn't risk you being followed and blowing all four of us out the water. That's why I sent them ahead and waited for you. That's why we're on a train that could be stopped at any point by the military. We're taking a massive risk."

Banjo looked suitably abashed. It was an irony that neither man realized that the younger man's actions had inadvertently aided them by making them split. To

Mummar, it was just an inconvenience to a plan that he
had meticulously timetabled, and that was now in danger of going off the rails, if only in part because they
were now on rails of a different kind.

Mummar's thoughts turned to the other two men,
who were now hitting the blacktop across state borders
in order to reach the target city by deadline time. They
were solid, closer to him in age than Banjo. The young
men who believed themselves gangsters were always
the weakest links. In that sense he was glad that he was
babysitting Banjo. The two men he had cut loose had
served time, like himself, and could handle themselves
in an emergency without giving too much away. He
wasn't so sure about Banjo. He did not doubt his word,
but his actions suggested that he was not in as much
control of himself as he may have believed.

He looked away from his companion and out the window at the landscape that was speeding by. He was unaware of the other passengers on the train—had been
since they had boarded—and paid no attention to the
staff or the rolling stock that would get him to his destination. It was as though the rest of the world did not
exist. There was only himself and Banjo…

And their ultimate goal.

CHAPTER ELEVEN

Bolan stood on the concourse at Pennsylvania Station, studying the boards and the arriving passengers. He didn't expect to see Fraser or Banjo magically walk in front of him. In fact, he felt a little frustrated at being here rather than getting down to some more productive activity.

"We have eight points within the complex where men with headsets and smartphones linked to the CCTV system can pick up anyone highlighted by the facial recognition program that has the data inputted from your people. Once we have them on a positive ID, then the nearest man can pick them up and tail them until you rendezvous and take over. Our orders are to defer to you at that point and let you lead the way. We're there as backup if you want, but I got the distinct impression that you don't want it."

Bolan nodded. "Don't take it personally, Andrew. The Bureau is best equipped to handle this part of the operation, and you were able to implement these measures damn quick, for which I'm grateful. Thing is, this is a job where 'need to know' doesn't even start to cover this op."

"I want to ask, but I'll refrain," the young man beside him replied with some humor. Bolan had met Andrew Low a few years prior, when he was just a field operative. The young man had risen swiftly within the Bureau, which was testament to his resources and also his ability to know what—and what not—to ask. Hal Brognola had used him several times for operations within New York City, and the Bureau always deferred to the big Fed when he came calling.

"You know what train they're supposed to be on?" Low continued, changing the subject.

Bolan checked his watch. "Due in fifteen."

"I'm surprised you didn't get that flyboy chopper pilot of yours to drop you on the top of the train and do a James Bond on their ass," Low said, deadpan. "It would have saved time."

Bolan shrugged. "Jack was busy. Besides, there might be others I need to track," he added on a more serious note. "By the way, that was some driver you sent to Stewart International. Got me here in one piece and one hell of a time."

"It would have been simpler if you'd chosen a better airport, but then again you don't tend to do simple, do you?"

"Andrew, you find a way of getting a charter flight that can land without getting noticed at LaGuardia or Kennedy, and I'll save your drivers some gas. I'd prefer to do simple…. It's these other bastards who make it difficult."

"Fair point. Damn these terrorists for making life hard."

Bolan looked at him. "Okay, I'll give you that. We are looking for terrorists. Beyond that, I can't tell you much."

"Because it's too secret even for the Bureau?"

"Because I don't know much more myself," Bolan replied. "We knew they were in D.C. One cell has been eradicated, but we only uncovered the identities of two of the other cell when they broke cover to run. We know it's a four-man cell. Add to that, we know we're two men blind and we also have no idea of target specifics. Only that it's here in the city."

Low nodded. "I get it. Now, if you'd told me that…"

"You live here, Andrew. What would you go for?"

Low shrugged. "The last time they hit NYC they went for something that was not just a big collateral target, but had a symbolic resonance. The Twin Towers were something that was so identified with this place. Short of bombing the Empire State or the Chrysler, maybe Central Park…though what that could achieve, only God knows."

"According to them, He does," Bolan said sourly. "I know our boys have looked at military targets, but that could be damped down, and besides there's nothing that major. They're looking for a big splash. The targets they had lined up for D.C. were national monuments and had governmental importance."

Low exhaled sharply. "Supreme Court, maybe. Manhattan Municipal Building or city hall, perhaps—though those are not national."

Bolan checked his watch, then the Amtrak boards. The train on which the GPS had tracked the hot phone was about to pull into the platform. The soldier turned to Low and was about to speak when he was stayed by the look on the young man's face: it was a mix of realization and disgust.

"Cooper," he began, knowing Bolan only by the cover name he had used for some time, "I think I know what they'll go for. Freedom Tower is almost finished construction, and the World Trade Center Museum is about to open. You hit those and the memorial, and you don't just cause collateral damage—you know how many are visiting the sites already?—but you hit at the heart of what we lost on 9/11. You twist the knife in front of the whole world."

Bolan's lip curled. "Should have seen that.... I've been thinking of something that could cause economic or military damage as well as personal and symbolic. But why not that? Hit there and you break spirit. Any domino effect from that is a bonus. We need to get on their asses." He indicated the Amtrak board.

Low nodded, almost visibly shaking from the temporary inertia his disgust had caused him. "Keep frosty," he said softly into his headset. "Train's in—start recon."

Pennsylvania Station was never still. Even at the quietest times people were always flowing in and out and across the concourse. Some times of day were, inevitably, busier than others. This was such a time. Bolan was grateful for the men who were linked to the CCTV and carefully positioned, as it was by no means clear which streams of human traffic were headed where. So much the better: the last thing he wanted was for Fraser or Banjo to recognize him. He had nothing concrete on which to base the assumption that they would, but his instincts told him that Fraser, at least, had seen him from his window.

As the people streamed past them, each lost in their

own worlds and wrapped up in their own preoccupa-
tions and problems, Low and Bolan stood like islands,
still and calm, waiting for word.

It was not long in coming.

"Third sector, Devlin reporting," crackled over the
headset. "I've got the two targets in sight. They're
headed for the subway and they're not onto me. I have
taken up position in train and am following."

"This way," Low said simply as he set off through
the crowds, carving a path toward the section of the station that was being covered by Agent Devlin. Bolan followed in his wake.

They caught up with Devlin as he reached the street
and was headed toward the subway entrance. His eye
caught Low's and he indicated briefly with an inclination
of his head. Bolan followed his line of sight and saw a
man he recognized—even from behind—as Banjo disappear down the stairs leading into the subway station.

Without a word, he took up the tail that Devlin had
begun, bidding farewell to Low with a tap on the shoulder as he passed him.

As he descended into the station, he kept passengers
between himself and the two targets. It was like being
back on tail in D.C. again. So far, much of this mission
had consisted of the mundane, broken by sudden bouts
of violence. He felt sure that he would have to step up the
pace and wrap this one up swiftly. He watched as Fraser and Banjo purchased subway tokens like any other
passenger. He followed suit, again just like any other
passenger—though he doubted that many other subway

users were carrying a Micro Uzi and a Desert Eagle, which he had equipped himself with on arrival in NYC.

BOLAN STUCK WITH them as they traveled the system, taking the Port Authority Trans-Hudson train headed out to New Jersey. The soldier wondered about the kind of timescale they were now working on, and why their base of operations was so far removed from the city center. Had Low's guess about the possible target been wrong? Had they realized they were being followed and were seeking to deflect and either evade or eliminate their tail? He hoped not, not with two men still unknown and at large, for it was pretty certain by now that Banjo and Fraser were traveling alone.

They disembarked at Hoboken, and Bolan followed them as they walked from the station to one of the restored brownstones that littered the town. The residents of Hoboken had always kept their buildings in good condition, which was one of the reasons the area had been such a target for the newly affluent and the hip and trendy of the '80s when they'd sought to move from the inner part of the city to the Jersey side of the Hudson. As a result, the town now had an odd mix of families that had been resident for several generations, and newer arrivals, who were either financial workers or artists from downtown in search of a little space.

It made this a perfect environment for the targets to blend in. It was a more racially mixed area than many parts of New York. The other thing it had going for it was the Stevens Institute of Technology, one of the oldest technology colleges in the United States. Knowing that Banjo and Fraser traveled light and without any ordnance, and suspecting that their two missing colleagues would do the same, it made a kind of sense that they would come to a place where students and science could combine. There was a bell ringing somewhere in the back of Bolan's mind. He watched the two men enter a brownstone; then he headed for a bar down the block, where he ordered a beer and hunkered down in a booth to scroll through the material on his smartphone without interruption.

He found what he was looking for. Heider's political connections before his conversion to Islam included a radical student body whose leadership included ex-students of Stevens. One of whom was now a research fellow in mining engineering. Not an obvious connection. His student past had been privileged information even back then, so the college would have no indication of past affinities. Mining engineering was not a subject allied to ordnance per se; there were, however, some points where the two could touch.

Had this been one of the people Heider had seen on his last trip to NYC? It was all circumstantial, but it added up so far, and, frankly, it was all he had to go on right now.

Bolan stood and left the bar.

"You know something, Bear? I was thinking on the way down here that this was a mundane mission and that I needed to step up the pace and tidy it up. Guess I got that one wrong. I feel like I'm in a bad P.I. movie."

"What happened yesterday was more like *Die Hard*

goes Hong Kong," Kurtzman replied. "And I'm not sure Hal would appreciate your 'stepping up' from that."

The first thing Bolan had done on leaving the bar was go to the nearest car-rental company and rent the least conspicuous car he could find. Having scoped the neighborhood, he realized that the majority of the people in the brownstones, either by income or by choice, favored smaller Japanese models rather than U.S.-made vehicles.

The Nissan was a silver hatchback, two years old, and fitted nicely into the background as he found a spot and parked up for the night. After, of course, setting up a surveillance cam and taking the time to go and get coffee and food to last him the long watch to come. Again, the makeup of the neighborhood served him well. Numerous coffee shops and cafés were in walking distance, most of which favored healthy food over junk.

The surveillance had been productive in one sense. Several people had come and gone during the evening and early part of the night. One of them, presumably returning from Stevens, was Piet Schrueders, the research fellow with links in his past to Heider. So his assumption had been correct and Schrueders was involved—either willingly or not—up to his neck. So much so that Fraser and Banjo had headed for his apartment for a meet up.

He relayed this information to Kurtzman and finished with a request for any information filed for Schrueders, any additional intel would help build a complete picture for the takedown.

"There's one last thing," Bolan added. "I think the other two members of the cell have arrived. At five twenty-three a camper van rolled down the street. Two males, one Caucasian and the other African American, left the vehicle and entered the brownstone. They looked to be in their mid-twenties. I took some stills, and there are the surveillance-cam images. I've uploaded them so you can run them to see what you come up with."

Bolan killed the connection and got out of the Nissan, stretching as he did so. He checked his watch: seven minutes after eight. Schrueders would be leaving for work soon if he was going to Stevens today. If he wasn't, that could mean his involvement was very deep, and could presage the beginning of the endgame.

Time to call Brognola and put some precautions in place. He hit the speed dial number as he walked down the empty sidewalk, keeping an eye on the brownstone as he soothed his aching muscles with exercise.

"Striker, I need to hear your explanation of what went down. I've got the President breathing down my neck and half the authorities in D.C. asking awkward questions. It hasn't got back here yet, but the big man has an idea it's tied in with what he's asked, and that's making things—"

"Difficult," Bolan finished. "Hal, I know. If I could have mopped up more discreetly I would have, but things have moved fast."

"I know, I've had updates from Stony Man. Last one's just come through. You don't have to go over that. I just—"

"Hal, listen," Bolan interrupted. "There's something I haven't told Bear yet. It's not confirmed, but I think it's possible, and I think we need to implement some precautions with maximum discretion. I want to nail these bastards, but I need a net in place."

Brognola was silent for a moment. "What is it?"

The big Fed's attitude had changed in an instant, and the soldier breathed a sigh of relief. He knew from long experience that Brognola had faith in his judgment, but he also knew the pressure the big Fed would be under right now. Briefly, he outlined his conversation with Andrew Low from the previous afternoon.

"That would be a logical conclusion," Brognola concurred when Bolan had finished. It was a simple statement, delivered in a tight voice that told the soldier of the anger and outrage that the big Fed was keeping in check. "I could get a shutdown on the site immediately."

"Not a good idea," Bolan replied. "I need to confirm I have the complete cell before taking them down. Any movement that puts their mission in jeopardy is going to make them run. It's not just the four of them, either. This guy Schrueders is involved, and there may be others they're either using or in collaboration with. I want all of them. I'm not going to let that scum desecrate the site and harm anyone who gets in their way. But there's always a chance I won't make it, so I want backup in place."

"I understand," Brognola said. "Problem I have is that as soon as I raise the question, military and security will want a total shutdown. That would be easy. Getting the level of discretion you require without the kind of objection they'll raise…" He let the statement hang.

"I know it won't be easy. But it's necessary."

"I know you won't let me down, Striker."

Bolan disconnected and checked the surveillance cam on his smartphone. A quick scroll through the imaging showed that none of his targets had left the brownstone during his brief absence. He bought himself another coffee and made his way back to the Nissan.

No sooner had he settled himself than three of his targets left the brownstone together.

PIET SCHRUEDERS HAD passed a sleepless night. There had been many of these since Heider had tracked him down. It was ten years since they had been part of the same group, protesting and mounting raids on capitalist institutions. Schrueders had realized that no amount of such protest would make a difference. In truth, as his education progressed and his talents ensured that giant engineering corporations took an interest in sponsoring his PhD and MA, he began to realize that he was rather taken with the fruits of capitalism and the idea of amassing a sizable bank account that would enable him to indulge his whims and passions. One of which had once been politics. That had changed.

He was lucky in that he had never been arrested on any demonstration, and any actions he had been part of had never been traced back to the source. He was clean on record, if not in conscience. He took advantage of that to distance himself, which had been aided by Heider's imprisonment. He had moved to Hoboken and taken up a fellowship at Stevens, secure in the knowledge that his past was well and truly buried. He could not have known that he was on a list of known associates, forever marked on a file.

When Heider had tracked him down, he hadn't known what to do. He was thankful that his partner did not live with him. What Janice would have made of the radical arriving at his door, he shuddered to think. Although the reaction of a girlfriend turned out to be the least of his worries.

Heider had learned a lot about the art of blackmail, and he had practiced it on the frightened Schrueders. The engineer had never been the most committed or courageous of his comrades back in the day, and Heider had played on those fears. Schrueders saw his life collapsing before him unless he did one small thing. Then he would be left alone. Even though he knew that this last statement was probably far from the truth, he was desperate enough to blind himself to believing it.

He was not surprised when Fraser and Banjo had arrived the previous day. He had been expecting them, although he was taken aback that Heider was not with them; a creeping fear spread down his spine when his queries about Heider's whereabouts were met with a blankly hostile, "He ain't coming," from Fraser. They told him that they were expecting two compatriots who should arrive sometime in the night. They gazed around his apartment with a mixture of disdain from Fraser, who had introduced himself as Mummar, and envy from Banjo, who almost seemed to be pricing the contents for larceny. Certainly, the way that Mummar spoke, he had little time for the creature comforts of soft furnishings, state-of-the-art home cinema and media players and expensive prints on the walls that Schrueders had amassed with the rewards of his trade.

He sat on the edge of one of the sofas, facing Schrueders across an antique mahogany coffee table, and spoke in a low monotone of the kind of explosive and detonating technology that Schrueders would have access to at Stevens.

"We want state-of-the-art—small, powerful, portable. We can pay you, but that ain't why you're going to do it. You'll do it because of what Heider knew."

Schrueders had shivered at that: the past tense made him certain that death followed these men.

"Why can't you make it yourselves or buy it from an illegal arms dealer—isn't that what you people do?" Schrueders asked desperately.

This had actually elicited a smile from the otherwise taciturn Mummar.

"You forget that you were one of 'us people,' and that's why you're going to help," Mummar said softly. "We had a few problems with our supplier and can't make a reliable connection on our timetable. As for making it ourselves, we need more power than we can manufacture quickly. Don't worry about us giving you away. We're not coming back. You be careful, and you'll be fine. Face it, you're our one-stop shop, Piet, like it or not."

Schrueders chose not to like it, but kept his mouth shut. As far as he could see, there was nothing he could do except comply and hope to God that he would never be found out. Part of which meant that he wanted them to be successful, even if he had no idea what their objective was. He chose to shut that out of his mind, despite his protesting conscience.

When the two others had arrived—introduced to him only as Amir and Hus—they had greeted him with a mixture of indifference and disdain. Indeed, for much of their conversation thereafter he had been ignored as though not even present. There was a part of him that preferred it that way, as they had things to discuss of which he would rather have no knowledge. By the same token, he felt sure that he really should keep an ear open for what they would require of him.

Schrueders had retired for what little rest he could get as the men talked on in his living room. But he had been unable to sleep, staring at the ceiling and wondering how fate had decreed that the past he had worked so hard to divorce himself from should now catch up and bite him in the ass.

It was light when Mummar appeared in his doorway.

"Wake up, man. You've got work to do. First thing is to fix breakfast. Then you call in sick."

"The condemned man ate a hearty meal," Schrueders murmured to himself. Then, louder, "If I'm not going to Stevens, how can I be of help to you?"

"Two things, brother. First, you ain't the condemned man. Not in that sense. We're the ones who won't be coming back. So all you've got to do is keep your nose clean, okay? Second thing, you are going to Stevens today, but you ain't going to work. Best they don't expect you, not what you're going to be doing."

Schrueders found himself in the kitchen, making breakfast for men he had never seen before and would be unlikely to ever see again in this lifetime, wondering just how he was going to achieve what they demanded of him. Scrambling eggs while he contemplated this seemed strangely surreal. He could hear the four men in the living room discussing the kinds of explosives and detonators that he had gone over with them the night before, and the best way of transporting them to location without being easily detected.

All the time, he did not think of the possible victims, only of distancing himself from any outcome.

When the four men had eaten, Mummar told him that before going to Stevens, there was need for the boys to do a little shopping.

"Been discussing the kind of carryalls and bags needed for this shit…This ain't no shoe bomber or underwear bomber shit, man. This is bigger. We need something that can conceal it, still be wired to us and can pass undetected."

"The kind of size and weight you're talking about, and the kind of power it needs, you're not going to be able to wire it to your bodies," Schrueders said hesitantly, trying in his imagination to compare the explosives seen in the lab and in the field with how they may look on a human being. The more he considered it, the deeper his conscience receded. "I guess the kind of rucksack that a backpacker would carry would be the correct size. You could pack it into something smaller, but it wouldn't be so comfortable."

"Screw comfort," Hus said in a harsh, cracked tone. "Get enough of that where we're going after. Just don't want to get stopped by the Feds before we get there."

"Is that likely?" Schrueders asked, a note of panic creeping into his voice.

"Relax," Banjo said with a sneer. "It ain't you they know anything about. Or us, really. But they know something's going down, so we got to be cautious like a fox."

"We want to look like nice little tourists, just seeing some sights in NYC, and you're the man who's going to help us do that," Mummar said. "We don't have what we need, so you're going to take Hus and Amir to the mall."

BOLAN CURSED AT the fact that the targets had split into two groups and there was only one of him. Just as well there was the tech he needed. He left the Nissan with the surveillance cam that was set on the front of the brownstone, linked to his smartphone. Leaving a beat later so that it wouldn't be obvious, he waited for Schrueders and the two men with him to reach the end of the street before he fell in behind them.

As they had left the building, their descent of the stone steps from the front door had given him an excellent angle to take some pictures, which he had downloaded to Stony Man for ID. It had been just a little too dark to get good images on the phone when they had arrived, but this was so perfect it could almost have been set up for the purpose.

There was no mall in the middle of Hoboken, but there was a shopping area that was located in the middle of the forty-eight-street grid that comprised the circumference of the town. It was here that Schrueders took the two, as yet unidentified, terrorists. Bolan stuck close to them as they shopped for hand luggage: rucksacks, duffel bags and other carryalls. In one sense it seemed bizarre to him that he was tailing terrorists who seemed to be comparing hand baggage like a pair of tourists. Yet all the while, his mind was sizing up the kind of explosive charges that they could pack into the different sizes of bags that passed through their hands.

Bolan watched Schrueders closely. He was nervous, his hands moving in tics and spasms, clenching and unclenching. His record had shown no affiliations with any Islamic groups; indeed, nothing since that deeply buried affiliation of his youth. The soldier was certain that Heider had blackmailed Schrueders into this action, and it was something that the man wanted no part of. This was something that should make him easier to deal with when the time came.

Having made their purchases, they left the shop. Instead of heading immediately back to the brownstone, as Bolan would have expected, they made a detour. They passed the clock on Eleventh Street and seemed strangely like the tourists they presented as their front.

Schrueders seemed to be growing more and more nervous, and it was strange to see the way in which the two terrorists berated him as they reached their destination.

Bolan could see why the engineer was almost visibly falling apart. He also doubted that Banjo—and Fraser in particular—would be impressed. Bizarrely, the three men entered Carlo's Bake Shop. The picturesque frontage gave way to a bakery, where customers milled among a myriad variety of baked goods.

There was no way that this was a scheduled stop or anything to do with their mission. Bolan, fascinated and also needing to know just what was going on, opted to take a risk and follow them into the store.

As he entered, able to lose himself even in such a small space because of the number of shoppers, he could hear Schrueders and the two terrorists. The engineer's tones were clipped, whereas the others sounded more relaxed.

"We should be getting back. We only had to get these—"

"Relax. This is the only chance I'm gonna get, and I don't want to miss it. This place is famous, man." The younger of the two terrorists spoke, looking around with fascination. The older of the two eyed him with contempt and spit out his reply in harsh tones.

"All the shit going down and you think of your stomach. Man, you gonna get fat."

"I'm not gonna get that chance," the younger man said ruefully. "So you ain't gonna deny me this. I love the show, and I always wanted to see if their stuff is as good as it looks."

Bolan realized what had drawn them there: the shop was the one taped for a reality show that he'd seen a few minutes of when he'd visited Leo Turrin in the hospital a while back.

Strange to think that even one of the most fanatical fighters had a side like this to him.

While the younger terrorist did something as mundane as buying cake, Bolan assessed the situation. There was no chance of taking them down here without collateral damage. It looked as though the four-man cell was operating independently, with only the help—albeit unwilling—of the engineer. So five men to eliminate. It was just a matter of keeping them in view so that they could be taken.

He left the three men to their purchases and exited the shop, taking up a position across the street so that he could wait for them unseen. As he did so, he checked the surveillance cam feed and saw that Fraser and Banjo were still ensconced in the brownstone.

There was also some information from Stony Man concerning the two unknown terrorists, unknown no longer. Hussein Ali, the older of the two at twenty-eight, was of Turkish descent, and had been resident in Washington since the age of six. He had no known gang or criminal affiliations. He'd had been born Muslim but had been generally nonreligious until conversion to the cause by a firebrand cleric. Since then, he had gained a reputation for protesting and for an online presence, but he had never been arrested and had been clever in treading a fine line with his internet presence.

The younger man was Amir Khan, whose parents had come to the United States from Uganda in the seventies after Idi Amin had decided to cleanse his country of those who had put growth and wealth into its struggling economy. Most had ended up in the United Kingdom, as they held British passports from their Indian roots. Some, like Amir's parents, had looked at the struggling economy of the UK at that time and had opted for the promised land of America. They had been let down. Years of struggle and failing retail businesses had left their six children in menial jobs and sometimes on the wrong side of the law. This was the environment Amir had been born into, and it hadn't taken long for his resentment to crystallize into gang life and the opportunity for revenge against the West offered by radical Islam, a West he felt had let his entire family down.

And yet he had been fascinated by something as American as a reality show about a bakery? Sometimes, Bolan really felt there was little logic to human nature.

The three men left the bakery and made their way back to the brownstone, with Bolan in discreet pursuit. He returned to the Nissan and seated himself, taking advantage of the coffee left on the dash, even though it was now cold.

It was now past eleven, and he figured that they were on a tight enough timetable that they had to make a move sooner rather than later. He was correct. Within twenty minutes of the three men entering the building, they were out again, this time with Fraser and Banjo with them. The five men made their way to the camper van. They looked tense, as though an argument had broken out between them.

He followed them to the Stevens Institute; they used Schrueders to gain access. Bolan could only hope that the engineer kept it together long enough to get them where they wanted, as he looked as if he was falling apart.

The soldier had a plan of Stevens that he could access on his phone. He had a shrewd idea of their destination, given their needs and Schrueders's position. Get them there, and that was where he planned to isolate them and take them out.

The last thing he needed was a wild card.

CHAPTER TWELVE

Stevens Institute of Technology was located in the midsection of Hoboken known as Castle Point, and had been founded in 1870. This location was presumably why it had a castle gatehouse that, with its rounded and turreted tower, looked like nothing so much as an attempt to hark back to a past that had more connection with another country than the New World. It was cute and quaint and completely useless for security. Even more so when the staff members who were supposed to run security let Schrueders through with no question and were only briefly distracted by the soldier's cover story of being an IT tech who had been called in to work on a malfunctioning network.

Bolan was glad he was finally able to use the cover he had researched at length for a previous assignment and had then barely used before hell broke loose. At least those hours speed-reading manuals had not gone entirely to waste. On the other hand, in a technology institute that had as big a rep as Stevens, shouldn't the security have been a little suspicious at an outsider being called in to fix a problem that could—and should—have been easily fixed in-house? No matter. He was in.

"HANG A LEFT, then second right," Schrueders muttered as he sat hunched on the front bench seat between Fraser and Amir, the driver.

"Look cheerful, bitch. We don't want anyone getting suspicious," Ali muttered savagely from the back of the van.

"Like they wouldn't already," Schrueders murmured. "I call in sick, then show up at the gate, and now I'm going to completely the wrong block."

"Strikes me they don't know their ass from their elbow," Mummar replied. "They got plenty of CCTV," he continued, peering under the horizon of the windshield to get a better look, "but they ain't got much in the way of patrols, and they don't seem to be busting any of their sizable guts to chase after us. Lazy-ass security, man."

"That's because nothing ever happens here," Schrueders said in a melancholy tone. "That's what I like about it."

"No need for anyone to ever know that anything has ever happened here," Mummar retorted. "Pretty sure that we shook the guy who wiped Heider's cell. After we leave here and get the mission complete, there'll just be the dispatches from home. Nothing left to trace us back here. You can go back to your life, Piet. No worries."

"Apart from my conscience."

Mummar laughed. It was harsh and grating. "Man, we all got pasts. And we all got pasts that come back and bite us in the ass."

Amir pulled the van into a parking space as Schrueders, unable to answer through the pall of gloom that had settled over him, indicated the block they needed. They got out of the van and made their way across to the block entrance, looking around but not noticing the Nissan that had pulled into a space around the block. They didn't notice the man in black who waited a few moments before getting out of his car and following them at a distance.

BOLAN WATCHED THEM as they walked across the road to the building housing the labs for experimental explosives and mining equipment. The four terrorists were clustered around the cowed scientist, who couldn't help but look like a man on a death sentence. Bolan wondered how long he would last after they had what they wanted. Was he worth saving? Maybe. The information he could supply under interrogation could be of use. The question was whether it would be prudent to try to separate and save Schrueders at the expense of simply taking out the cell as a whole.

Stevens was built in the midtown section of Hoboken and sat on a serpentine outcropping at the foot of which was Sybil's Cave, at one time a tourist spot for its waters but long since closed up and awaiting redevelopment. The cave at the foot of the cliff led to the shorefront of the river, which could serve a dual purpose: a means of escape for the terrorists and an escape for Bolan should his mission attract too much attention.

It was the middle of the day during a semester, yet the campus was not as busy as Bolan might have expected. There were small groups of students he had passed on the way in, and around this building there were a few people going in and out. It was a low volume of traffic, which he preferred. The fewer innocent bystanders, the better.

The five men had made their way into the building. After a discreet moment, he followed them.

The double doors leading into the block were unguarded, and although there was a security system, Bolan had no need to hit the keypad as a pair of students exiting the building held the door for him. He thanked them and watched them go, wondering if the man and woman deep in discussion had even noticed the man they had just let in.

He left them to it, walking down the corridor and taking in the CCTV. Several doors were closed. Behind some of them he could hear activity, while others were silent. The doors were heavily reinforced, and those sounds he could hear were muffled. It gave him pause to consider the possible explosive power that lay behind them.

He was now in the last corridor of the building; from here there were only the fire doors. There was one room, the door firmly closed.

Bolan acted as though there were no cameras recording his movements. After he had gone, there would be no reason to go back over the recordings: whatever he would do to end the terrorist threat, he could not risk it in this building. He knew that now, having been given an intimation of what was behind the doors. As for this moment, he doubted that anyone was actually monitoring what was coming up on any of the screens. But now there were more pressing concerns. He took a contact mike from one of his pockets and attached it to the door. He donned its earpiece. Beyond the door he heard hushed breathing; he could almost feel the tension.

And then the silence was broken.

SCHRUEDERS OPENED THE locked cabinet and took out the packages wrapped in oilpaper. Carefully he placed them on the nearest workbench, having cleared the space of retorts and burners. The four terrorists hung back. Seeing this now in front of them, each in his own way felt the enormity of what they were about to do, for themselves and for those they intended to harm.

Schrueders unwrapped one of the packages. Inside was a slab of what looked like partially dried concrete. It was greasy and sweating.

"That's it?" Amir said softly. There was a mixture of fear and awe in his voice.

"That's it," Schrueders replied. "It's not much to look at, is it? You wouldn't think that it took several years to get this compound. Several years of trial and error, tests that went fugazi. To get that—" he indicated some test tubes that were in the cabinet and contained a colorless liquid "—to this."

"Is it safe, man?" Mummar asked in an undertone.

Schrueders looked at him with an amazed expression, for one second the research fellow showing rather than the prisoner. "Safe? Of course it's safe."

"But it's sweating, man, That ain't good…"

"This is not dynamite. If that sweats, it means trouble. This, on the other hand, is another matter. The liquid within helps keeps the compound stable. As a pure liquid, it's volatile. In suspension, it's stable as long as it doesn't dry out. Then it's combustible. You need to keep it in the right state of suspension. That's the beauty of it. The detonators are not the usual type. They're timed individually, and they work by drying out the moisture. No complex electronics, no need for any combustion. Just a simple and inevitable chemical reaction."

Ali smiled and leaned in to look at the uncovered block. "It's perfect. How much of it do we need?"

Schrueders blew out his cheeks. "A block this size will take out half a ton of rock. Sybil's Cave would be cleared by it."

"Sybil's what now?" Mummar frowned.

Schrueders shook his head. "It doesn't matter. The point is that if you want to take out something the size you're talking about, you still need a lot of this stuff. That's why you need the rucksacks. It's powerful, but you're talking a lot of tonnage."

"You got enough here for all that?" Banjo asked.

Schrueders nodded. "You'll clean out the department, but there should be enough. The only thing I need to do is make it look like a break-in to cover my ass."

"What about the CCTV?"

"They're slack around here. It's a backwater, we don't get trouble…. Ironic, really. I can actually walk right into the office and wipe the files without anyone noticing." He laughed bitterly.

"Man, this country deserves what it gets," Mummar muttered.

BOLAN HAD HEARD all that he needed to. Fraser had a point, though not in the way he intended. The country deserved more than the idiots it had running security in places like this. He couldn't rely on anyone to pick up the slack, so he had to make sure that things were tight: too tight for the terrorists.

Right now, he didn't care what happened to Schrueders. The man had proved himself to be unworthy as a human being by disregarding his fellow man and throwing his lot in so readily. His primary aim right now was to stop them leaving campus.

He detached the mike and made his way swiftly back through the building until he was out the main entrance and headed toward the camper van. When he reached it, he took the Tekna knife from its concealed sheath and applied the blade to all four of the tires. That would stop them using this vehicle. There were no others within a couple of hundred yards, and the first in line was the rented Nissan.

Very few people were in this area of the campus. Bolan wondered if he should quickly try to evacuate the building he had just left. Better not, he concluded, as he had no idea how many people were actually behind those closed doors and how long it would take to explain himself, no matter what cover story he chose. Best to let them stay there, allow the terrorists to leave and then try to herd them in the direction he wanted. Scanning the grounds, he had the perfect spot.

All he had to do was wait. They wouldn't be long. He walked back to the Nissan and slipped behind the wheel.

He saw the four terrorists exit the building without Schrueders.

HE HAD CAREFULLY taken all the explosive packages from storage and laid them out. The detonators he did likewise, demonstrating how they worked and how to set them. He was very careful in doing that, as he had no wish to either blow himself up or to give them the opportunity to do so before he got rid of them. Ali, Mummar, Amir and Banjo watched him attentively.

Once he had accomplished the task, he helped them pack the explosives into the rucksacks they had brought with them, taking care to keep the detonators separated until the time came to set them. When they had done that, he looked around, then picked up a stool and walked toward one of the windows. He paused, as though remembering something, turned back and used the leg of the stool to smash one of the glass cabinet doors.

"What are you doing, Piet?" Mummar asked softly.

"Thinking ahead. If you drop me at the gate on my way out, I can make sure I've wiped the CCTV as of now, and by the time your mission is completed it'll be like we were never in this room. Meantime, if I smash it up a little, then it'll look like you broke in here. Well, like someone did…"

"Piet, Piet, Piet," Mummar said sadly, shaking his head as he moved toward the engineer. "There's no need for you to worry about that. No one's going to associate you with what happens."

"Yeah, maybe, but there's still going to be the matter of accounting for the missing load," Schrueders said, a tremulous note creeping into his voice.

Mummar smiled; it was cold. He closed in on Schrueders and embraced him, whispering, "No one's ever going to think you were involved, Piet. At least not as anything other than an unwilling hostage."

Schrueders did not reply. As Mummar let him go and stepped back, the engineer's eyes glazed over and he pitched forward, falling against the terrorist as Mummar moved back, allowing him to slide to the floor in a slowly spreading pool of blood.

Mummar bent over the engineer and used his jacket to wipe the thin tool he had used. It was the shaft of a Phillips-head screwdriver, sharpened to a point.

"You can't beat the old prison ways," Ali said admiringly. "There's no knife I know that you can conceal and palm so easily."

"Damn right," Mummar said. "We've got what we wanted. Let's go."

BOLAN WATCHED THEM as they made their way back to the camper van with purpose. He knew immediately what had occurred. No matter—it gave him one less thing to worry about. They reached the van and he saw them curse as they realized what had happened. Amir walked around, checking all the wheels, gesticulating angrily. Bolan watched Mummar calm them and start to issue orders. He might be saying nothing of any great import, but his action stayed their dissent and acted as a focal point. The soldier admired that. Without Fraser they would be headless chickens and easy to pick off as such. Fraser was what made them a unit.

So he was the first to take out.

Bolan slid out from behind the wheel of the Nissan,

at the same time bringing the Uzi to hand and setting it to short bursts. One tap, three shots.

He had the driver's window wound down, using the sill as a rest, with the door itself providing cover.

The four men were still standing by the camper van. They had made no attempt to take cover, despite the obvious fact that whoever had damaged the vehicle was an enemy, and one in close proximity. The Executioner had little doubt that this was what Fraser was trying to drum into them, to get them to focus.

A pity for him that they weren't the soldiers he was, for he would suffer the consequences. One tap, three shots: Fraser took them in the head and upper chest, and he spun under the momentum of the bullets. He was dead before he hit the ground.

For a second, the remaining three terrorists were frozen like potential roadkill in the headlights, trying to locate the direction of fire while working out where they could run.

And then they broke. Bolan cursed as instead of staying together, they moved in separate directions. Because of where he had the Nissan located, none of them were stupid enough to make a break toward the main gates. To the rear of the building they had just exited was the edge of the peninsula that led down to Sybil's Cave and the drop down to the banks of the Hudson. He had wanted to drive them that way so that he could take them out with a minimum of trouble for himself and a minimum of danger to any innocent bystanders. They should have stayed together and mounted a rearguard action. If Fraser had been alive, then that was what might have happened. But with the most disciplined and trained member of the cell now eliminated, they'd lost their heads.

It had always been a possibility, but not one that he had seriously considered, which he now saw as a miscalculation.

Ali and Banjo had separated but were both headed in the same direction, toward the rocks that led to the caves. They were too far apart to try to take out in the same action, but as their destination could only take them one way, and away from any innocent bystanders, they could wait.

Amir was the immediate danger. He was carrying a rucksack full of explosives, and he was running toward an area of the campus where there were people, whose attention had been alerted by the gunshots.

Bolan cursed as he picked up speed and raced after Amir. The terrorist turned and stumbled, falling as he pulled a gun from his pocket. The stumble saved him as the Executioner had sighted and fired; the three-round burst plucked at the air where the terrorist's body had been moments before.

Amir fired back wildly. The shots strafed the air around Bolan. The soldier stood and took aim again. There was little point in trying to avoid shots so wild; in doing so he stood more chance of being hit. He loosed another three shots at Amir, hearing sirens in the distance as he did so.

The soldier was an excellent shot, yet somehow the desperate motions of the terrorist as he tried to scramble to his feet acted with providence. Fire that should have snuffed out his life was denied by the desire to stay alive.

Two of the three bullets hit home, but only in the thigh. The third thudded harmlessly into the turf.

Amir screamed, blood pumping from the artery in his thigh that had been hit. Bolan moved toward him, sighting in for one last shot. Behind the prone terrorist he could see that some people were hurrying away from the firefight, but unbelievably some were rushing toward it. To them, it looked as though Amir was the victim of a random shooting from a man who was now moving toward him for the kill.

They were partly right, Bolan figured, but in the way. He had to finish this before they were too close. He did not want to put them in the line of fire, nor did he want them to detain him. Each moment he spent on Amir was another moment that the remaining two terrorists were gaining ground.

With purposeful strides, Bolan closed in on his target, hands clamped on the Uzi for a steady shot as he picked out the terrorist's head and chest. Amir had a major artery ruptured. He didn't have long left, but there was still damage he could inflict.

Amir, as the world closed in on him in a tunnel of darkness, was well aware of that. His time was up, and he would not be able to fulfill his mission. Paradise would not be waiting for him, unless...

There was one thing he could do to help his comrades on their way. He could try, with his last moments, to take out the man who had eliminated the other cell, and had now eliminated half of his. That might buy him eternal salvation.

Absurdly, one of the last things that went through his

mind was the memory of the confections from Carlo's Bake Shop. In a life of wasted opportunity, it was one of the few things that he could recall as an untainted pleasure. It was little enough, but it would do to take him into whatever came next.

With the last ounce of strength he could muster, he twisted his gun arm so that the muzzle was directed into the rucksack. He squeezed the trigger....

Bolan could see what he was doing, but he could not fire as his own bullets would have hit the rucksack. All he could do was curse and throw himself to the ground as the explosive in the rucksack detonated, blowing Amir into the hereafter.

Bolan opened his mouth to equalize the pressure and flung his arms over his head as he hit the ground, hoping that the explosive power would not be enough to take him with the terrorist.

CHAPTER THIRTEEN

"I know you said you wanted to step things up, but this is taking it a little far, even for you."

Bolan had no reply. It had taken him nearly an hour before his hearing had returned and the buzzing in his ears had started to subside. He ached all over. The shock wave had felt like a gang of Marines had jumped him, swinging baseball bats. He was lucky that there had been no stone or glass near enough to the blast to generate substantial debris. The earth thrown up had been reduced almost to a fine dust. It was only because his reaction and recovery time had been tested by hundreds of battles that he was able to get away from the scene before anyone else had time to react. He didn't know it at the time, but he beat the sirens by a matter of minutes. The campus was soon swarming with police. They had found Schrueders, but there was nothing left of Amir save a hole in the dirt.

Getting away from the scene had been paramount. Any thought of chasing down Ali and Banjo would have to wait until he was clear of the campus. To be detained while searching near the caves would do nothing other than waste time with detailed explanations and denials, then finally verification.

He knew where they were headed. He would have

lost the trail down by the Hudson's banks, but he could pick it up in the heart of New York City. He would need help, though.

Brognola would not be happy, and he had a right not to be. Bolan should have taken out all four of the terrorists while on campus. He should have waylaid the camper van before they had even had the chance to enter the research facility and just eliminated them. But he'd wanted to know if they had any other connections and how they planned to carry out their mission. That hadn't been necessary; he had created this situation himself.

But what if there had been others who could have taken up the task? They would have no lead on them. He had taken a gamble, and it had only partly paid off. He would have to take the consequences when the time came. Right now, it was more important that he finish cleaning up.

That was why he was now in midtown Manhattan, in Andrew Low's office. The Fed eyed him over the desk as he put down his phone.

"Forty men, positioned around the museum and the construction site. We should really close it to the public."

"I agree. We should. But if we do, then we alert Ali and Banjo and drive them underground. And not only do we lose them, but we also lose the explosives they have in their possession. We need to get that back. We need to flush them out."

"I guess so, but what do we do if they're cornered and do what Amir did?"

Bolan smiled mirthlessly. "We don't let it get that far."

"THE PORT AUTHORITY of New York and New Jersey have been told that we're positioning men on-site, but as far as they're concerned it's just a matter of a protest that's being flagged as part of the ongoing antiglobalization campaign. Not violent, but a possible public obstruction."

"Pity to use these people as a shield," Bolan said wryly. "Agree with them or not, they're sincere…but then so are the bastards we're trying to snare."

"Exactly. I don't want to freak the locals too much, just account for our presence," Low commented.

The two men had left Low's office almost as soon as the order to supply the human resources had been issued, and they were now standing in the middle of the memorial site, which honored the 2,983 victims of 9/11, whose names were inscribed on seventy-six bronze plates. Each of those names represented a memory that would be sullied by the terrorists they sought. By a kind of domino effect, everyone who had ever come into contact with the deceased would be directly insulted by the actions the terrorists planned.

The names of the victims from the North Tower and those of the passengers and crew of American Airlines Flight 11, which had hit the North Tower, were located around the perimeter of the north pool, while those of United Airlines Flight 175, which had hit the South Tower, were with those of the victims who had been in that tower, around the perimeter of the South Pool, along with those who had been in the immediate vicinity of the Twin Towers. Here, too, were the names of those who had perished as first responders during res-

cue operations, along with those who had been killed at
the Pentagon, either on-site or as passengers and crew
of American Airlines Flight 77, and those of United
Airlines Flight 93, which had been brought down near
Shanksville, Pennsylvania.

The sheer weight of the numbers, and the widespread
locations in which they had perished, weighed heavily
on his mind as the soldier paused for thought. This was
perhaps as many people as had been lost in desert warfare over the succeeding decade.

As a soldier, Bolan faced death every time he went
into action. It was what he did, his raison d'être. The office workers, cleaners and service workers who had been
in the Twin Towers or their immediate vicinity on that
morning were not part of any combat. They had been
going about their everyday business.

There were those who would say that the actions of a
covert nature that Bolan took part in were the acts of a
criminal, that the United States was not at war and that
there was no necessity to take out the men who would
plant bombs or, indeed, be walking bombs. If they said
that about any overseas actions the nation took part in,
then there was debate to be held. But as he stood con-
templating what the site represented and the lasting reminder of the senseless slaughter it would stand as, he
felt that anyone who saw his actions—and those of operatives like him—as criminal might like to stand here
and feel what he could feel. Maybe they would like to
stand next to a suicide bomber as he arbitrarily ended
their existence as these people's had been.

There were a number of workers still on-site, and as

Bolan prowled the area, he wandered out of the construction area and into the areas that were populated by the public. Here, he made his way as if drawn to the Survivor Tree, which had been replanted in December 2010. It was a Callery pear tree that had originally been planted on the site back in the 1970s. It had been there all the while that construction had gone on and had made it through. It had been at the center of what had happened, and somehow it had managed to survive the event. It had been buried under the rubble on the site until October, when recovery workers had unearthed it as part of their work. It had been eight feet tall, badly burned and had only one living branch.

That had been all that was needed. Taken to Van Cortlandt Park in the Bronx and carefully nurtured by the New York City Department of Parks and Recreation, it had been replanted on November 11, 2001, after being cleaned of the ash that had weighed it down. No one had expected it to survive, but it was more than a tree: it was symbolic, and it was as if in some strange way the hopes and desires of the country had been wrested in it. It survived a storm that uprooted it, and even after its replanting it had survived Hurricane Irene, standing tall while everything around it was lashed by the elements. It had been described by one of the survivors 9/11 as something that "reminded us all of the capacity of the human spirit to persevere."

It now stood thirty feet tall, and as Bolan looked up at it he realized two things: first, that this place had significance that went way beyond the material. Second, the tree itself had such a symbolic weight that it was a natural point for one of the two terrorists to head for.

He took out his cell phone and called Low. "The Survivor Tree—it's the obvious target for one of them. Concentrate on that as the center of the sweep and move out. The memorial site, too. You take out the work that's been done, you cause damage to the plates that will go round the pools. Then you hit right at the heart of the nation. The collateral damage they can cause with that amount of explosive is just a bonus."

"Good call," Low's voice murmured in his ear. "That makes sense, and it gives us a point of origin."

"Any reports coming in that match our targets?"

"Possibly. We are sure that they're on their own, right?"

"I am," Bolan stated. "Schrueders was the only point of contact they had once they reached New York. There was no indication of any other contact, and during surveillance they acted like they were alone. They have no backup. Why?"

"There's one report I've picked up that might be about our boys. I think so. They must have picked up public transport part of the way—"

"Plenty of places they could pick it up once they got down on the boardwalk along the Hudson," Bolan said. "They only came part of the way?"

"Uh-huh—I guess they didn't want to be tracked as easily as they can be by rail. They got partway into Manhattan and then jacked a car."

"Are we sure it's them?"

"The victim was alive. She was just pulled out of her

car and flung on the road. Lucky she wasn't run over by oncoming traffic. Bastards didn't care."

"Hell, at least they didn't shoot her, which might have been a mistake from their point of view. Was she was able to ID them?"

"She's still in Emergency, but it's superficial and she was able to furnish NYPD with a description. That tallied with our boys, and I was able to take CCTV from the nearest junction and blow it up. It's not admissible, but I'd say it was them."

Bolan paused for a moment. He knew that Low was not a man to make any commitment unless he was more certain than most people would be.

"You know what? I'll go with that. Have we been able to pick them up?"

"Oh, yeah. I love CCTV at times like this. We've been able to pick them up in the last five. You want to go meet them?"

"Oh, yes. If we can divert them somewhere a little less populated before they get here."

"Shit, Cooper, this is NYC. There's nowhere left here that's 'less populated.'"

"You get me a car and let me worry about that," Bolan said with finality.

BANJO AND ALI had been terrified by the explosion Amir had set off. The enormity of the blast had sent them sprawling as they ran, and they had a moment of blank fear that it would trigger the explosives they were carrying. The exhilaration that they were still alive should have given them pause for thought. Was their own imminent sacrifice really what they wanted? Instead, it only made them thank God that they were still able to make what they saw as the ultimate sacrifice.

With the man who had been following them taken out of the game, at least temporarily, by the explosion, they had a head start that they intended to use to full advantage. There was irony in the fact that they took the path that Bolan would have ideally directed them, moving toward the outcrop that led down to Sybil's Cave and out to the waterfront.

Although it had been partially opened a few years before, the cave was not open to the public and they had to break their way into the old pathways leading downward. There was no security on duty, which was perhaps just as well for those who would have been faced with two men who were desperate and unthinking. Ali and Banjo charged through the barriers and wire fencing around the construction areas with their guns in hand and in full view.

Neither spoke to the other, with no communication in their flight, no plan. They ended up on the waterfront because they had nowhere else to run. It was only when they were on the riverbank, with the sirens blaring in the distance above their heads, that they had time to pause. They looked at each other with eyes wide and staring, chests heaving with the effort of their flight and with the tension that surged adrenaline through their blood.

"What in God's name happened there?" Banjo gasped. "Who is that asshole?"

"Trouble," Ali panted, before bending over to vomit

a thin stream of bile. "We're on our own now, man. Just us. We've got to see this through."

"How? How are we supposed to do that, man?" Banjo gasped as he doubled over, trying to suck air into his lungs. "That asshole knows what we're up to—he followed us from D.C. Ain't no way we're going to shake him, man."

Ali forced a grin. "Listen, you think that he managed to survive that? Amir did that to buy us some space, man, and I figure he did us a favor. We owe him, man, so let's stop worrying and just get on with it."

That was easier said than done. Both men were doubled over by the effort of their flight, pain creasing their abdomens with every breath. They felt conspicuous, and they looked it as they made their way along the bank until they were able to ascend to the boardwalk. They were covered in dirt and dust, disheveled and walking like men who were exhausted and paranoid. They felt as though everyone coming toward them and walking past them knew who they were. They were attracting attention by the way that they held themselves.

By the time that Bolan was back on his feet and making good his exit from the grounds of the institute, the two terrorists had brushed themselves down both metaphorically and literally. They were now acting and looking like tourists as they boarded the train that would take them across the river and into Manhattan.

The carriage was half-empty when they boarded, and with the rattle of the tracks they were able to stand in an area where they could converse softly and not be overheard.

"You think that asshole was working alone?" Banjo asked.

Ali shrugged. "Maybe.... Does it make a difference?"

" It could—if he was reporting to the Feds, then they'll know who we are and they'll be looking for us. They might have guessed what our target is. How are we going to pull this off, man?"

"You need to chill, brother. We don't know any of that. What would Mummar do, man? He'd make us split into groups and make reconnaissance of the area. Feds ain't that hard to spot, even if they're undercover. All we need to do is get into the museum and the memorial site and then blow, brother."

"Yeah, right...all they go to do is shoot us down before we get there."

"Man, they got to catch us first. Listen, Mummar would have the four of us split into two, but that don't apply now. We need to stick together, watch each other's back, man. We need to try to keep out of sight, find a way to get there without being picked up easy. Like, first thing we need to do is get off this train. They'll be watching all the public transport, train and bus. What we need is to get some wheels, man."

Banjo nodded. As the train pulled into the next station, they moved to the doors and got off, making their way through the exit while scoping the immediate area. There was only one uniformed cop in sight, and he didn't give them a second glance. If their descriptions had been circulated, they hadn't reached as far as this officer.

Banjo and Ali walked past him, every fiber of their beings screaming for them to look back to see if he had noticed them. But they didn't. As they walked down the sidewalk they waited for a shout, for a shot to whistle by them. There was nothing, and it was only when they were around a corner and out of sight that either of them felt able to relax in even the slightest degree.

It was then that they saw the opportunity that they needed. It came upon them before they had the need to plan it, and to Ali it seemed as though it was a sign from providence.

Ahead of them, a white Ferrari swerved its way through the traffic and pulled up at the curb. The road-side door opened, causing oncoming traffic to swerve and sound off angrily, and a middle-aged woman got out, flipping the bird at the passing cars that honked their horns at her. She walked around the car, tottering on her heels, and headed to a hot-dog stand, where she ordered a chili dog from the vendor, who was torn between serving her and looking at the near pileup she had caused in stopping suddenly.

"This is us, brother," Ali murmured.

Banjo gave him a startled look. "You are joking me, right? We take that car here with witnesses, and with that hot-dog guy to get in the way? And that car, man."

"Listen, brother, that car might stand out, but it's going to be fast and that's what we need. Don't matter if they know what we're in, as long as we can maneuver fast."

Banjo was unconvinced, but he had little opportunity to argue as Ali moved forward. He had to fall in or else be left behind.

The woman had her chili dog, and paid the vendor

with bills and coins that spilled from her purse. She seemed to be drunk, and Ali grinned sardonically. He was doing the people of Manhattan a favor. It would be one less drunk driver for them to worry about, one less DUI for the police to arrest. Of course, they would have other things on their minds before too long, but that was just too bad.

The woman wandered out into the road, having no regard for the oncoming traffic other than to curse at it as she pulled open the door. She didn't notice the two men with rucksacks heading toward her, picking up the pace as they got closer. Neither did the hot-dog vendor. He was busy serving another customer and had paid the drunk woman no more attention once she had left him too much cash, cursed and wandered off. It was only when he heard her yells, screeching above the traffic noise that he looked up.

What he saw made him pause, openmouthed: two young men stood near the car. The one on the sidewalk yanked open the passenger door of the Ferrari and dived in, while his companion on the other side took the woman roughly by the arm, pulled her away from the vehicle and threw her onto the road. She screamed, tumbling almost under the wheels of an oncoming SUV. It was only by deft driving and braking that the vehicles close by managed to avoid running over her. Those directly behind them somehow managed to avoid rear-ending those cars that had braked.

Ali paid her no heed and had no concern for what happened to the woman. The only thing he was grateful for was that she had left the keys in the ignition and so he had no need to scrabble through the detritus of her purse as it lay on the road. He slid in next to Banjo, who was yelling at him to get going, and slammed his door shut. He fired up the engine and with the briefest of looks at the traffic coming from behind, gunned the engine and squealed away from the curb, slipping the car into gear and hitting the first bend he came to at high speed.

Neither man looked back. They did not see the pileup of traffic, the woman screaming hysterically in the road as she finally registered the fender of a car up against her, the warmth of the metal on her skin. They did not see the shocked hot-dog vendor yell as he finally realized what was happening, drop his customer's order and run uselessly after them. They did not see some passersby use their cell phones to call 911, while others used their phones to record what had just happened. More than that, they did not see the unblinking eye of the CCTV cameras recording traffic movements, high above them, that caught the whole thing in digital image.

None of that mattered. The only thing that meant anything to them right then was that they had transport and that it was fast. Sure, it was easily identifiable: any vehicle would be to the authorities. What they needed was something that had speed and maneuverability, something they could use to keep one jump ahead of any Feds until they were able to get to their target area and detonate the bombs they carried with them.

The mission had started out being about stealth and subterfuge. They had intended to travel to the target areas, pick their positions and make their sacrifice without anyone being any the wiser until after the event.

That was before the man in black had screwed all their plans. Now, having to take the position that the authorities were wise to their plan and also had the means to identify them, their modus operandi had changed. This was no time for subtlety. They had to stay out of the hands of the authorities and assume that the target area would be protected. Rather than slip in the back door, they had to charge the front door and hit the button before they could be shot down.

A daunting prospect for some, no doubt, but not for men who already knew that their destiny was death.

CHAPTER FOURTEEN

Bolan took over the vehicle from one of Low's men. It was another Nissan, this time blue rather than silver.

New York traffic was always the same: insane on the verge of gridlock. The city might have cut the crime rate over the past decade to the point where it was actually one of the safest cities in the States, but it still had problems with its drivers and their attitudes to both other drivers and pedestrians. Car horns blared at the slightest imagined transgression, and as Bolan had half an eye on other traffic and was so prone to slowing at moments others saw as opportune, he attracted more than his fair share of attention.

Ignoring the drivers around him, the soldier made his way through the grid system of streets until he was in the area of Manhattan in which the Ferrari had been carjacked. It was maybe too late to pick up the scent, but at least he would have a starting point from where he could begin tracking his prey. Ideally, he could pin them down before they made the memorial site.

That assumption was based on his knowing which way they had traveled. The hot-dog vendor was still at work, the incident of less than an hour before reduced to an anecdote to be recycled many times. Bolan passed him without giving him a second glance, then turned in to the curb, taking in the scene with one knowing glance. Moments later he pulled into the traffic once more.

Bolan reached the turnoff where the Ferrari had left the street. He took the turn and hit the speed dial on his smartphone, which he kept on hands-free and speaker.

"Cooper, you're at the point of entry, right?" Low asked.

"Just turned off," the soldier replied. "You get that track on the imaging?"

Low told him yes. His men had gathered intel from the CCTV on the blocks surrounding the area where the incident had occurred. From that, they had been able to compile a route that was now relayed to the soldier.

"How far in front are they?" he asked when Low had given him the data.

"Here's the thing. They were twenty-five minutes in front until they reached the last location given."

"Were? What's happened?"

"Not sure. Somewhere between two setups, they've just run off the road and into thin air."

"WE JUST GOING to gate-crash the site and blow ourselves to paradise?" Banjo asked with a note of desperation as Ali weaved erratically in and out of traffic, driving as though their enemy were hot on their tail rather than an unknown distance away.

"Yeah, sure, why not? And they'll just get some kind of antitank shit and blow the hell out of us before we get within half a mile," Ali snapped. "Use your head, brother. We need to be smarter than that."

"Then why are you driving like you're on the fast

train to paradise already, man? We'll get busted or killed—or both—before we're anywhere near—"

Ali laughed harshly. "We've got no time to waste, brother, but we've got to be smart. I need the speed to get us to a place and a man who can help us."

"You know someone?" Banjo asked, keeping one nervous eye on the traffic as Ali cut off a yellow cab to take a corner and almost took out three pedestrians.

"I don't, but Mummar did. He told me in case of emergency that this is what we should do."

"He told you? Why didn't he tell me, man? He think I'm useless or something?"

Ali hit Banjo on the side of the head. "Don't be stupid, brother. You knew shit I didn't, and I knew shit you didn't, and Amir knew shit neither of us did. He trusted me with this because I'm Turkish, not black or Indian. He knew that I could understand this dude better than either of you brothers."

"Which dude, man? You ain't making any sense."

"Shut up and let me see where I am, brother," Ali barked as he peered under the horizon of the windshield to catch a street name. Grunting with pleasure, he threw the Ferrari into a turn against the traffic that caused squeals of brakes and blaring of horns but somehow left them miraculously untouched as they left the main drag and hit a maze of side streets and narrow alleys running between buildings. A sharp left into a narrow way between two five-story blocks took them off the grid of CCTV and into unknown and unseen territory.

Ali slowed the Ferrari suddenly, throwing Banjo forward against the windshield.

"Huss," the terrorist said, "you want to send us skyward before we're ready?"

"Chill, brother," Ali cautioned as he peered among the trash bins and pallets that littered the alley, counting the doorways until he came to the one that made him nod to himself. He took the Ferrari toward the far end of the alley until he came to a loading bay that was deserted. He turned the vehicle in, killed the engine and got out, beckoning Banjo to follow.

"C'mon, help me cover this," he said, busying himself with pallets, cardboard boxes and tarps used to cover delivered goods, taking them and placing them carefully over the Ferrari so that its shape and color were disguised by the tarps, weighted carefully with the other pieces of trash. "Work of art, man," he said to himself when they had finished.

"Cool, if we don't make paradise we can go to the Museum of Modern Art and show off our style," Banjo said with heavy sarcasm. "Now you going to tell me what you've been talking about?"

Ali beckoned him onward. "I'll do better, brother, I'll show you," he said with a sly grin.

The terrorists walked down the alleyway, Ali noting carefully each doorway until they came to the back entrance of the building he sought. When they reached the right door, he stayed his companion with an arm and tentatively tried the fire door. It was unlocked and gave way easily. Ignoring the worried and confused look that Banjo shot him, Ali led his companion into the dark recess that lay behind the door. They were in the stairwell of the fire escape, and their feet echoed on the stone

stairs as they ascended two floors. Ali led Banjo through
the access door and into a hallway that was in complete
contrast to the dank dark one they had just exited.

A brightly lit corridor stretched either side of them,
carpeted in rich red shag. The walls were painted ochre
and yellow and were hung with paintings and framed
photographs of the desert and gleaming white archi-
tecture with spiraling minarets. Fluorescent lighting
gleamed overhead, leaving no shadows on the half-glass
office partitions behind which men and women in Western dress worked on terminals. No one seemed to notice the two men who had just entered, even though one
man strode right past them holding a manila folder. He
gave them the briefest of glances before hurrying past.

"Security, man—they'll be onto us," Banjo murmured, taken aback by the fact that they had not already been questioned.

"Of course they will, brother. Probably expecting us
already," Ali said with a smirk.

Banjo glared at him. He was getting more than a little
pissed at the way Ali was acting like he had a great secret but was unwilling to share it. Banjo's nerves were
already jangling from the morning's events, let alone
from psyching himself up to the ultimate sacrifice. This
was a stupid thing, but it was bugging him out of all
proportion.

He was about to say something when he was stopped
by the sight of the man with the manila folder coming
back toward them, beckoning as he did.

"This way. Quickly," he snapped. Ali followed him,

and after a pause, Banjo did likewise, feeling lost and bemused.

They were led into an office where an Eastern-looking man—maybe Turkish, like Ali, figured Banjo—sat behind a terminal. He ignored them as the man with the folder ushered them in, then left, closing the door behind him. It was some moments before the man looked up.

"So you're all that's left of Mummar's great mission?" he said slowly. He waited for either of them to reply, and when he was met with silence, he shook his head. "I had hopes for Mummar. He was a good soldier, a good planner. It's a pity that asshole Heider blew things open, and it's an even greater pity that Mummar took a hit trying to cover your asses."

Banjo had heard enough. He exploded. "Who are you, man?"

"Sit down and shut up," the man snapped. He did not move, but his voice and bearing had an authority that made both the terrorists obey without giving it a second thought. Once they were seated, he continued. "Now report—I know what happened at Stevens, but I want to know how you got here and if you were followed."

Banjo stayed silent and listened while Ali filled the man in on the events that had happened since their escape at Sybil's Cave. It was obvious that he found the chain of events annoying, particularly when it came to the point where they stole the Ferrari.

"Why did you pick such a high-profile car?" he asked, containing his rage. "That will make it easy to trace and for the authorities to put two and two together. You have made your mission more difficult by doing that."

"I don't think so, brother," Ali said. "The car was fast and could get around these streets easily. Time is our enemy as much as the Feds. We needed help, and the best way to get it—"

"Was to come here, and in so doing lead the authorities directly to me," the man interrupted, his tone rising with his anger. "The only thing I can hope is that you managed to somehow slip off the CCTV grid. Even if you did, it would take only a cursory check to show that this business is in property nearby, and to again put two and two together. You really do not realize what you have done, do you? We have invested a lot of time and money into the network. It has not been easy, but we have come a long way—too far for it to be endangered by your idiocy."

"Network? Man, what the fuck are we talking about?" Banjo exploded again. "Who are you?" He turned to Ali. "And why are we here?"

The man behind the terminal sighed. "You stupid child. Your friend is not much better. He was given this address for extreme circumstances, and these are not— to my mind—extreme. But now that you are here I must help you while making sure that our mission is not compromised. You know of course that every cell across the U.S.—across the world—is independent. That is how we keep power. You cannot cut off the head to slay the beast as we are all heads. But all cells need financing, need help to establish themselves. This is mostly done through a chain, so that again links can be cut adrift without weakening the whole.

"Yet this all costs money, and it all needs arms. This

is where I come in—import and export. We are a Turkish company. Except I am not Turkish, and our registration is a formality. Since 1979 we have only had a presence at the UN, and then only under duress for most of the time. We have no embassy, but then we do not need one— certainly, we could not mask our activity so well if we did. But now you have endangered all that by leading the authorities almost directly to our door."

He brought his fist down hard on the desk; the sudden ferocity of the movement made both Ali and Banjo jump. "You had better hope they do not find us, or your deaths will not be glorious, and they will certainly not be swift."

"Man, the only thing we want is a swift death—a glorious martyr's death. That's why we're doing this. But we can't do it without some help now because things have just gotten really screwed up."

Banjo was babbling, and despite the anger the man behind the terminal felt—which he kept from his expression—he could see that Banjo was sincere, if a fool. He wanted to achieve his mission but did not have the training to cope with the stress and the need for flexibility that the field brought with it. That was something he would have to talk to his paymasters about. This situation could not arise again. But in the meantime, there was work to be done. He rose from his chair.

"Very well. You are children and you have the ways of children. But you have the fire of belief within you, and it is my job to nurture that flame so that it may flare and burn brightest at the most opportune moment."

Banjo looked at Ali. He wanted to ask what the man

was talking about, but he could see from the expression on his companion's face that things were actually going their way. No slow death, after all.

Beckoning them to follow, the man—who had so far made a point of not giving them a name or asking for theirs—led them down the corridor toward the far end of the building. They passed offices where people ignored their presence, either through training or through a genuine disinterest, it was hard to tell. Ali wondered if everyone in this company was part of the organization, or if they really thought they were working for an import-export trader.

At the end of the corridor was a door set in the wall. Opening it revealed the only office on the floor that was not part of the open plan. Leather-bound volumes lined the walls; a large plasma screen was incongruously set into the center of one wall. A desktop monitor showed real-time share indexes from all markets, with a printer intermittently churning out hard copy. There was a picture window beyond the mahogany desk and leather chair, looking out across Manhattan. At this level the sight line was not clear; other glass and steel buildings stood between the window and the river. There was an incongruous gap, still, where the Twin Towers had once stood. Ali calculated that they were only a few blocks from their objective. He was certain that they would be expected, though he had little idea how that opposition would manifest.

"Is that you, blood?" Banjo asked, indicating the nameplate on the mahogany desk. It read: Mohammed Rezla Pahlavi, CEO.

The man's lips quirked for the first time into a sem-blance of a smile. "That's what I call myself. A small joke at the expense of the West, like the Empire style of the room. I don't expect any of the idiots I do business with to understand. That just makes it more amusing."

"So what can I call you, man? I don't like not address-ing you. It seems all disrespectful," Banjo continued.

"I appreciate what you say. You can call me Rez, if it makes you feel better."

"Brother, what would make me feel better is if we cut the crap and you helped us get to where we want to go," Ali said peevishly.

Pahlavi sat down and used a remote to trigger the lock on the office door before switching on the plasma screen. Instead of the rolling news and business chan-nels that may be expected in such an office, it instead showed a changing feed from the CCTV centers of Manhattan.

"Traffic control is very important the larger this city gets," he began incongruously. "It is necessary to have a clear picture of what is happening within the grid. Of course, should an engineer be able to hack into this sys-tem, it has a dual purpose. In the first instance, he is able to relay the data from the cameras directly to a third-party source. That enables this source to keep a record of what is occurring, and so be one step ahead. When you combine this with other intelligence-gathering sources, as erratic as they may be by nature, then one can build a clear picture. This is why we knew you were arriving. Your presence has been half traced, half guessed by the American authorities. Choosing to take such a conspicuous vehicle was an idiotic move. It brought you into focus, enabled them to trace you with a degree of certainty that was present before. It also gave them a trail."

"Yeah, now I see why you were pissed at us," Banjo said quietly. Ali said nothing.

"Your perception does you credit, even if your companion will not acknowledge his error," Rez murmured. "It is fortunate that you went off the map, as it were. They could trace you to near here. Too close for us to feel comfortable, but if we can move you out, then not enough to directly endanger us."

"Dual," Ali said in a harsh tone. When Rez raised an eyebrow at him, he reiterated, "Dual, you said. So what's the second?"

"Ah, I see. Yes, there is a secondary purpose. It is only to be used in extreme circumstances, because it has the risk of being traceable. But it is imperative that this mission be achieved, so that risk is worth taking. A good engineer, having hacked into the system, can then disrupt the information flow. This can buy time and also space. When any part of the system is down, there is no way of keeping an accurate trace on activity. We can give you a smoke screen that will enable you to get to your target objective."

"All right!" Banjo exclaimed, as excited as a kid who has just been told he's going to the Super Bowl.

Ali, however, was not so overwhelmed. "That's good, brother," he said slowly. "But what's so important about two dudes from D.C. blowing shit up that you'll endanger all this?"

BOLAN PARKED THE Nissan down a side street. He'd get a ticket, but Low's people would pay as it was their vehicle. Come to that, he doubted that federal authorities had to pay parking fines. Maybe it would get towed away, but that was doubtful. Still, the idle thought gave him an idea. He hit a speed dial number on his cell.

"Striker, nice to hear from you. I thought you were relying on other sources of intel these days," Kurtzman said.

"You know you're the only one who can really hit the spot, Bear," Bolan replied. "You've been keeping up to speed on me, after all. So do you know exactly where I am right now?"

"I do, and if you think that just using me to avoid a ticket—"

"That's what I like, thinking outside that box. You know why I'm calling. If they left a car like that parked illegally, someone's going to ticket it. If I'm lucky, they've been real careless, and I'm assuming that all ticketing is through handsets that feed back wirelessly to a mainframe?"

"There are some systems in operation like that. I'll get onto them and with a make like that it'll show immediately. We're only talking a block radius, right?"

"It would have showed up on CCTV if they'd come back into frame. They're here somewhere. Given time I could find them, but I don't have that. Any help…"

There was a moment's silence as Kurtzman pondered the circumstances. Then he said, "Nothing comes straight to mind, but there are some sources that are off-off-record. Rumors and nothing more. Let me ask a couple of questions. Should be quick. Meantime you scout the ground."

Bolan thanked him and disconnected. All around him people went about their business, unaware of what was in their midst.

What was in their midst? Why would the terrorists have disappeared off the map? No way would they just be sitting in a hot car, wasting time, no matter how freaked they might be. They had come to this point for a purpose.

Bolan looked around. They were only a few blocks from the Twin Towers memorial site, and the area was mostly office space with a few stores to service them. In this area it was mostly finance and diplomatic. No official diplomatic sources—even those of suspect nations who still had U.S.-based representatives—would touch them for fear of taint. Finance, then. They could be in one of the buildings housing finance and trading companies. That narrowed it down a little, but not enough.

The soldier brought up the grid of the area on his smartphone. He was itching for combat, to draw a line and find some resolution. But he had to be patient, methodical. There were three alleys and service streets between the point where the Ferrari had last been caught on camera and the point where it had seemingly vanished from the next corner-mounted relay.

Three routes could take him to the other side of the block. The cameras on that side had not picked them up, either. They had to have stopped in one of the three.

There was no way of narrowing them down as yet.

He just had to pick one and recon. The nearest one was the obvious choice.

It wasn't promising. There was little space for anyone or anything to take cover. A narrow sidewalk on each side serviced the fire exits and delivery bays for the buildings that sat deep from the front of each sidewalk. Large, wheeled garbage bins stood on the sidewalks, ready for the week's collection. He was able to recon the alley swiftly, as the delivery bays were empty and mostly unused. A few vehicles were parked there, but none was a Ferrari.

He reached the far end and came out on the street parallel to the one from which the Ferrari had vanished. He'd drawn a blank, but on the plus side he had been able to review the area quickly. Hopefully, the others would be searched as quickly.

He walked down to the second service street and began his search. This one snaked into a dogleg angle about halfway down, and the buildings on either side were not of uniform size and length. He felt encouraged. This would be a more obvious place to seek refuge.

Perhaps because of its shape, the street seemed to hold more crevices and angles in which to hide. The wheeled garbage bins intruded into the roadway, leaving spaces in which a parked car could be concealed. He proceeded with more care. The delivery bays down here had been kept less tidy, with crates and cartons left on loading docks, and the area was littered with plastic sheets and tarps.

There were a few vehicles down this street, too, but again no Ferrari. He was halfway down and wondering if this was going to be another dispiriting blank when he came on the delivery bay where Ali had parked. A feeling of satisfaction swept over Bolan as he saw the tires of a car beneath the canopy of a tarp that had been weighted down with crates and cartons.

It wasn't a bad attempt at camouflage under the circumstances, he had to admit. The car had been parked as far into the shadows of the dock as had been possible, and the terrorists had covered it as best they could with what was available. A casual passerby would not have spotted the vehicle, even less so been inclined to investigate what it might be. It was just too bad for the terrorists that they had the Executioner on their tails.

He felt his smartphone vibrate and answered it. "Bear," he said. "Your timing is immaculate."

"I take it you've just found our friends, then?"

"Not quite, but I have found the Ferrari. It's in the delivery bay of a building—"

"The Simonsen Tower, by any chance?"

"This is all coming together. What have you heard?"

"There are whispers about an import-export business run out of the building. They have two floors and are supposedly Turkish. But they also ship a lot under Liberian flags. They have links to the Somali government, with a lot of business coming their way."

"That's interesting, under the circumstances. Anything concrete?"

"Only the block they're housed in. It's all smoke and mirrors. They have holding companies for their holding companies, and it would take an army of accountants an infinite number of years to trace it all back to the source.

However, if you believe in coincidence, there are some interested parties who have noted an upsurge in terror activities in certain African nations following the arrival and departure of ships run by this line. There are certain lines of financing out of the main company that seem to just disappear into thin air. And we all know money doesn't just vanish."

"They sound like they might be worth looking into. They certainly sound like the kind of people who would have an interest in two frightened would-be bombers."

"Striker, there's nothing at all to suggest they've ever been involved with anything in the U.S. But they do seem to be careful."

"Leave it with me, Bear. If there is anything to link them, it'll soon be out in the open. Priority is seeing if our friends are in there, but I get the feeling that if there is a link, then Ali and Banjo have just uncovered one big can of worms. Let Low know what's going on so he can get people on it."

"Will do, Striker, and I'll tell Hal, too. You know how cranky he gets when you leave him out of the loop."

"THERE ARE THINGS that it is best you do not know," Rez said smoothly as he hit a button on the intercom. He spoke into it without his eyes leaving the two men before him. "Ajad, I think it is time that we implemented the new emergency procedures."

A mumbled, static-blurred agreement responded to his words. Ali and Banjo exchanged glances. Rez caught their expressions.

"Do not worry, gentlemen. This will all be for your benefit. Watch."

All three of them turned their eyes to the plasma screen. As the feed flickered and changed, the constant wall of images began to be broken up. Some camera feeds pixilated until they were nothing more than flickering patterns of light, while other feeds cut out entirely; a few seconds of black screen represented their sudden breakdown.

"This will continue for the next thirty minutes. We know from our own work and from monitoring their repairs to the system that it will take them that long to trace the fault. By that time we will have withdrawn our hacker from the system by the back door. This should give us long enough to mask your progress to the target."

"That's fine, brother, but they aren't just using CCTV to look for us," Ali spat. "Have you thought of that?"

"Do you really think we are that simpleminded?" Rez asked. "This is just one part of the operation. They have men looking for you? Fine, we give them a distraction. A lot of distractions. Calls that will place you at many places within the borough of Manhattan. Calls that will need at least a cursory check. We will send out operatives to create diversions. Packages will be left and reported, harmless, of course, and also untraceable. We do not want to distract the media from what you are about to do, after all. But we do need to keep the authorities on the defensive."

For the first time since they had arrived, both Banjo and Ali looked happy.

"Now you're talking, brother." Ali grinned. "I like your thinking."

"While I am surprised that you know what thinking is," Rez murmured. "No matter, you are willing and committed, which is all that anyone can really ask." He got up from behind the desk, killing the plasma screen and then beckoning them to follow. "Come with me. You will leave the building separately and take different routes. I will brief you as we descend."

He led them out of the office and back down the corridor, past the fire door they had used to gain access and to the elevator at the far end. As they waited for the car, he murmured instructions.

It was unfortunate that his words did not carry just a little farther, as there was next to no noise coming from the open-plan offices, and in such an instance his meaning may have been clear to—and thus avoided a lot of trouble for—the man who had just carefully clicked open the fire door, the man who was just too late to catch the terrorists and their adviser before they entered the elevator.

CHAPTER FIFTEEN

Bolan cursed as he saw the three men get into the elevator. He had climbed the fire escape swiftly, keeping an eye out for any surveillance equipment, and had carefully opened the fire door, hoping that he would not be observed. It was a blind entrance, and with time at a premium, he had to take a chance.

He was unlucky on two counts: the first was that he heard the murmured voices of the three men and saw them turn as the car doors closed; the second was that his entrance had not gone unnoticed.

He was about to withdraw, hoping that they had not seen him as the doors closed, when he heard the barked voice and saw the security guard coming out of an office down the corridor, by the elevator.

"Hey, you! What do you want?"

Bolan could just turn and run, which had been his original intention in order to try to meet the elevator on the ground floor, or he could respond to the guard. That would cost him valuable time, but the risk was that the guard would then alert the soldier's targets. The guy was coming head-on: it would be hard to evade him. With luck, he could get take care of him in a few seconds.

"This isn't Kaufman Brothers, is it? Wrong floor, man," he said, affecting surprise as he looked around.

The door was half-open by now, pushed back to give him more space to pull back if necessary.

The guard did not answer. He drew his gun with a speed that suggested he was better trained than the average security guard, and two shots smacked into the door by Bolan's head. The guard's firearm training wasn't of the quality of his reflexes, thankfully. By the time the metal of the door had buckled by the heavy-duty shot, Bolan had already moved.

The impact was heavy: a .357 round fired from a SIG Sauer by the look of the gun that was dwarfed by the guard's fist.

Bolan couldn't withdraw. The stairwell was ricochet heaven, and he would be going down and at a disadvantage in returning fire. Attack was the best form of defense. The soldier had CS gas grenades, but no time to grope for his mask. It would have to be his accuracy that saved him. He snatched the Uzi from its holster, set it to short bursts and rolled across the width of the corridor. There was an open office door at an acute angle, and he aimed for it to provide cover.

The guard was static, concentrating on firing. Two more shots boomed in the confined space, smacking into the pile of the carpet, barely muffled. Bolan ignored them and concentrated on coming up with the Uzi in position. A tap and three shots stitched the guard across the chest. A startled look crossed his face as he crumpled to the floor. As he went down, a second tap made sure that he would not get up again.

Attack had been necessary to avoid the men in the elevator being alerted by the guard as he pursued the soldier, which could cause more problems than a mere few moments' delay. This, of course, presumed that the guard was the only armed man in the offices.

Bolan turned to scan the office space behind him. Two women and a man were cowering behind their desks; one of the women was screaming. They might not be innocent, but they certainly were not armed. The soldier left them and raced for the fire door, which was still open.

It wasn't going to be his day. Two more shots came from one end of the corridor, and they were echoed by two more from the opposite end. He was pinned back in the office, unable to reach the stairwell.

The time for subtlety had passed. He took a grenade from one of his pockets, pulled the pin and pitched the bomb down the far end of the corridor, toward the door. Without waiting for it to detonate, he spun and fired off two bursts toward the elevator end of the corridor. He caught sight of two men with handguns firing at him. They were in suits and were snapping off their shots so that they flew high. One of them was caught by a burst of fire, crumpling, while the other man drew back into cover.

As he moved back into the relative cover of the office, Bolan took another grenade and pulled the pin, arming the deadly orb before pitching it toward the elevator. The explosion might damage the shaft, but there was little chance of it being occupied by anyone other than the targets. The office workers were at a safe range.

He hunkered down, ready for the dual blasts that

shook the whole floor of the block. A moment's concussive silence filled his head before his ears cleared and he was able to hear screams, groans and alarms going off on this floor and others. He checked the people in the room. They were stunned but otherwise unharmed. People from the offices wandered the corridor outside. Some were dazed, others in shock. There was no gunfire directed at him, and barely any attention was paid to him as he moved toward the shattered office door. Whatever opposition he may have expected had been eliminated in the blasts.

A quick glance back to the elevator showed Bolan that the doors had been caved in and hung over the shaft, where shattered cable ends could be seen. Truth was that he'd missed the opportunity to take out the targets when the elevator hit the ground floor. If he was lucky, they had still been in the car when the blast hit and were trapped. That was not something he'd bet on, though. He needed to call in assistance, and while he did that he'd check out the office at the end of the corridor.

What had seemed to be a simple wooden door that should have been a hole in the wall still had some remnants showing that it had been reinforced.

He was curious as to why; it might be important. That view was underlined by the fact that three armed men had been at that end of the corridor, taken out by the concussive force of the blast. Bolan stepped past them, hitting the speed dial number on his phone that put him through to Low. He outlined the situation briefly.

"Emergency services are already on the way," Low explained. "You don't set off two grenades in Manhattan without attracting some kind of attention. I already sent men, figuring it had to be something to do with our boys. You're shouting at me, by the way."

"Sorry, concussion," Bolan said briefly. "You sound miles away. If our targets are trapped in the elevator car, then we may need to be careful because of the explosives they carry. If they were already out, I need a trace ASAP."

"That may be a problem," Low replied, running through the number of decoy calls that had so far been received and the disruption to the CCTV network. As he did so, Bolan found the remote for the plasma and brought up the CCTV images.

"I think I've found the source," the soldier said simply. "The decoy calls might stop, but the CCTV feed is being screwed up by remote. Get a tech here with your men. And another thing," he added, picking up the nameplate that had been blown across the desk and onto the floor. "Our Turks sure aren't Turks. My guess is that they're Iranian."

"What makes you think that?" Low queried.

"The arrogant bastard running this show is using the name of the last Shah. Some joke."

THE THREE MEN were in the lobby of the building when the grenades blew. The doors of the elevator car they had just left buckled out as the force of the blast was directed downward, the stresses on the buckling shaft twisting the metal. Banjo looked panicked, as did Ali. But although it took Rez as much by surprise, he showed that he had a depth of experience that the two American terrorists would never have.

While all those around them were either frozen by shock or hurrying blindly in whatever direction they faced, Rez grabbed the two bombers by their jackets and propelled them toward the main doors of the building, past the reception and commissionaire, where confusion reigned, and pushed them out onto the sidewalk.

"Whoever your man was, he's right on your asses. You have to stay strong and do this. The diversions are in place. Don't look back, don't think, just act. Do what I told you, and you'll be fine," he snarled. "Now go."

Banjo and Ali, unable to even say their goodbyes, let alone have any kind of argument with Rez, stared wide-eyed at each other before moving off in opposite directions, moving jerkily like men who had no real control over their actions.

In many ways, that was the case. They were now pawns in the game that Rez had set in play. Their operation as an independent cell had ceased the moment they'd walked into the building. They were men who were now part of a much larger machine, as was the man who called himself Rez.

The Iranian adjusted his jacket and started to walk down the sidewalk as though he had no connection to the building he had just left. In the confusion, he figured that he wouldn't be noticed. There was a safe house he could head to. He had a new passport there, and as an Egyptian businessman he could leave the country within twenty-four hours. In forty-eight, he could be back in Iran.

He paused briefly to take stock, then moved on.

THE EXECUTIONER HAD only a short time before the emergency services would arrive. That would mean the NYPD, and they would want to detain him. Low had men on the way, but that would take time that Bolan could not afford. It would be better if he got out before anyone had a chance to ask awkward questions.

As he left the office, he passed confused and injured office workers. At any other time and under most other circumstances, he would tend to those who were injured and perhaps innocents caught in the cross fire. Not this day. There was no time, and it was not an imperative with paramedics on the way. He took the fire escape, vaulting the stairs so that he could reach the exit onto the side alleyway as quickly as possible. A few moments more and he reached the sidewalk, looking on as a crowd began to gather around the front of the building. He could hear sirens approaching at speed.

He noticed a familiar figure detach himself from the crowd and cross the street; the traffic was slowed by the commotion outside the building.

"Well, well, the Shah," Bolan murmured as he crossed the street, skirting traffic, and fell in behind his man.

The two terrorists were nowhere in sight. He could leave them for the moment to Low's men as their destination was known and it was their route that needed to be picked up. Manhattan was small enough to navigate quickly when the need arose. The man in front of him was more immediately important. His company and position provided a link between the isolated terrorist cell and a larger network. Maybe he could be made to talk; maybe that wouldn't be necessary.

The man turned down an alley similar to the one at the building they had just left.

Bolan took his Desert Eagle from its holster. He wanted to take the man alive if possible, but if there was no choice, then he wanted to make sure he took him down. He quickened his pace to catch up, gaining ground. They were alone as they moved down the alley, and he wanted to take out the man before they reached the far end. So far, he seemed preoccupied and hadn't noticed the footsteps echoing his own.

It seemed that much of the past few days had hinged on encounters down back alleys, and so it proved again. Bolan would never know what had made the man ahead of him suddenly realize that he was being followed. It was enough that the man suddenly turned with a gun in his hand.

The distance was enough for him to snap off a shot but not quite enough for Bolan to jump him before that could happen. The Executioner threw himself against the wall, flattening to make as small a target as possible while firing a shot. He went for center of mass, as it was the biggest target. His quarry returned fire with a shot that went high and wide as he was thrown off balance by the slug that hit him on the upper-left side of the chest.

As Bolan moved toward him, the prone man showed remarkable strength and fortitude in raising his gun to fire again. The soldier could take no chances. A second shot to the head, at a relatively close distance, eliminated the threat.

Checking that they had not been seen or that or that anyone had entered the alley, Bolan quickly rifled through the dead man's pockets. The streets at either end of the alley were busy, but like all these service roads, this one was dead—an ironic word choice, Bolan mused as he quickly emptied the man's pockets. A wallet contained only some currency. There was, however, a smartphone. The man had not had time to wipe it, and hopefully it could be taken apart to provide some kind of intel.

There was no time to think about that now. Bolan checked again, and with no one seeming to have noticed or heard the brief exchange of shots in the chaos of Manhattan, he stood and walked away from the corpse, pausing only when he reached the far end of the alley to check for bystanders.

It was a pause for thought that he could take out a man with two shots in the middle of the city and not even be noticed, but at least this time it served him well. He slipped the dead man's phone into a pocket and used his own to call Low.

"I've got another cleanup for you," he said briefly. "Any sightings?"

"You're making my day difficult," Low muttered. "But yes, we've got one of the bastards on track."

ALI HAD BEEN given his route, and he was determined to stick to it. After the explosions in the office building, he was terrified. He had never been afraid of dying before. He realized now that was because he was always the better fighter. His life up to this point had consisted of taking on weaker opponents, such as gangbangers, and so the idea of someone being stronger was a concept he could not comprehend. His life had never been in serious danger, and so the notion of blowing himself to a martyr's glory was so abstract as to not seem real. But the way the elevator had buckled and the shaking of the floor beneath him and the noise—even muffled by the two floors between himself and the explosions—had brought something home to him.

Dying would be painful. It would be scary. And right now he wasn't sure that he wanted to do it. But he knew that any such doubts were pointless. The man in black would get him, and if he didn't and there was the chance to run, then he would always be looking over his shoulder. One way or another, he was going to die. Rather than a glorious death, this now seemed just a quicker death.

He took the bus, staying aboveground as he had been ordered and staring sightlessly out of the window at what would be the last people he would ever see. For the first time, he wondered who they all were and what their lives were like, all the while knowing that it didn't matter.

BOLAN TOOK THE subway. Low had told him that there had been calls claiming bombs had been planted. There were men swarming the system, and every call so far had been a hoax. Bolan figured the strategy—hoax and CCTV interference—was to cause chaos, but any bombing would distract from the big gesture. To keep the system running wouldn't be the risk it might appear from the outside. Of course, if it was a wrong call…

No, it couldn't be. There had been no whispers, no indication of activity. This was standard crank stuff, not even expected to be taken seriously.

Bolan left the subway and headed for the northern edge of the memorial site. The Feds had picked up Ali's trail. He was on a bus that was headed for the area. It was worrying that there had been no sign of Banjo, but the net of Feds was tightening all the time under Low's direction. He would be found. First things first....

The soldier saw a bus pull up, then Ali disembarked among a group of passengers. There were too many people around him for an immediate approach. Had he had time to prime the bomb yet?

Bolan kept his distance as he threaded through the crowds, closing in on his man. On leaving the subway he had inserted an earpiece for his phone, so he could accept any incoming calls hands-free. He had a feeling he would need it.

Ali was still half a block from the memorial site.

One of the bombers would head to the museum. Would it be Ali? And what about Banjo? All that went through Bolan's mind as he scanned the crowds on the street. He had to find a way to isolate the bomber so that he could take him down with a minimum of risk to passersby.

The incoming call took his attention for a moment.

"We've got Ali covered. You, too. I have men encircling you. Do you want them to close in?"

Bolan looked around. He recognized a couple of the faces in the crowd from earlier. Feds. "No. Wait for my cue," he instructed.

Ali was nervous. Everything about his body language told the soldier that. It made him difficult to second-guess. The bomber stopped and shrugged the backpack off his shoulder.

Bolan knew he was about to prime the bomb, that in the confusion of the past couple of hours he had failed to do it. This might be the only chance Bolan would get.

"Stay frosty, Andrew," he said softly. "Keep your men away."

Ali looked around. He needed some degree of privacy to prime the explosive. There was very little here. The only thing he could do was go into the lobby of a building and use the restroom. It was what Bolan would have taken as an option, and the soldier swore softly to himself as he saw Ali do just that.

One wrong move and the whole building would go down.

The building was composed of office space, with a concierge receptionist who had been preoccupied with a courier, allowing Ali to slip by. A security guard saw him and moved forward as Bolan entered the lobby. The soldier swore softly.

"Get someone in here and take care of the staff. I don't want to have to run interference," Bolan ordered down the open line.

Ali had entered the ground-floor restroom. Bolan picked up the pace and got there a half step ahead of the guard.

"Leave it," he snapped as an arm came across his chest to stop him. The guard turned with anger on his face; then he met the soldier's stony visage. There was an authority there that made him pause long enough for one of Low's men to approach, ID at the ready. The guard was confused by this turn of events, but he backed off more from lack of any other course of action than from choice.

"Clear the lobby. Keep everyone out," Bolan ordered. There was no time to clear the block, but at least he could avoid further intrusion. Taking a deep breath, he entered the restroom.

Ali was under the lights illuminating the sinks. They were set in marble, with mirrors lining the wall. That was to Bolan's right. To the left were the stalls and urinals. As far as he could see, they were empty, which eliminated the chance of a bystander being in the way.

Ali had set the fuse on the basin; the gray lump of explosive was sitting beside it. No connection had yet been made.

Bolan had the Desert Eagle in his hand. "Move away from the sink," he said softly, watching Ali look up at him in the mirror. There was an expression of abject defeat in the man's eyes.

"Brother, what are you going to do? I'm dead anyway. For the glory of God or by the hand of another if I fail."

"Not necessarily. Cooperate and you can live. Die now and you don't achieve your aim."

Ali smiled sadly. "I can still take out this building and everyone in it. That's something." He returned to trying to prime the bomb. His hands shook as he picked up the fuse component. He caught sight of Bolan raising the gun in the mirror.

"Are you quick enough, brother? Hit the explosive and you're gone. I drop the fuse it may be enough."

Bolan appeared not to take his eye off Ali. In truth

he was casting a glance to the surface of the sink. Trembling hands could drop the fuse component on the explosive. There was no time for him to hesitate.

One squeeze and the Desert Eagle boomed in the enclosed space. Ali's head took the full impact. Nerveless and unknowing hands dropped the fuse component onto the surface of the sink.

Bolan moved before Ali's lifeless body had even hit the floor. There was little left of his head at that range; the mirrors and tiles were sprayed with brain and blood. It made the floor around him slippery, but Bolan had a sureness of foot born from necessity.

The liquid fuse shattered on the sink, the contents spreading across the surface. That should have been enough to trigger the necessary reaction with the explosive.

Bolan was quicker than Ali had hoped. Before the spreading liquid reached the gray mass, Bolan scooped it up and stepped back, breathing heavily with relief.

"Come in and clean up," he ordered through the open line. "I've still got one left to take down."

CHAPTER SIXTEEN

The activity around the building had caused enough commotion for a small crowd to be gathering beyond the lobby. Low was waiting outside the restroom and took the explosive from Bolan as the soldier strode toward the sidewalk.

"Can't you clear this crowd?" he snapped. "If Banjo is in the vicinity, then he's going to know there's a problem and exactly where it is."

"This is NYC, Cooper. You can't just disperse a crowd or stop it forming at will," Low replied testily. "It shouldn't have got this far."

The soldier was angered by that statement, but only because the Fed was right. Everything about this mission had been cockeyed from the get-go: pitched into a hunt for terrorists because of intel he had stumbled on, asked to tackle it by the guy in the big house and having to act like some kind of counterintelligence agent when his real strengths were preparation, planning and execution of military action. He had been forced into actions that would not have been his first choice, and by the nature of having to track them and gather information at the same time, he had missed a golden opportunity to take them down in one move.

He bit back the anger he felt and said, "Circumstances

aren't always as we'd like them, Andrew. Save the recriminations. Tell me you've got something on Banjo."

"Maybe. A crane operator on the construction site
reported that one of the tourists had wandered on-site
and he had to warn him off. The man went without any
argument, but his description would fit, although to be
truthful it would fit a lot of male tourists."

"How easy is it to wander on-site?"

"It isn't, generally. Security is good, but there have
been occasions when deliveries have been made and
gates left open and unguarded, if only for a few seconds."

"Accidents happen, I guess, but maybe not with such
synchronicity. Have you picked him up?"

Low shook his head. "The operator didn't report it
immediately. I guess he didn't think it was that important. I've got men around there now."

Bolan sighed. "Downside of not creating panic, I
guess. It would be just right for Banjo to hit there. You
could put money on it. You could put your life on it," he
added with a grim humor.

BANJO WAS SCARED and alone. He had never felt this way.
If he had known that Ali felt the same way, it may have
been some comfort to him. He, too, was scared of dying,
but more afraid of not completing his mission. If he was
unable to do this, then whatever happened next was of
no consequence. The only thing that would matter was
that he had failed.

After parting company with Ali and Rez, Banjo had
taken the route that had been given to him. It was a more

direct route than that given to his erstwhile colleague, and although he was to proceed on foot, he had directions that cut across blocks and brought him to the memorial site while Ali was still caught in traffic.

Giving his situation more thought than the older man had and realizing that he would be marked and traceable by more than just the disrupted CCTV, Banjo had paused at the first possible opportunity in order to adjust his appearance. He moved the rucksack so that he wore it on his front, and pulled the hood as far over his head as it would go. They were small things, but it would make him harder to spot, and perhaps be enough to throw a street-level observer.

The fact that he had made it to the memorial site without being stopped or—as far as he could tell—tailed appeared to bear him out. Once he was there, he scoped out the site to see how easy it might be to get on to the construction site. When Mummar had briefed them on that in D.C.—something that seemed to be another lifetime ago, not just a matter of weeks—he had given them schedules of work and timetables for shift changes in security. Banjo had no idea how he'd gotten them and hadn't thought to ask. He had just memorized them as instructed. And as he checked his watch, he had seen that he had arrived within ten minutes of a change, a gap that would give him the opportunity to slip onto the site.

It had all been going according to plan until that construction worker had challenged him. The man had to have had a photographic memory for every worker on the site, the way he had been able to ID Banjo as a stranger. Play the innocent, act the stupid tourist who had wandered in by accident and stop the man from creating a disturbance.

It had caused a delay, but not one that ruined the plan. Banjo had not been detained, and he still carried the bomb with him. His plan of action now was to prime the device and find a way of getting on-site before the timer set it off. If all else failed, he knew it was powerful enough that as long as he could get near the site before the set time, even if he was shot the power of the bomb would cause the kind of collateral damage intended.

Calmly going through those options, he had sought somewhere to wait until he could carry out the next stage.

He chose a diner about a block from the site. It seemed suitable, somehow. If he had been on death row, he would have been granted a last meal of choice. Well, in a sense he had put himself on a kind of death row when he had opted for a suicide mission. All he was doing was granting to himself the same as any state would.

Banjo ordered waffles, chicken wings and coffee. He sat at a table away from the window, keeping as low a profile as possible, sipping at his coffee and savoring the taste. The same was true of the food when it was delivered to his table. For a few minutes, while he took each mouthful and tried to impress the flavors on his memory, he could forget what was about to happen.

But all too soon the meal was finished. He had a refill of coffee and sipped it while he looked at the rucksack by his feet. There was a restroom at the back of the diner, and he picked up the rucksack and made his way to the small room.

The men's restroom was a confined space. One urinal, one sink, a hand dryer and a stall. There was no lock on the door into the restaurant, so he went into the stall and locked it, using the closed lid of the toilet and the top of the tank as workspaces. It was hot and tight in the stall, and he could feel the sweat drip off his forehead and down his nose as he worked.

Banjo took the block of explosive and placed it carefully on the lid before taking the fuse and laying it on the top of the tank. He worked slowly and methodically, concentrating on his memory of the method Schrueders had shown them in the lab. He heard men come in and out of the restroom. One tried the door of the stall, then mumbled an apology and went out again.

Finally, Banjo had the bomb primed. Carefully he placed it back in the rucksack, then stood for some moments looking at the innocuous piece of luggage sitting on the lid. If the rest of the people in the diner had known…but this was not the time for such thoughts. Dismissing them, he took a deep breath and clicked the lock on the stall.

Showtime.

"HE'LL BE BACK here. He has to be. The question is simply one of which avenue of approach," Bolan said as he stood at the main gate to the construction site.

"I have men positioned in a cordon around the area. He won't get by without being picked up. How are you going to play it?" Low asked.

"By ear, the only way I can," Bolan said. "We have to assume that the bomb is primed. I can't guarantee getting that lucky again. The question is whether it's a timer or self-detonated. If it's a timer, then we're up against an unknown limit. Self-detonated and we have to take him out before he can trigger it. And without hitting the backpack…. Believe me, I've seen what that can do."

"Simple, then," Low murmured.

"Just tell me if you scope him and put me on his tail," Bolan said calmly. "Keep your men back. This is up to me."

"It's taking a lot on yourself—"

"I have to. It's what they pay me for. Besides, it's my responsibility," Bolan added.

He looked around. The site had been cleared of personnel. Once Banjo was inside, it was all on Bolan. If the bomb was detonated, it would cause immense damage—collateral and psychological—but at least it would be in a position where fewer people were hurt. It was a no-win no-brainer, but it was the best they could do at this juncture.

"We've got someone…looks like our man. Heading this way from the north side of the site," Low murmured, listening intently to his earpiece.

"Pull back, try to get your men to sit back once he's passed them and let the bastard in," Bolan said as he moved onto the site. "Let me do the rest."

BANJO WALKED AROUND the perimeter. His skin was crawling, and not because of what he was about to do. He had always had a kind of sixth sense about setups. It was as if his subconscious knew how people acted and could tell the difference. He couldn't express what was wrong. Something about the way it had been so easy to get here from the diner a block away. Something about the way in which the construction site had been so empty, as if even the security had been warned away. Something about the way in which only one gate had been left open. It was too easy. He was being set up.

Whoever was behind it—and he was sure it was that bastard in black who had taken the others down—knew that Banjo would guess this. But they had also worked out that he had no other choice but to continue.

He wondered if Ali was anywhere near, or even if he was even still alive.

Banjo wandered across the site, looking around him all the while. He was carrying the rucksack casually over one shoulder and giving not a single thought to those whose memories he would defile. He was thinking instead only of the glory that would be awaiting him. He could taste the coffee—cream, three sugars—and the waffles and chicken; the flavors melted together on his tongue.

He looked up at the sky. Even though it was progressing to evening, and overcast, to him it seemed as if the sun was burning brightly at the height of a blazing blue sky, beckoning him to the heavens.

He put the rucksack on the ground and looked at his watch.

BOLAN WAS IN cover. He had positioned himself as centrally as the available cover would allow, figuring that the optimum position for any bomber entering the site would be dead center, where the core of the memorial was situated. Banjo's movements since entering had done nothing to change that view.

Watching him, the soldier was disturbed by the way in which he was moving. There was something slow, almost dreamlike, about his progress across the site. He had guessed he was being set up, but he didn't care. Why? Because he was confident that he could trigger the device before he was taken out? Or was it simply the almost beatific state of the fanatic about to realize his dream?

Bolan had the Uzi trained on the bomber as he reached the center of the site and put the rucksack on the ground. He withdrew both hands from the device. If he knew he was being watched and had to trigger the device manually, then there was little chance he would be careless enough, having gotten this far, to remove all contact and risk being taken out before he could fulfill his mission.

It had to be a timer by the way in which Banjo looked to the skies and then at his watch.

Timer. And set so that he had come onto the site close to the time. Even if he had been taken down outside, if the bomb was not defused, it would still cause the required level of devastation.

Time. However much of this there was left before the blast, it was a sure bet that it was small.

Bolan was about 150 yards from the bomber. It was a fair distance for the Uzi, but he had the skill required for accuracy at this distance. He only had one shot.

One tap: three shots. Banjo's head was now angled downward, and the rounds stitched the man at an angle from the rear. The side of his head disappeared and he fell forward, jerking briefly. The rucksack was by his outstretched hand, but nerveless fingers would never grasp at it.

Before Banjo was down, Bolan was out of cover and racing across the gap between the dead bomber and himself, the Uzi still ready to deliver another tap should there be any sign of life.

Banjo presented no threat. He had gone to his martyrdom hoping that he had set events in motion that would assure him of that. It was up to Bolan to make sure that this was not achieved.

"Cooper." Low's voice was in his ear, his tone on the one word speaking volumes.

"Banjo's neutralized. The bomb may not be. Stay back and keep clearing the area," Bolan barked.

As he did so, he carefully began opening the rucksack. Inside, there were the constituent parts that he recognized from his encounter with Ali: the gray block of explosive and the container with the clear fluid that acted as the catalyst. The container was attached to the block, and there was a division between them that appeared to be in the process of dissolving.

Bolan had some experience in defusing conventional bombs. He was no expert, but he had the ability to take a conventional timer to pieces and to disconnect wiring. This had no wiring. It was simple and incredibly effective: take a catalyst, set the container to dissolve using a solution of the right acid and, by judging thickness of separation and strength of solution, you could produce an accurate timer, one that was hard to disconnect with-

out the acid causing a break in the separator and so has-
tening the catalyst.

He didn't have much time, and he had no experience
to draw on, but he was damned if he was going to let it
end this way.

With an exaggerated slowness and care, he took the
complete bomb from the rucksack and placed it on the
stone of the pool, giving him room to work.

The detonator was attached by means of a small tube
that had been inserted into the block of explosive. When
the acid ate through the container for the catalyst, it
would dribble down the tube. To simply hold the block
above the level of the container would prevent that, but
on his own it presented the problem that he would then
be forced to break the connection with one hand. To snap
it off still risked some of the catalyst spurting along the
tube. It may only take one drop to start the reaction, for
all he knew.

No, it would have to be this way.... He extended the
tube until it was straight and as far away from the block
of explosive as was possible. He could see that the acid
solution was nearly through the separation, and so he had
a matter of seconds. The pressure of the liquid in such a
confined space pushed against the weakened separator.

He took the gray block in one hand and the tube in
the other. He pulled them apart sharply. The stress on
the tube caused the weakened separator to split, and
the pressurized catalyst spit down the tube and harmlessly into the pool. He held the gray block away from
the ground and breathed heavily, not daring to think

what might have happened had one drop of the catalyst reached the block, as had been intended.

When he spoke, his voice was dry and cracked. "You can get a cleanup team in here now. The bomb has been defused. The terrorist is dead."

He got to his feet and stood, looking down at Banjo as he waited for Low and his men to move in. When the Fed arrived, Bolan handed him the gray block without a word and turned to walk away.

As he did so, he felt for the smartphone in his pocket that he had taken from the joker who'd named himself after the last Shah. If he was Iranian, as that suggested, then the trail from Somalia to D.C. to New York still had to reach its end.

He took out his own phone and hit a speed dial number. When Kurtzman answered, Bolan spoke without preamble.

"I've got something I want you to take a look at, Bear. If I'm right, then this isn't over just yet."

CHAPTER SEVENTEEN

"Interesting things, smartphones. Especially if they're owned by someone who is a little lax in keeping them tidy. They can yield an incredible amount of information."

Bolan grinned. "You sound like Bear. Did you memorize that to try to impress me, Hal?"

The big Fed returned the grin and paused by a bench in the Mall. "Shut up and rest your feet, Striker. You're going to be getting some action soon enough, so take the opportunity to take a load off."

Bolan joined him on the bench and they watched a phalanx of joggers pass by before continuing. "So it was helpful, then?"

Brognola nodded. "Although helpful is a relative term in view of the cleanup this mission facilitated. You could have been a little tidier, considering where you were."

"What can I say? When you're on the defensive from the beginning, then you tend not to worry about keeping things clean. You just want to do the job."

"Luckily for you, the Man sees it the same way. There was some heat coming down, but you'll be pleased to hear it wasn't anything I couldn't deal with," Brognola said wryly. "However, the Man brushed all that away when he heard what you did at the memorial. You have no idea— No, scratch that, of course you know what it would have meant if that had been a successful terrorist attack. That's the second time you've dug one out and the second time you've just put more work on your plate."

Bolan shrugged. "What can I say, Hal? It's what I'm here for. So I'm guessing that the smartphone yielded something interesting."

Brognola nodded. "You were right about one thing. Anyone who uses the name of the last Shah as a cover is an Iranian with a sense of humor. Your boy had a number of other names, but his DNA and prints were on national security databases. He has quite a record, but had been MIA for a while. Guess we know why. There were a few known fundamentalists on the information gleaned that we had nothing definite on, and a few that we had been keeping close. It's easy to pretend you're Turkish when you're Iranian—let's be honest, most of us in America would be hazy about the difference unless we were really familiar with people from those countries."

"So he'd been using the business as a cover to aid terror cells. Glad to have nailed him," Bolan said with some satisfaction. "But what else did it tell you?"

"There was information on the phone that led us on a trail back to Iran. We have some names of men who are not in the government but are closely allied to it. They've been very busy funneling cash to groups, individuals and also known arms traders. We could do with them shutting up shop. Make that cyberspace they're using for their channels dead, you know?"

"And of course we can do nothing officially as we've had no links with Iran since the end of the seventies,"

Bolan finished. "I don't get it. Yeah, they hate us, and with Afghanistan and Iraq they've felt under threat, but why now? Why not ten years back? Or has it taken us that long to stumble on it?"

"We can be slow sometimes, sure, but not that slow." Brognola sounded slightly aggrieved. "Believe me, Striker, this is pretty recent. We think we know why now. Have you heard of the Parchin report?"

Bolan thought about it for a moment. "Parchin is a military facility that houses a large part of the Iranian army's armament capacity."

"I figured you'd know that, Striker, but what about the report?" When the soldier replied in the negative, Brognola continued. "The International Atomic Energy Agency has been investigating Iran's nuclear capabilities for some time. Which, let's face it, is kind of hard when the country in question refuses to cooperate with inspectors and wants them to just use the information that's given out as the official line, which is that they have a nuclear capability and that it's purely for power. Now, that's kind of rich when you consider how much of their coin comes from petrochemicals and how much they've been holding the West to ransom over that during the past three decades."

"Hey, they're just thinking ahead," Bolan replied wryly. "Of course, the fact that a by-product of all that research is the kind of weapons-grade plutonium that would come in useful for a nation with rampant paranoia and a lurking regard for annexing their neighbors is purely coincidental. And I'm thinking that the perfect place for all this to be taking place would be the Parchin facility, which is why the IAEA are particularly interested. Am I guessing right?"

"I would say so. Now, as you're only too well aware, Iraq and Afghanistan, no matter how necessary they might have been at the time, have been going on a little longer than desired and have been a little more messy than we would have liked."

"This generation of soldiers' Vietnam," Bolan replied with feeling. "We're just unraveling those messes, so the Man isn't going to want a potential third situation like that to arise."

"Precisely…and although the United Nations is a wonderful body, it has to be said that sometimes there can be too much talk. Better to act swiftly on what we know, and keep it discreet."

"You think I'm discreet after D.C. and NYC?" Bolan queried.

Brognola shrugged. "That was, like you said, a different matter. The attacks at the memorial would have been a bitter blow, but more than that, they would have been one major distraction when Iran wants everyone to look anywhere but Parchin right now. And the fact is, a mission like this is what you're good at."

"Okay, seems like I'm going back in the field. Am I going in through Afghanistan or Iraq?"

Brognola laughed. "Sending you in via a place where we have a presence would be a bad idea. We know how carefully they watch those borders."

"Pakistan or Turkey, then? Although I'd be guessing we're a little wary of the former, and the latter might be suspect over their use as a cover in this instance?"

"Y'see, that's what I like about you, Striker. Tactical thinking. No, my friend, we're going to send you in from the least likely angle."

Bolan grinned. "Oh, man, Russia's president will love that if he ever gets wind of it."

BOLAN STOOD ON the shores of the Caspian Sea, looking toward the peninsula of Iran. Just over seventy-two hours had passed since he had been sitting in the Mall with the big Fed, and he had to admit that Brognola had acted with alacrity. The Executioner had been put on a regular diplomatic bag flight to Moscow, where he had entered the American Embassy as an IT and security consultant being sent to liaise with a Russian corporation regarding the installation of new servers that were to be supplied to the embassy complex.

Although nearly everyone on the embassy staff knew only the cover story, the CIA station chief had been clued in, and she made sure that Bolan was not asked any awkward questions during his brief stay at the embassy.

In fact, Tanya Morgan had already arranged for Bolan to be housed at the expense of the Russian corporation, and Bolan spent less than two hours at the embassy before being taken to a hotel, where he spent the night before Morgan arranged for him to meet Roman Schevchenko.

Schevchenko was a wiry, graying and seemingly diffident man who was almost shy when introduced to the soldier. It was only when he had dismissed his guard and was alone with Bolan in the boardroom of Teklis

Software, his corporation's core company, that his inner steel was revealed.

"I will not waste words with you," he began. "If I am found out, it will be difficult for me. I have a London home, but even there I will not be safe. But like many I became a made man despite men like my country's president, not because of them. America has been good for men like myself, and we do not want the East to gain any more power in this corner of the globe than they already have. This is why I offer assistance when none can be forthcoming in official channels. I take risks, but I have always taken risks. You call us oligarchs. Others call us gangsters. I call us realists."

"What can you offer me?"

The Russian smiled. "To the point. I like you, Mr. Cooper. A man like you would do well here. But no matter. I will arrange the armament you need and also the method for getting you into Iran. I have contacts who will supply me with the required hardware through channels that cannot be traced. You just give me those requirements. You have communications equipment—" he waited for Bolan's assent "—then that is good. Enjoy the next twenty-four hours, Mr. Cooper. I will have everything ready for you by then."

Bolan had supplied the required list and had returned to the embassy briefly, where he used the security-cleared channels to touch base with his contact cover and relay progress. From there, he made his way back to his luxury hotel.

Morgan had liaised with him the next morning at his hotel room, and word had come from Schevchenko that he was required "on-site" for a product conference. Bolan knew that meant that things were ready to move. Schevchenko greeted him, introduced him to the guide who would get him into Iran and to the next point of contact and handed over the requested ordnance as well as a war chest of Iranian currency.

Bolan was grateful for the gesture of the war chest, but he had enough money for what he needed to do. He declined that offer.

Wishing him good fortune, the Russian bade him farewell.

In the back of the black sedan with tinted windows that usually ferried Schevchenko around the city, Bolan and his guide—answering only to Yuri, and then only when posed a direct and relevant question—left Moscow and headed for the Caspian shores.

Schevchenko had a luxury home on the shore, complete with its own jetty and yacht. When Bolan arrived, he noted that the vessel was being moved and moored farther out in the water, making room for another craft. While they waited for its arrival, there was a chance to grab a few hours of necessary sleep. It was uncertain when he would be get another chance to recharge.

And now he looked across the water to where the coast of Iran beckoned, waiting for the vessel that would ferry him there. As he and Yuri waited in silence, in the fading light a fishing boat traveled slowly toward them. In blacksuits, with duffel bags containing their weapons, the two men would look incongruous on a fishing vessel. Better hope they didn't get stopped before they landed, then, Bolan mused as the boat came in to moor on the jetty.

The crew was Iranian and looked at both men with something approaching suspicion. As Bolan and Yuri were beckoned aboard, the soldier felt a sense of unease.

"They're looking a little hostile," he murmured to Yuri. "Are you sure we can trust them?"

"No," the Russian answered blandly. "No more than you would expect. They are paid money, and they need the money. If we do not arrive, word will reach my employer. If it does, they know they will be dead. We cannot trust them, but fear is useful in such situations."

"I see," Bolan replied with an equally bland expression. Although he was far from reassured by the Russian's words, he could see the logic and so was reasonably reassured as the vessel cast off and headed for the coast of Iran.

The two men were shown to a cabin and shut in after a few perfunctory words from the skipper. He spoke in neither Arabic nor—as would have been expected—Farsi, but rather in Armenian. Bolan's grasp of the language was nonexistent. Yuri translated. In essence, he told them to stay put and keep quiet. They would not be welcomed above deck as they may be observed by other vessels, and if there was any engagement they were to remain where they were unless it was an emergency.

"Good thing you understood the language," Bolan said when the skipper had left them.

The Russian smiled. "I also speak Persian as though I was born Iranian. I speak many languages fluently. That is why I am a good employee. On the other hand, if these fools think I speak Russian and Armenian alone, and do not understand them the rest of the time, then that is not always a bad thing."

Bolan nodded. "Good point. You're a smart man, Yuri, and you had me fooled. I had you down as a muscle-bound lunkhead."

"You flatter me. I suspect that you are not entirely truthful with me."

Bolan smiled. "Maybe not, but we've got a good stretch of sea ahead of us, and if we're going to work together, then you're going to have to show me how smart you are and tell me what you've got planned."

Yuri shrugged. "I plan nothing, Mr. Cooper. It is not my place. However, I have been fully briefed. When we set ashore, we will be met by men who are loyal to opponents of the regime."

"There are men like that?"

"Please, do not be disingenuous. Even the most devout Muslim is not necessarily a proponent of separatism and radical religion. Some, indeed, are fond of the Western world and its ways, particularly those that are based around the petrochemical dollar. They look at their counterparts in other Arab nations and weep. Did you know that ten percent of the oil in the world and fifteen percent of the natural gas can be found beneath the sand and rock of Iran? It must be very hard to watch all that money and potential fun going to waste on prayer mats and minarets."

"And, of course, your boss just happens to be in a position to help them realize those Western dreams if they should be in a position to overcome the more fundamentalist regime."

Yuri shrugged. "My employer is a man who has built a business empire. In the course of that endeavor, he has learned many strategies and has made the acquaintance of people who can help him to realize those strategies, as well as those who would benefit from his assistance. With such resources at stake, it would be a poor businessman who could not act as a broker to aid the smooth flow of money and resources from one country to another."

"Even if the ruling faction of one of those countries would not choose to see it that way," Bolan added wryly.

"Of course. This ridiculous hostility is why we are forced to access Iran via an indirect and more time-consuming route. Avoiding detection is something that is an unfortunate necessity. However, it would be best if we took advantage of the time that is granted to us to get some rest, as we may not have an opportunity to rest at length for some time."

"You take second watch. I'll take first," Bolan said.

Yuri grinned. "I would have offered to take first, Mr. Cooper. I do not exactly trust these men like brothers, either, you know."

THE VOYAGE ACROSS the Caspian Sea proved uneventful, and both men were able to rest and keep watch with no disturbance whatsoever. The area was patrolled by Iranian boats, but the presence of a fishing trawler that frequented these waters on an almost daily basis did not arouse anything beyond the barest acknowledgment.

The vessel was able to make the far shore of Iran in the expected time, with nothing to cause a ripple of excitement taking place.

It anchored about five hundred yards from the sandy, flat shoreline, and a small dinghy with an outboard engine was lowered over the side. The skipper told them in broken Armenian that one of his men would take them in and then return with the boat, and in truth he seemed glad to see the backs of them as they descended.

A surly fisherman piloted them on in silence. They bucked on the shallows and he killed the motor, staying the boat enough for the two men to alight in the surf before turning it around, firing the motor and heading off toward the trawler without a backward glance.

Bolan and Yuri now stood on Iranian soil, looking at the rising plains and seeing nothing. This was one of the few areas in Iran that was not mountainous or hilly, and although this meant that they could not be easily ambushed on arrival, it was spare enough to make both men feel exposed.

"So where's the cavalry?" Bolan asked, looking around.

Yuri checked his watch. "We're ahead of time. Fifteen minutes."

Bolan nodded. "Then I suggest we find cover of some kind so we can wait unobserved." But where? Among the flat sands and softly rising plain, there was little they could use. They dug out a hole, covered it with plastic sheeting they carried in their duffel bags and camouflaged it with a layer of sand. It would be useless in daylight, but in the dark it would be easily passed over by patrol boats skirting the shore, or from the air.

It was a long fifteen minutes. Bolan did not check the time, but his own tingling nerves told him that their contacts were late. If their part in this action had been discovered, then it left the two men exposed and without backup. That was not a pleasant prospect in a country that had little to do with the outside world and was locked down within its own borders.

While the time dragged, Bolan thought about the mission: he had a twofold task. The first was to infiltrate Tehran with the help of regime opponents and take out the politician in the guardian council who had been instrumental in providing funding to radical cells across the United States. The information that had been taken from the smartphone he had captured in NYC had been specific. One man had been the driving force, though whether he had been operating with full approval of his government was open to doubt. The way in which the Iranian political system operated, with its unwieldy mix of Islamic tradition and parliamentary democracy, made it sometimes hard to see where ultimate responsibility lay. All politicians and administrators were answerable ultimately to the supreme leader, a cleric to whom even the president had to present policy and legislation for approval. Yet it was doubtful that the cleric had a full grasp of everything that went on within a system that the melding of East and West had made labyrinthine.

The named official was the one to eliminate, and in a way that made it clear his assassination was a warning: further action would not be tolerated.

That was the first part of the mission. As if that were not enough, he was to try to enter Parchin and recon the base for any signs of the development of nuclear weapons. If there was some, again a warning shot was to be fired across the bow, a cease-and-desist order, making the regime aware that their activities had been noted. Anything overt that could be traced back to the United States would cause an international incident. Something that looked like an accident was required.

As soon as he had achieved the first part of the mission, the second would have to be undertaken with maximum speed. He felt sure that Yuri was a man who could be trusted to be efficient, but what of those who were already late for the rendezvous?

He could hear the distant whine of an engine as a vehicle approached across the plains. If it was their pickup, he resolved that as the mission progressed he would adapt and improvise on the given strategy in whatever degree it took to ensure that only he and the big Russian took risks, and only risks that they could weigh adequately.

The pickup vehicle was a flatbed truck that was used for transporting fruit. Pallets and crates were still tied in the rear. Two men occupied the cab. One was smiling, the other taciturn. They reminded Bolan of an old vaudeville act from TV movies when he was a kid. The smiling man—Mahmoud—apologized profusely for the delay, claiming that they had been avoiding police in the city and so had taken a roundabout route. Akhbar, the silent one, was impassive and stone-faced, staring about as if expecting hordes of military to overrun them at any moment. Mahmoud spoke to them in Farsi and was obviously familiar with Yuri. He greeted him warmly and had no hesitation in using his native language.

"We're wasting time," Bolan snapped, interrupting the fulsome apologies. "Let's get going. Where are we headed?"

"Rasht," Mahmoud replied, his tone suddenly more sober as he took the measure of the soldier. "It's just down the coast from here but too busy to risk landing. Since the revolution, more and more people are in the cities. We used to be a nation of land dwellers, and now we are all children of the cities. They say that over half of us now live in cities, and by the time I die—God willing I live a long life—then nearly nine-tenths of us will be crammed into concrete and clay. It is not a great city, but it is where my brother lives and where he does his business. We will go to his home and you will meet him. I am just your deliveryman."

"That was more than I really needed to know, but thanks anyway," Bolan murmured, noting Yuri's grin.

"Forgive me, my friend, I talk too much. I have to, as Akhbar here does not."

"I doubt he gets a chance to get a word in," Bolan said.

"He could not, even if I was silent," Mahmoud said, his face clouding. "He did too much talking against the government when he was a young man, and they silenced him by coming at night and slicing out his tongue. That was twenty years ago, when your Desert Storm put fear in us all, but not always for the same reasons. That's a lot of talking I have to make up for."

The rest of the journey lapsed into an uneasy silence, and Bolan was relieved when they reached their destination.

The sun was starting to rise as they entered Rasht, and the city was coming to life. Bolan and Yuri hunkered down in the cab, sandwiched between Akhbar and Mahmoud, with their blacksuits covered by borrowed clothes. That was why even the slightest delay had caused the soldier concern. Before sunrise it would have been harder to see into the cab of the truck, and there would have been fewer people on the streets. Now the populace was beginning to rise and go about their business, and as a result there was also a larger presence of police and military on the streets.

Mahmoud negotiated the narrow streets with skill and speed, landing them in the courtyard of a building that rose around them on three stories. The white reflected the already rising sun, while the cool stone of the courtyard housed palms and shrubs in tubs and beds. As the truck entered, two young men slammed large wooden gates shut behind them, securing them with a gate bar. A middle-aged man came out of the main building to greet them. He shook Yuri's hand.

"We meet again. I always hope it will be under better circumstances, but they never seem to come."

"Perhaps they may. This is the foreigner Mr. Schevchenko wishes you to assist."

"You speak our language, or do you wish me to converse in English?" the man asked Bolan in tones that bore little trace of any accent.

"Your language will be fine. In your country, it would

be only courteous," he added, noting to himself that Yuri had avoided mentioning his nationality. He knew his accent would give him away in English, but perhaps less so in his halting Farsi.

"Come inside. We will eat and discuss what is to be done," the man said warmly, leading them through and into the cool interior of the building. Inside, it was suffused with a muted electric glow, and the cold morning air was dispelled by hot-air heating. The two young men who had closed the doors followed them and took the borrowed robes from Bolan and Yuri, vanishing into the depths of the building, as had Mahmoud and Akhbar, only to reappear bearing trays of yogurt, tea and fruit that they placed on a table in the center of one room. There were low, Western-style couches around, and the man beckoned them to sit and partake. Both men were glad of the chance for a repast before the next stage of their mission. While they ate, they listened to what the man had to say.

"I do not know if you know who I am," he began. "Yuri, of course, is familiar with me, as we have conducted business of one sort or another on many occasions. I am Nouri Razmara, named after my great-uncle, who was assassinated over sixty years ago so that the corrupt government of the time could replace him as prime minister. Since then, this country has always been in the grip of dogma, whether it be the politics of the Shah or the religion of the Ayatollah. There is no place for freedom in either of these extremes. All I—and the men with whom I am allied—seek is the freedom that you have in the West. We could be a great player in world affairs—instead, we are ostracized and marginalized."

"That is your point of view, and I see no reason to argue over the matter," Bolan said carefully. "But I fail to see what this has to do with the matter in hand or the arrangements that have been made. That is my only concern."

Razmara waved dismissively. "Of course, you are right to be concerned only with what is necessary to you. But it is vital I try to communicate to you the dedication we have to your mission. It is a difficult one. Parchin is a fortress, and so in its way is Tehran. We have put much thought into this. Of course we could buy the muscle, as I think you would say, but we could not guarantee their tongues short of cutting them out. And that would attract unwanted attention," he added with some humor. "We have used only those who we know well. That means that they are not necessarily fighters, but they can support you."

Bolan nodded. Razmara spoke as though he expected some dissent from the soldier, yet this was exactly the way that Bolan would have chosen to play it.

"All we require from you is the transport, the backup and the route out after we have achieved our objective. It is best that the fewest people possible are involved in the actual action. One, we would not wish to endanger men who live here or their families should reprisals take place. Two, we are trained and your men are not. That would make them a liability, no matter how well intentioned, as I'm sure you know. Three, the nature of this work means that the fewer people on the ground for this, the better. Are we clear about that?"

Razmara nodded. "That is good. We can continue with no problems awaiting us from the inside. The outside will present a problem enough."

"I hope that's something you have addressed," Bolan said quietly. "Now, how about you outline your plans for getting us to the locations and the arrangements that you have made to ease our way on arrival?"

"Of course," Razmara agreed. "After we have finished here, the first move is to transport you to Tehran for the night. As you may be aware, the city is to the southeast of Rasht, and the roads between them will get you there in a matter of hours. Once there, we have a safe house for you until the night falls."

CHAPTER EIGHTEEN

"There are millions of people in this city. It has some of the most advanced scientists in the world, with the capabilities to work on the Hadron Collider and to be one of the foremost nations in the world when it comes to cloning animals. A massive producer of gas and petrochemicals and a nation that has had a nuclear program since the fifties."

Bolan stood at the window of the fourth-floor apartment in the center of Tehran, a modern building that overlooked a mosque that could have been built in the past year or in the time of Mohammed, so traditional and permanent was its design. He spoke softly, and when he paused Yuri looked up from cleaning his BXP10 and interjected.

"You sound almost as though you work for the Iranian tourist board," he said with humor. "Your point is what, exactly?"

"That the people back where I come from have no idea about this nation. About what it really is and the danger it could truly represent if it chose. For the past thirty years or more, since the last Shah was deposed, because of the fundamentalist nature of the rulers, the American media and the people—hell, maybe even the government for all I know—has looked on Iran like it's some kind of dirt-poor, shuffling-in-the-dust Arab nation. We fight and worry about their oil, but never really take that into the equation. This is a nation that mixes the radical and dangerous in technology with a worldview that seems at least a millennium out of step with the rest of the world. It's very deceptive and very dangerous because of that."

"Then I guess it's your job to make your superiors aware of this when you return. Perhaps they do know, but choose not to represent that to the people?"

"That wouldn't be the first time, or the last. I just hope that this idea of sending out a warning without triggering another Iraq or Afghanistan war works. If it requires more overt action, or causes Iran to react unduly, then there may be problems."

"Now that, my friend, would be a very bad thing," Yuri commented, gesturing to emphasize his point with the detached stock of his submachine gun. "My employer and those like him rely on the flow of goods and services to remain free. The regrettable upheavals in the two nations you mention have severely restricted trade, and my employer and his comrades are great exponents of the Keynesian theories of free trade. Besides, I had family who served the Red Army in Afghanistan." He mock shivered. "An awful place, I am told. I suspect that the past thirty years have done little to improve it. For that to happen here—"

"Is very unlikely. If the rumors about Parchin are true, then it could all go in another direction far too easily. No, for our respective reasons and our respective employers, it would be best if we achieve the right result over the next thirty-six hours."

Bolan turned away from the window and the city going about its business below them. Apart from the heat and the fact a large majority of the men and all the women were in traditional Muslim dress, they could have been in any major capital. The apartment that served as a safe house was owned by a businessman whose company was involved in import and export of machinery involved in refining and engineering. That had made it easier for him to run a sideline in the import and export of another kind of hardware than it may have been for Razmara. The businessman, who maintained his anonymity to the soldier and his compatriot by expediently sending two lackeys to greet them, had plundered his illicit stock to leave them weapons that could be added to their own ordnance.

Razmara had swapped the flatbed truck for a Mercedes with tinted windows that had once again been driven by Mahmoud, with Akhbar the silent shotgun. The roads between Rasht and Tehran were of good quality, and with the vehicle being that of a respected businessman who often made the journey between the two cities, they made good time with little to no chance of being intercepted. Once in Tehran, the driver had negotiated his way to the apartment building near the center of the city, where he had taken them into the underground garage.

"Nouri makes this trip often—our contact, who wishes to remain unknown to you because of his own nervousness, is both a friend and colleague. It is stupid that he feels safe with you not knowing his name. If you are captured and tortured, you know more than enough to lead to him anyway, but…" Mahmoud shrugged.

"I'll try to make sure that doesn't happen," Bolan commented.

After ascertaining that they weren't being followed, and with suitable traditional covering so that their faces would be masked to the building's security cameras, Mahmoud took them to the fourth floor by elevator, where he bade them farewell and good fortune before leaving them in charge of two taciturn and nervous young men who displayed the armament left for them before making their excuses to leave. But not before leaving them with a tablet that carried maps, photographs and video of their target, his home and the surrounding area.

In truth, the soldier was glad when they departed. It left the two professionals with a chance to familiarize themselves with their objective and also to ensure that their equipment for the evening's work was primed.

The ordnance they had been left was a mixed bag. Yuri was delighted and amused to find that a Dragunov sniper rifle had been left for them, disassembled.

"I trained with one of these when I was a military man," he reminisced, caressing the detached barrel. "It is a fine gun, and accurate to a hairsbreadth when you know how to use it."

"But completely inappropriate," Bolan interjected.

"Of course," Yuri mused. "It is a shame that we cannot carry out a distance hit on our target. That would make the getaway a lot easier."

"Not when we have to find somewhere secure to set up a four-foot-long gun and then take it to pieces and ship it out without giving ourselves away," Bolan explained.

"You are right, sadly," Yuri agreed.

They had also been left a couple of 9 mm RAP-401 pistols, of South African manufacture; some C-4 plastique and detonators; two HK PSG1 semiautomatic rifles that chambered 7.62 mm NATO rounds with a number of twenty-round box mags; and two Benelli MT3 combat shotguns with folding stocks. Bolan was not averse to the latter, their twenty-seven-shot per round .33 caliber pellets of double 0 buckshot being useful for maximum damage and confusion in confined spaces. It seemed a shame not to take advantage of the ordnance that had been left for them, but it presented them with two main problems.

The first was that, for this part of the mission in particular, they did not want to be weighed down, which was why the ordnance they carried with them had been picked for the optimum balance of effectiveness and weight. The second was that although it would have been in some senses better to travel light and pick up ordnance along the way, it would be traceable. Even though it was contraband, it would not take much in the way of forensics to trace them back to the importer who was running piracy. They could not guarantee they would return from their mission or not be forced to leave some of the hardware behind them. From there, the network of dissidents would soon be uncovered. Bolan did not want to be responsible for the chance of so many deaths.

Yuri did not want to have to explain such an eventuality to his employer.

So the soldier and his companion stuck to the ordnance they had brought with them in the duffel bags. Yuri was fond of the BXP10 SMG, which he had trained with during his army days, so familiar with the weapon that it seemed like an extension of his arm. He also carried a Glock 23 semiautomatic pistol, its 13-round mag of 165 gram SpearGold Dot jacketed hollowpoint rounds being, to his mind, of maximum efficiency. He carried spare ammunition for both, as well as for the SIG Sauer P229 that he carried as a single-shot weapon.

Bolan, for his part, had chosen the Uzi that he had been using more of late. Its lightweight and faster draw contrasted well with the heaviness of the pistol he favored, the Desert Eagle Mark XIX. He had always liked the .44 Magnum version, but he had gone with the .357 for the mission. Although he had no real desire to use the weapon that evening, its efficiency would be useful in an emergency. Last, he'd chosen a BXP10, like his comrade. The MAC-10 knockoff was a solid, reliable weapon.

Their duffel bags also contained monocular night-vision headsets with infrared and heat functions, wireless security cams and fiber-optic cameras with small monitor attachments that could prove vital. They carried small quantities of Semtex with detonators, and CS and flash-bang grenades, as well as nose plugs. Finally, and perhaps the weapon that they might need most on this stage of the mission, they both carried Benchmade Stryker automatic knives with four-inch blades.

With some regret they placed the ordnance left for them to one side and went about the task of readying their own weapons for the night's mission. Once that was done, it was time to study the intel that had been left for them on the tablet.

Bolan had to give it to the men who had been charged with gathering the data. They were thorough. There were schematics of all telecoms and electrical cabling for the block on which the target's house was situated. The building itself was a four-story apartment building similar to the one in which they were holed up. Its schematics and blueprints had been laid down for them, showing all the possible points of ingress and egress, as well as the security system that had been installed. It was much the same as the building they were in.

These were buildings for the business and political classes, and as such they were designed to keep people of money and influence safe from attack or robbery. They were not impossible to crack, but without the full picture it would be easy to trigger one of the many alarms and bring police or military down on Bolan and Yuri.

Finally, there was footage shot from phones and also—somehow—lifted from the internal CCTV, showing their target as he went about his business. Timed, and with a written report filed alongside, it showed any regular routines the man had in his personal and professional life, allowing Bolan and Yuri to build a picture of each day of the week. Being that this was a Tuesday, they homed in on the target's regular routine for such a day, along with the forecast for any changes brought about by government business that had been plotted for a week ahead. Unless he had something in his personal life occurring that would cause a major change, they had as clear a picture as was possible of his activities for the day, both as they studied the intel and in the hours ahead, when they expected to achieve their mission.

While they studied, they ate the fruit and spiced vegetables that had been left for them, along with tea and yogurt, a light meal high in sugar.

Eventually they completed their self-briefing. Outside, night had descended. It was time to head out.

"THIS IS IT," Bolan said softly. "You take the front and draw the security. I'll take the garage entrance and make our man."

"Obviously, I get all the glamorous jobs," Yuri said flatly. "Don't think I will forget this. How long do you need?"

"Fifteen minutes maximum. If I can't finalize the mission by then, we'll have to withdraw and take a different approach. But that's not going to happen."

Yuri's face cracked in a smile. "I don't suppose it is. You go now."

Bolan left the Russian on the street corner and made his way to the garage entrance at the rear of the building. The streets were devoid of people at this time of night, especially as the last call to prayers had rung out from the muezzin and the men had returned home to their meals and families.

All except for Lotfy Mussivand. The government official lived alone, and Bolan and Yuri had watched him enter the building, exchange words with the concierge and security and then take the elevator to his apartment. From the intel they had received, they knew that the man was a serious individual who was dedicated both to his religion and to the furtherance of his regime's influence. The word *fanatic* sprang to mind. Apart from prayer and religious meetings, Mussivand had little time for any kind of social activity and was not married. He was in his mid-thirties, and Bolan was surprised that this had not caused comment or affected his career. But it was good this night.

Dressed traditionally in clothing that had been left for them and that covered their blacksuits, both men had been able to pass for Iranians with just a little makeup to alter their complexions and beards added to their clean-shaved faces. They had waited until the mosques had discharged the devout onto the street before leaving their safe-house apartment by the back way, blending in easily with the sudden crowds. Their ordnance fitted easily onto the web harnesses over their blacksuits, with the loose-fitting clothing overtop. As long as they were not stopped for any reason, they were sure to reach their destination with ease.

The streets were heavily policed, but there was no indication that was anything other than usual, and they were able to walk from the safe house to their target without challenge. The time it took enabled the streets to clear and the sun to fall, leaving them with the space and cover they required.

Disguised as he was, Bolan had no worries about the cameras picking him up. The only danger they presented was if the concierge and security came to investigate. Hopefully, Yuri would do his job.

The entrance to the garage was by a key-operated electric eye. Bolan did not have the necessary key. He had to find a way of getting in that was quick but also quiet enough so as not to attract attention. Blasting the mechanism with a small lump of Semtex would have been his first choice, but it was not an option.

From the blacksuit he slipped out a small tool kit that contained a socket spanner. The plate over the electronics was secured by four bolts that were almost flush. If he was lucky, the socket would have just enough purchase. Third time and the socket caught, loosening the first bolt. The second and third were easier, with the fourth proving to be as awkward as the first. Bolan withdrew the plate and shorted the electric circuit within. The lock clicked, and he was able to pull the gate open just enough to enter, but not before he had replaced the plate and secured the bolts just enough to keep it in place, lest any passerby notice the damage.

Once he was in and the gate was closed at his back, he hurried across the underground garage until he reached the elevator, hoping that it was not also key operated, as sometimes happened in such buildings. There had been no mention of it in the schematics, but it was the kind of tiny detail often overlooked.

After checking his watch to see that opening the gate had cost valuable minutes, Bolan cursed to see that the garage-level elevator entrance had no call button and *was* key operated. The same would no doubt be true for the emergency stairwell. He was about to check that out when fortune favored him: he heard the elevator car rattle down the shaft toward the garage level. He secreted himself behind a concrete support pillar, bringing the knife to hand and hoping that whoever was descending was alone. Right now, the last thing he needed was a fight that would use up more valuable moments.

The doors opened, and from his vantage point he could see that a lone man exited the car, his attention focused on his phone as he fumbled for his keys. Bolan contemplated for a moment whether he should hit the man with the hilt of the knife and render him unconscious, or whether he could actually risk leaving him to go about his business—after all, it was not his fight.

The broken gate cinched it. The man would be sure to raise the alarm. Bolan watched the door of the elevator start to close and cursed as he was forced to step in the opposite direction. Two strides and he stood at the man's shoulder. One blow and the man crumpled without even realizing he had been hit, his phone and keys clattering to the floor.

The elevator door closed, and the soldier snatched up the fallen key in order to trigger the door before the cage could ascend again. He had hit the man hard enough to keep him out for a while. And the soldier hoped he'd be gone by the time he came to.

YURI APPROACHED THE front of the building as Bolan vanished around the corner. His job, as he saw it, was simple. He had to distract the men inside from the security cameras and if necessary create a diversion. His hand reached into the pocket of his robe and through the hole he had cut so that he could access directly into his black-suit. He clutched the SIG Sauer P229, ready to draw it if necessary. A single-shot weapon would make less noise, but it did leave him more open to attack than a swift burst with the BXP10.

He entered the building and saw three men gathered in the lobby. One was the concierge; the other two had the look of security men. To have two security men in a building was unusual, and it bespoke of the importance in which Mussivand was held. All three eyed him with suspicion as he entered, not recognizing him as either tenant or regular visitor.

He made a supplicatory gesture and greeted them traditionally. They returned the greeting in a hesitant manner. Yuri continued, "My friends, I am wondering if perhaps you can be of assistance to me. I am searching for this address, and I have become lost." He pulled a piece of paper from his pocket and placed it on the surface of the reception desk. The concierge leaned forward to take a look at the address the Russian had scrawled at random from the street map on the tablet. It was two blocks away, far enough to not find with ease, yet not far enough to render his presence here suspicious.

"You have taken a wrong turn, my friend," the concierge told him. "Where did you start from?"

Yuri named the street in which the safe house was located. The words were out before he could bite his tongue, and he cursed his stupidity. He had not meant to incriminate those who had aided them. There was another reason, too, one that the concierge seized on as he looked oddly at Yuri.

"But if you came from that area, then how could you have passed this place and arrived here without noticing that you had done so?"

Yuri did not immediately answer. He was aware of the CCTV monitors that were behind the concierge's desk, where he could see Cooper leaving the elevator on the fourth floor. He was also aware that the suspicion of the man in front of him had alerted the security guards, one of whom stepped a little close, while the other lined himself up between the Russian and the door to the street. The guard who had come closer was now peering over the desk at the piece of paper, his line of sight uncomfortably close to the CCTV monitors.

"How can you not know this?" he repeated, looking Yuri square in the eye with a penetrating gaze that seemed to search for any sign of untruth.

"I am not from Tehran," Yuri replied calmly. "I have come from Rasht and am not familiar with this city." It should have fooled any lie detector, as it was nothing less than the truth, if a little on the economical side. He should not have put himself—or Cooper—in that position. He felt that he had spent too long running errands for Schevchenko and was out of practice. That he would attend to if they got home in one piece.

The guard studied him. He kept his face as immobile as only a Russian ex-soldier could. His eyes locked with the guard. He could read in the man's face that he believed him. He truly believed that he had ridden the wave…until the other guard moved forward from the door.

"Hey, who is that?" Yuri heard the guard behind him

move forward, could almost feel him as he leaned over to look at the CCTV monitors.

Ah, well, he figured, it had been a nice idea to try to keep this peaceful and quiet, to avoid fuss. A nice idea, but one that hadn't come through in the end. As the guard and the concierge had their attention diverted from him for a moment, he stepped back so that he was near the door, pulling his hand from the folds of his robe and leveling the SIG Sauer.

For a moment the two guards and the concierge were frozen, caught between the CCTV monitor and the sudden move in front of them. The guards were armed with Kalashnikovs that were shouldered, and there was no chance for them to unsling them before Yuri snapped off three shots, moving his arm only slightly to reposition and ride the kick. The three men had inadvertently clustered so closely together that they had made his task simple.

Chest shots for all three dispatched them with no time wasted. He glanced out the front of the building. It didn't seem as though the noise had attracted undue attention, and he thanked fortune for the thick plate glass of the lobby. Moving quickly, he dragged the man in front of the reception desk around so that he could be piled with the other two corpses. They could not be seen from the elevator or the street, but it would not be long before they would be found. Yuri looked at his watch, noting that Cooper still had five minutes to clean and clear.

Yuri strode across the lobby and locked the glass doors, one eye on the elevator. Five minutes to stand guard and stop anyone or anything that crossed his path, preferably without any more commotion than had already been stirred.

It was not the best job he'd ever had.

CHAPTER NINETEEN

Bolan had made his way from the elevator and into the corridor of the fourth floor without interruption. Tehran was a busy city, and this would be an equally busy building as it housed families and single men of some wealth and importance. However, timing was everything, and to enter at this moment, when men had just returned from the mosque or had gone immediately about their business, meant that there was the kind of lull that happened three or four times a day. It was a moment of slackness in the day's activity that gave enough of a window to enter without being observed.

Bolan scoped out the CCTV security cameras as he entered the corridor. They would be picking him up, but he hoped that his companion was fulfilling his own task and that this would not matter. As he approached the door to the apartment where Mussivand was resident, it struck him that he had come halfway around the world to carry out the same kind of mission that he had been charged with in D.C. There was an odd symmetry to the way in which this part of the mission had unfolded, and it was not a symmetry that he found pleasing. He was a soldier by trade, not an assassin, which is how circumstance had cast him this time around.

At least it would not—could not—be like this when they made their way to Parchin.

This was assuming, of course, that they got that far.

He stood outside the door to Mussivand's apartment. He would have expected a man of such importance to have a stronger bodyguard presence than intel had shown. It was a measure of how secure this regime felt in its omnipotence that guards on the building were considered enough.

The soldier slipped a skeleton key from one of the slit pockets of his blacksuit and stuck it in the door lock. With a bit of a judicious jiggling back and forth, he felt the lock click softly and yield.

With a gentleness that belied his intentions, Bolan edged the door open wide enough to allow him to slip into the apartment. It had been difficult to keep the sound of his entry silent in the quiet of the block, but apart from a few scrabbling sounds of metal on metal and the click that signified entry, he had been able to keep it to a minimum.

Inside, the ambient light from the street blended with the soft light from candles, which bathed the apartment in a kind of twilight glow. Bolan did not shut the door completely. A quick exit and the unnecessary noise of the lock closing were uppermost in his mind.

He felt under his robes for the sheathed Stryker knife. It was best to have it in hand before proceeding any further; especially as he could feel his nerve endings tingle, years of experience feeding a sense that something was not right.

Could someone have betrayed them? Was he expected?

The carpet beneath his boots was thin, the flooring beneath of a hard wood. It was difficult to make any kind of footfall without some noise, but he was as expert as anyone in making the impossible possible. He moved down the hallway of the building, familiar with the layout from the schematics that had been on the tablet in the safe house.

The main living area was dead ahead; bedroom second left, bathroom first left. On the right was a second bedroom that was used as a study. The kitchen led off the main living area. Three storage closets were located within the apartment, with the doors to them in one bedroom, the main living area and the kitchen.

The light was flickering despite the stillness of the air-conditioned atmosphere. Something was making the candles flicker: movement of some kind? Pools of shadow and the scent of sandalwood were his overriding impressions. If there was someone moving within the apartment, he was damned quiet. Too quiet. It was not the movement of someone who was going about his nightly activities with the lack of awareness he would have expected. This was the movement of someone who knew he was not alone.

The doors to the first bedroom and the bathroom were closed. The flickering of the shadows in the hall originated from either the study or the main room. Bolan proceeded with caution. He flattened himself to the wall so that his own shadow did not merge with those already cast.

As he neared the door to the study, he could hear breathing. Faint, regular and controlled: the breathing of a soldier in wait.

"Come in. I know you are out there."

Bolan stayed where he was. It was not often that your prey invited you in, and if they did they sure were prepared.

"Do not waste my time. I know you are there. I do not know who you are, but then I do not care. You should not be here—that is all I need to know."

There was a note of arrogance in the man's tone that pricked Bolan's attention. He was sure he had the upper hand, which might be all the soldier needed.

"You expect me to step into a hail of fire?" Bolan asked in Arabic.

"That is not a native accent," Mussivand replied calmly, switching from Persian to Arabic. "An American? European, perhaps? You understand Farsi but choose not to speak it back to me.... Would that perhaps betray you?"

Bolan checked his watch: two minutes. It would be a simple hit if he could be sure that the man was unarmed, but nobody sounded that arrogant without a gun in his hand.

"You might as well speak," Mussivand continued. "It will do you no good to try to prevaricate. If you try to enter the room, I will shoot you, and if you try to escape, you will find your avenue of escape cut off by the military. I have, of course, alerted them."

Bolan cursed softly. The one thing that had not been included on the schematics was a direct line to the military. Of course, that made perfect sense, and it was probably wireless, which would be why it had not shown up on any plans. It also explained the light security presence in the block.

Bolan sheathed the Stryker knife and reached for a grenade. If they had military on their tail, any pretense at subtlety had to go out the window.

"Okay, so you're smarter than me and well prepared," Bolan began. "American, yes. We know about your funding of al Qaeda cells in the U.S., and we've closed you down—"

"For now," Mussivand interrupted smugly. "But we will soon find another route. You cannot stop us. I am just a little surprised that you traced it to me, and that you have the temerity to attempt such an outrage. You will, of course, be paraded through the streets and shown off to the media for your crimes before you are executed. Unofficially, before you can be exchanged, of course."

Bolan smiled mirthlessly as he fingered the Semtex he had taken from a pouch on his web harness. It was a small amount, but enough to cause the collateral damage required in such a confined space. He primed it with the detonator and continued talking to buy the seconds he needed.

"The idea was that I come here and take you out with no trace as a warning to your government, or whichever faction of it is backing you in this. A nice, quiet assassination. But I guess it's not going to be that way."

"Indeed not. Step into view, after divesting yourself of all weapons," Mussivand demanded.

"Oh, come on. You don't think I'm that stupid, do you?" Bolan sighed before tossing the primed Semtex into the room and throwing himself to the floor as far away from the doorway as possible, his mouth open and hands over his ears to prevent concussion and deafness.

The explosion was sudden, and it seemed to shake the whole building with its ferocity. Whatever quiet had existed before was now shattered as alarms and sirens wailed, meshing with the voices of those who were startled by the rending of the evening's quiet.

Dust from the study room filled the hallway, and the candles extinguished by the blast threw the apartment into darkness.

Bolan had the Desert Eagle in hand as he looked into what remained of the room. Furniture had been splintered by the blast, the windows blown out and the decor ripped around the walls. Mussivand was sprawled across the floor, his body ripped and torn by the blast, his limbs at unnatural angles. There was no doubt that he was dead, and no need for Bolan to finish the job. A Beretta 93R lay near his lifeless arm.

Bolan turned away and went out the door, heading for the stairs. This was not a time to risk the elevator. He still had the pistol in his hand, and as the door to one of the other apartments opened and a man appeared clutching a gun, Bolan snapped off a shot. The man was quick and ducked out of the way. By the time he was back in the frame and looking for the intruder, Bolan was gone.

YURI SWORE LOUDLY as the explosion echoed through the building. Knowing Cooper's plan, he realized that something radical had gone awry and that withdrawal was the order of the day. The front entrance was not a viable option. Sirens already sounded and alarms wailed, triggered by the effects of the blast. A man leaving the building by the front would be running straight into the arms of the approaching authorities.

He would have to use the back way. Hopefully he would meet up with Cooper, and equally hopefully he might just avoid authorities who would be slower to approach the rear.

Yuri raced to the stairwell, making no attempt now to hide the BXP10. As he hit the emergency stairs, he could hear someone descending at speed. He hoped it would be Cooper, as he paused with the SMG angled up.

"C'mon, what are you waiting for?" Bolan said with a mirthless grin as he came to a sudden stop at the dogleg angle of the stairwell, his Desert Eagle fixed on the Russian, stayed only by the same reflexes that had stopped the Russian from firing without thought.

The two men hit the stairs that led to the basement garage. Yuri, in the lead, held up his arm to stay the soldier as they reached the exit door. He opened it carefully, scanning the garage space.

"Okay," he snapped, leading the way out, BXP10 at the ready. "I hope you can improvise, Cooper."

"I sure can," he said, fishing the stolen car key from a pocket.

Yuri looked momentarily puzzled, then shrugged as the soldier led him across to the still-unconscious would-be driver, prone on the concrete.

"Get the gate," Bolan ordered. "The electronics are out, so you need to slide it across."

While Yuri complied, Bolan fired up the engine of the vehicle, whose lights blinked when he hit central locking. Bolan thanked his luck for technology, remembering the days when he would have had to waste precious time finding which car the key fitted. Yuri rushed back and clambered into the car, and Bolan took it out into the street.

"We'll have some time," Yuri commented. "There will be CCTV of us, but they might not immediately access that. What happened back there, by the way?"

Bolan outlined the events briefly as he drove.

When he finished, Yuri shook his head. "I thought I was being rash in shooting the security. You go big when you go, Cooper."

"Sometimes there just isn't any other way," Bolan replied as he took the car in the opposite direction to the safe house. "Fact is, Mussivand is dead and the necessary people will know why. What they tell the world is another thing. Without me—or you—to hold up like puppets, they can't prove a damn thing."

"Then I suggest we get out of Tehran. And soon," he added pointedly.

Bolan took the car off the main road, eyeing with some concern the military and police vehicles that were speeding in the opposite direction.

"There will be footage of us leaving the building in this. We need to ditch it and head back on foot."

"Why not just go?" Yuri asked.

Bolan shook his head. "Listen, we need the ordnance

we brought with us if we have a chance of getting into Parchin. We can't risk compromising the people who have helped us so far. We'll clean out that safe house and hit the road."

"I can't argue with your reasoning, but I do wonder if we can get back to our equipment," Yuri said flatly.

"Won't know until we try," the soldier retorted.

While they had been speaking, Bolan had taken the car down a series of side streets until he was in an area where they could be sure that there was no CCTV. He beckoned Yuri as he got out of the vehicle, then took him down a small alley. More time spent in alleys, Bolan mused, but this time with a purpose. He stripped the beard from his face, wincing at the pull of the spirit gum, and smeared the dark makeup so that it covered his chin. He indicated to Yuri to do likewise and then swapped robes.

"We're about a half mile from the safe house, roughly two and a half klicks," Bolan figured. "And we need to get on the road before sunup. How well did you memorize that street map we were looking at?"

"Not well enough to guarantee we can get back without a few detours," the Russian replied wryly.

"Me, neither," Bolan said. "Time to hide in plain sight."

They hit the streets, looking a little different from when they had walked into the alley. They walked back to the main road and started to trek back through the city. As they approached the part of the city where the bombed apartment building stood, they hit a cordon of police that held up traffic. They could see in the distance the military and emergency services gathered at the front of the building.

"You live through here?" one of the police on the cordon asked Yuri as they approached.

"No, just on our route," the Russian replied as simply as possible in perfect Farsi.

"Then take another one," the policeman snapped before turning to answer a colleague who was yelling across to him.

Bolan and Yuri chose a route that took them around the block until they could come back toward a route they recognized. Their improvised disguises had passed muster when called on, and they thanked their luck.

They walked onto the block where the safe house was located, grateful that there was no one on staff to notice their arrival.

While they packed their duffel bags, Bolan flicked on the TV in the apartment to catch the news. There were early reports of an explosion and the death of an official, but there were no details. The TV images were the first time that Bolan had a chance to see the full extent of the damage that the Semtex had wrought. He realized how they had ridden their luck to this point and hoped it could continue just long enough to get out of Tehran.

"Ready?" Yuri questioned. He had cleared the apartment while Bolan had checked their route on the tablet and kept an eye on the news.

Bolan nodded and killed the TV. In the sudden silence, the noises of the evening that filtered in gave no indication of what was happening nearby. The soldier stowed the tablet in one of the duffel bags and picked up the key for the vehicle that had been left for the second stage of the mission. Although they were headed away from the scene of the explosion, he was aware that he would be taking a possibly traceable vehicle through a city on alert.

They just needed that luck to last. He had no desire to implicate the men who had aided them at great risk.

"Let's go," Bolan said.

CHAPTER TWENTY

Parchin was a military base located in a position where the landscape gave it the optimum security offered by nature. It was the jewel in the Iranian military crown. The roads leading toward it were monitored closely, and for that reason Bolan chose to ditch their vehicle about four miles from the base, assiduously stripping and cleaning it of any incriminating evidence. The sun was rising as the two men started to trek the remaining distance.

Although they had entered the country via the Caspian Sea and so had made their initial travels over that small part of the country that was plain land, the majority of Iran was on a mountainous plateau, and that had aided the regime in making any military bases both hard to access from the land and hard to spy on from the air or from orbit. There were plans of Parchin that were available from what weapons inspectors and the IAEA knew of the base, but there were also stretches that were nothing more than blank spaces on a plan.

Their problem was twofold. First, they had unknown areas to penetrate and work in; second, they had to contend with the fact that as the premier military base for the Iranian armed forces, those parts of the base that were known had excellent security and the manpower and ordnance to put paid to even the most well-planned military strategy.

Their solution was also twofold. First, they were a two-man unit that was only lightly armed and had no intention to cause collateral damage unless it proved to be necessary. This was as much an intel-gathering mission as a military strike. Second, they had the one thing that the strict Iranian regime would never have really expected: an inside man.

"Truly, I am grateful for the power of finance," Yuri gasped as he took a mouthful of water while they sheltered in the cover of a small outcrop. "Never underestimate the power of guns and money, Cooper. Political and religious ideologies may have strength and fervor, but unless they have the money to buy big guns, they will always finish second."

Bolan scanned the horizon. "Gee, thanks for that critique of power structures in the modern world. I'll run that by my boss sometime, see what he says."

"If he has any sense, he will say the same as mine— the largest number of zeros at the bottom of the page is the winner."

"Sadly, I think you're right. Mostly…" Bolan continued to scan the horizon, looking for any sign of life in the arid, mountainous landscape. They had come across country, bypassing the roads and taking an arced route to avoid contact with the line of communication in order to keep cover. It had made the trek harder than if they had been able to run straight and parallel with the road. Lack of cover had made that an impossible task. Bolan was frustrated by the fact that this had lost them time and energy they could ill afford. With Mussivand dead, the shutters would come down, and they had only so long until they could get back to their rendezvous point on the shores of the Caspian.

Now they were waiting for their rendezvous: their inside man and the means to get them into the base.

"There he is," Bolan said softly. "Get ready."

Yuri followed the soldier's line of view. An Iranian army truck was approaching quickly. The Russian stowed his water bottle and joined Bolan in the cover of a group of rocks nearest the road.

The truck slowed, the engine coughing, before it came to a halt just over a thousand yards from where they were concealed. The passenger side door opened and an Iranian soldier got out, cursing loudly in Pashto. He kicked the side of the truck, gesticulating wildly, as he was joined by another man from the passenger side who tried to calm him. From the driver's side, a man alighted, shrugged and spoke placatingly as he lifted the hood.

"That's him," Yuri said softly, even though there was no chance of their being overheard. "Second cousin. I'd recognize him anywhere."

Bolan ignored this cryptic remark. He weighted the Desert Eagle in his hand and indicated that the Russian should take out his own handgun. As Yuri did so, Bolan murmured softly, "One head shot. That's all we've got. You think you can do this?"

"I have trophies, Cooper. Look to your own shooting," the Russian replied with a vulpine grin. "The one on the right is mine."

"Line 'em up," Bolan whispered, sighting his man.

"Ready…" Yuri murmured hoarsely.

"On three," Bolan replied, counting them in. The two pistols cracked, shattering the silence of the day.

The driver dived for cover. The other two Iranians were not so lucky. In middispute, both were cut off as the twin shots found their homes. One man lost the vast majority of his skull, while the other had less blown away, but still enough to destroy any kind of motor function ability as he hit the ground, arms and legs twitching.

Bolan and Yuri moved swiftly from cover. Before the driver had a chance to regain his feet and dust himself down, they had dragged the corpses off the road, stripping off the uniforms while avoiding covering them in blood. Using water from the truck, they washed the blood off the road and tamped down the sandy soil at the side to cover their tracks.

"We were not shooting at you, fool," Yuri remarked to the driver as he tried to squeeze into the uniform of one of the dead men. It barely fit in some places, not at all in others, but with some fortune they would be able to disguise themselves long enough to gain access. Bolan was luckier with his uniform, but it was still a far-from-convincing fit seen up close.

"Fool, I dived because you might miss, and how suspicious would I seem if not worried about bullets flying," the driver remarked, eyeing the two men. "You look nothing like Iranian soldiers. This is doomed."

"I like you, mostly because you are Mr. Happy and the opposite of your cousin," Yuri remarked. "You are being paid well. All you need to do is get us inside, then in the confusion head for the Caspian Sea. A new life in Russia awaits you, my friend."

"You make it sound simple," the driver spat. "Maybe it would be, but I cannot see you getting past the gates and nothing but a slow death for myself as a traitor."

"All you have to do is drive. Let me do the rest," Bolan said sharply. "If you're not with us, then we'll leave you here now to make your own way."

"That would be certain death," the driver said quietly.

"Then shut up and do what I say. That way we've all got a chance. Understood?"

The driver nodded with only the slightest hesitation. They climbed into the truck and started toward the gates of Parchin. In the rear of the closed truck they carried chemicals for the labs, and the soldier knew that the clearance this gave them would enable them to access the areas closest to the unmapped sections of the base. The problem would be getting past the main gate, as the two men with the driver on this trip would not bear close inspection.

"Stop here," Bolan ordered when they were less than a quarter of a mile from the base. The driver slowed and looked at him quizzically. The soldier continued, "Motion sensors extend for a klick. Cameras cover the same distance around. Beyond that, there is no known security that extends out beyond that perimeter. Am I right?"

"I know of nothing," the driver replied.

"Then let's hope you're right. Wait here. Yuri—with me."

The Russian complied, and he smiled slowly when Bolan outlined his plan. It was simple: the two men took the explosives and detonators that remained in their ordnance and went in opposite directions, priming and planting three bombs in each direction, spaced over a distance of five hundred yards each way on either side of the ribbon. They moved quickly, sweating with the effort to beat the clock. When they had completed their task and returned to the truck, Bolan beckoned for the driver to continue, keeping an eye on his watch. As the gates of Parchin came into view and the base opened up before them, he told the driver to slow a little, counting down time as they rolled over the road.

They reached the gates, where duty sentries were backed up by cameras and scanners that played over the truck. Their disguises would be pitiful if the sentries and the tech were given time to do their duty. This was where split-second timing would be essential.

Two of the bombs detonated in the terrain behind them, echoing across the empty land between and throwing up earth and rock. Before the sentries had a chance to react, a third bomb went off. As alarms sounded within the base, the sentry nearest to the truck waved it through, backing up behind it and closing the gates as a fourth bomb detonated.

Inside the base, forces mobilized to recon and engage with whatever was happening in the hills. As the driver took the truck into the base, he maneuvered to avoid troops and vehicles that were moving toward the gate. Behind them, the last two bombs went off.

The chaos of sudden mobilization was exactly what Bolan had been banking on. With a sudden concern for whatever was happening on the outside, a supply truck with a driver who had been eyeballed by the sentries as a regular and two men in uniform with no time to check credentials was easily waved through to enable defensive action to take place.

"You realize, of course, that they will soon find out what exploded and become suspicious?" the driver muttered.

"And you, of course, realize that if you continue to shit yourself with fear you will give us away and never get to see Russia, freedom and rubles?" Yuri growled. "Remember that, or else I will have to rectify the problem immediately."

The driver said nothing as he parked his vehicle in the bay surrounding the chemical labs.

"You make the delivery as usual and let us worry about everything else," Bolan said, trying to calm the rattled man. "If you're asked, we've been called to the gates and that's why you're unloading alone. Got that?"

The driver nodded, and as he climbed from the truck and began to mechanically go about his usual task, not daring even to look at them, Bolan beckoned to Yuri to follow him.

In their ill-fitting uniforms and complexions that did not blend in with the norm, they felt that they were too conspicuous. They had to get to cover as soon as possible.

Beyond the chemical labs was a section of the camp that was fenced off. That was nothing unusual, as on their way in the soldier had noticed that fencing and additional guard posts had been set up to delineate the different facets of military operation within the borders of the camp. What was significant about this section was that it was one of the blank areas on any plan of the known base.

Bolan wanted to get inside there as soon as they could. Beckoning the Russian to follow, he made his way to the mesh gate within the fencing that led to the low-level concrete buildings beyond. From the power plant that stood within the fencing, servicing the structures, he could guess that whatever went on behind the concrete facade required a large amount of power. Could it be what he was looking for?

They closed in on the gate. It was deserted, as the alarms going off within the camp had pulled the sentry from his post. It was only as they reached the gate and walked through to the compound beyond that the sentry ran up to them, barking at them to get out.

"What is your clearance?" he yelled as he came close.

"This," Yuri murmured, stepping forward and punching up with the Stryker in his fist. The blow caused the sentry's eyes to widen in surprise, and although his mouth opened, no sound could emerge. Without withdrawing the blade, and with his hand still in place, Yuri clasped the sentry in his free arm, supporting him as he continued toward the buildings with Bolan.

"Find me a corner where I can leave this bastard, Cooper. He grows heavy in death."

The soldier moved forward and helped Yuri support the sentry's deadweight, dragging him across the concrete apron in front of the buildings until they reached a doorway. Bolan heaved at it, and the door gave way to reveal an office beyond. It was deserted, the chairs pushed back from desks, terminals left on, with signs of a hasty departure.

"Good thing those explosions moved them out," Bolan grunted as he helped the Russian to heave the corpse onto one of the chairs.

"Shouldn't we at least make an effort at hiding him?" the Russian asked sardonically as Bolan moved toward a connecting door.

"No time. We need to get what we want, then get out," the soldier snapped.

Even though their uniforms were ill fitting and they looked out of place, in the general confusion they were able to move with a degree of freedom in the area as the other occupants were not concerned with the military surrounding them. That much was obvious from the way that Yuri and Bolan were ignored as they moved into a more populated section of the first building.

Bolan was no expert on science and its application in war—only in terms of its end product—but he knew enough to realize that this was a chemical-weapons lab. There was a covered and sealed walkway through to the section beyond, and as they headed toward it, Bolan could see that at the far end the doors were air locked on coded keypads. Within the rooms beyond, he could just make out men toiling at their task of creating chemical death, past the hazmat suits that were hanging from the air lock walls.

"We put something under them?" Yuri questioned.

"Can't risk anything reaching the air that might spread. No, we'll leave these people for now and drop a report into the UN weapons inspectors."

"Yes, like they will be of any use," the Russian spat.

"Knowing we know might be enough to deter them until we can find another way. It's the long game with these guys. C'mon."

The two men went back the way they had come and out through the lab and then the office. It looked like nobody had returned in their absence. But on second glance, that was the key problem: there was literally nobody.

"Where has the bastard gone?" Yuri asked, astonished.

"I don't know, but I think the bigger question is what can he do?"

"I was sure he was dead."

"We will be unless we move," Bolan bit off before leaving the building with his SMG ready. If it had been hazardous enough before this, now it was truly a question of keeping their backs covered.

IN THE CONFUSION of the explosions and the mobilization of the troops within Parchin, the absence of one man was not, at first, noticed. When his immediate superior did realize that he was a man short, a search was not foremost on his mind; rather, it was the charge he would bring against the soldier when he eventually turned up. This line of thought was dismissed when he drew back from directing his men into recon parties for the area surrounding the blasts to find the missing man dragging himself across the ground. Two men rushed to his aid.

As he reached him, the officer realized two things. The first was that it taken all the soldier's strength to get himself that far, and that he had nothing left with which to convey a message. The second thing was that this man had been guarding the gate into the hazard zone.

The officer stopped dead in his stride—as dead as the man before him—and suddenly pivoted on his heel, yelling orders to those men within immediate earshot before using his radio to report in.

He had realized that there may be no threat from the hills beyond, and that even if there were men there, they did not matter. The important thing was that Parchin had been breached. How, he did not know; that didn't matter.

There was someone on the inside, and he or she had to be captured.

"CHEMICAL SHIT IS one thing, but it's not what we're looking for, right?" Yuri gasped as the two men sprinted between the buildings.

"Nuclear warheads," Bolan stated between breaths.

"They wouldn't store them here?" Yuri returned as more a question than statement.

Bolan shook his head. "This is a military base, not a launching facility. I don't even know if they have the capacity. But they might have the research facility, and that's what we want."

"More proof for the weapons inspectors," the Russian said.

"And the IAEA. But we don't just report it if we find it. This one we knock out if we can."

Yuri nodded and did not waste any more breath.

There were seven buildings in the uncharted area. Two of them they had covered. A third loomed ahead.

Bolan beckoned to the Russian to take the left side of the structure. There were reinforced glass windows down the sides, and as the two men ran toward the far end, they could see the work going on in the interior. In here, there were engineers working on standard weaponry, taking it to pieces and reassembling it. There were scopes that had digitized elements, missile guidance and triggering systems that worked on computerized elements and cumbersome panels that Bolan recognized as the piloting systems of tanks. Each component that had been analyzed and replaced had also had some small chip or component added.

The two soldiers reached the far end of the building and came together at the entrance. Bolan shook his head. This was not what they were looking for. However, it did register that this may be a prototyping lab for the adaptation and enhancing of existing weaponry.

Four buildings remained, and time was tight. He knew that as much from instinct as from the change in the note of the sirens that were still blaring. If they could recon the buildings before the military got on their asses, they could look for a route out. In his mind's eye, he could see the plan of the base that he'd memorized before they'd reached the main gates. At the far end of the unknown area, where they were headed, there was an airfield that would have planes or choppers. They would need all the skill they could muster between them, and a lot of luck, but if they could reach that point they had a fighting chance.

But first there were still four buildings to negotiate. And just maybe they had hit pay dirt. The four were clustered away from the three they had just checked and were connected by covered walkways. The cinderblock buildings had windows that were heavily frosted and shatterproof, and as they drew nearer they could see that the buildings and interconnecting walkways were accessible by only one entrance and exit, which was protected by a keypad locking system and an air lock with CCTV coverage.

If there was anything of a fissionable nature within, then this was certainly the way to protect it.

As they neared the portal, Bolan indicated that Yuri should fan out so that the two men were separated and would stand on either side of the doors. The Russian looked at him, puzzled. Why didn't he just try to blow the door off if they were short on time?

Bolan knew what the Russian was thinking, and he knew that whoever was inside would figure the same thing. It was a certainty that despite the general alarm, a section of the facility this important would have a guard stationed inside whose orders did not cover responding to a general alarm. If he was there, he would be watching them, and Bolan would have bet that the guard or guards inside would be waiting for him to do exactly what the Russian had figured.

So if he didn't, then it would take some nerve under the current circumstances for the guard not to take the offensive, which was just what he wanted.

He signaled Yuri to hang back as they reached the doorway and shot out the CCTV camera. Breathing steadily, he counted to himself and placed his ear to the wall. Before he had reached ten, he knew from the sound coming through the noise surrounding them that his gamble had worked.

The lock clicked and the door swung open toward the Russian, who stepped back to clear himself some space. The head of an Iranian guard cautiously poked its way out and found Bolan standing to one side of him, the SMG raised. A short burst took the man's head almost off his shoulders. Before he hit the concrete, the soldier had stepped over him and into the air lock between the two doors, Yuri at his heels.

There was a second guard. Torn between raising his weapon and firing or slamming the second door shut, he hesitated for a fraction of a second. That was all Bolan needed. One tap on the SMG's trigger and the second guard hit the floor, stitched across the torso. Bolan stepped through into the first of the four buildings, indicating to the Russian that he should leave the doors open. Neither man knew the combination and they would need to escape quickly from what looked like the only route.

Once inside the buildings, Bolan could see that they were interconnected and had fissionable material within at least one of them. Radiation suits hung by the entrance into the building, and much of the lab equipment in this section was familiar to him from past experiences.

There was no doubt that nuclear research of some kind was going on there, and as Iran had declared their peaceful research to the IAEA without any qualms, something this secret could only be weapons based. He had already seen enough to confirm this to Hal Brognola when they reached safe airspace. The question was, what would he do about it in the interim?

Within this section of the facility there were five scientists, all of whom looked frozen in shock. Three men and two women. There were weapons on the walls, and he had no doubt that they had been trained to use them. His Russian compatriot obviously felt the same way.

"Please do not move, and then we will not have to shoot you," he barked clearly in Farsi. "You will answer our questions quickly, or we will shoot you anyway."

Not subtle, Bolan thought, but concise if nothing else. It did not, however, elicit the reaction that either of the men expected. One of the scientists stepped forward, her face flushed with anger. She was young, maybe an idealist, and certainly in no mood to lie down easily.

"You will put those weapons down now and wait for our militia. Any further actions would be pointless. You would be stupid to fire in here, as you could set off a reaction that would not only destroy you, but most of this base."

Bolan cracked a grin. "You're taking a hell of a chance, lady. That might be exactly what we want."

CHAPTER TWENTY-ONE

She drew back, eyes wide with shock and anger. Bolan moved forward and pulled her away from the lab bench. Yuri moved from behind him to cover the rest of the room.

"So what are you doing here?" the soldier asked.

"You wouldn't understand," she said coldly.

"Try me."

"We are developing a compact and protected fission-able device from the by-products of our energy suppliers in order to attach it to any kind of timer and detonator you would care to mention."

"Warheads," Bolan said coldly.

"More than that. A portable device that will be ade-quately shielded to cause no harm to those men used to transport them to wherever they are required. Suicide bombers like you haven't seen before. Such things do already exist, but the technology is patented and kept from us, as it is from India and Pakistan. The West does not wish us to have this."

"Can you blame us?" Bolan muttered, knowing as he spoke that his words were pointless.

"The woman speaks like a stupid film," Yuri said hurriedly. "I don't care what they're doing. She is play-ing for time. Let us do what we have to and then go."

Bolan nodded. "You might be right. I've confirmed what I was sent for. All we need to do is take out enough of this facility that they can't keep the experiments going before the IAEA are alerted."

"Then let's stop talking and do it," the Russian said in exasperation.

Bolan knew he was right, but he also knew that he was no physicist or nuclear scientist. He wanted to destroy as much of the equipment and facility as possible without triggering any kind of nuclear explosion, or even generating any leakage. He needed guidance, and the only people he was likely to get any kind of guidance from in here were not the sort to cooperate.

"Okay. Start shooting up the computer equipment and I'll lay some explosive charges to bring down the building."

"You won't do that. You do not want to kill yourself by cancer," the woman said with a sneer.

"Chances are we won't get out of here, lady," Bolan told her. "Might as well take it all down."

He pushed her away and reached for the Semtex he was carrying. The immediate area was filled with the roar of the Russian's SMG as he took out the computer equipment. If it brought the server down as well, then maybe they could take out that side of the operation in one blast. The noise forced four of the scientists back into a huddle, with only the woman standing firm. Her dark eyes were defiant and full of hate…but not fear. It told Bolan what he wanted to know.

"C'mon, Yuri, let's take them through to the next

building. We've got ten minutes to do all of them," he said, gesturing to the Iranians to move.

"Cooper, what if there is fissionable material here?" the Russian queried, trying to keep the nerves from his tone.

"Not in this building," Bolan stated, seeing by the woman's reaction that he was right.

The two men drove the scientists through the walkway and into the next building. But before they left, Bolan took the extra precaution of leaving a little bomb behind, something to delay pursuit.

As they entered the structure, they were met by a guard, who tried to fire at them through the encroaching crowd of scientific personnel—both those corralled from the previous building and those who had been working in this one—but he was deflected from his aim by the need to avoid friendly fire damaging his charges. Bolan had better nerves and better aim: one tap of the trigger was all it took.

This building was different. There were lead-lined cabinets with reinforced glass that held rods and equipment that screamed nuclear materials at Bolan. While the soldier covered the assembled personnel, Yuri took out the computer equipment and smashed electronic measurement tech that lined one side of the room.

"No way can we use explosives here," Bolan stated. "And we've got too many people, damn it."

"Send them back," Yuri replied. "Let them block the way a little."

Those who had been working in this building looked puzzled, while those who had been in the previous lab

and knew what would happen to them began to panic.
The panic spread among the remaining scientists. When
Bolan and Yuri fired at the ground near their feet, driving them back into the walkway between the buildings,
the only one not to turn and run was the woman. She
backed away from the gunfire but kept staring at them
coldly as she retreated.

When they had been driven back, Yuri moved quickly
to slam the door behind them, firing into the keypad on
the lab side of the door.

"It will slow the Iranians down. We can't turn back
now, anyhow," he said simply. Bolan agreed, and the
two men moved toward the third block and whatever
fate awaited them.

With no one from the facility to activate the lock,
they were now faced with the problem of gaining access to the third building, a puzzle solved for them by
the stupidity of the guard, who rushed out to meet them
in a meaningless display of bravado that enabled them
to cut him down and progress quickly.

The third building was populated by scientists who
appeared to have a similar remit to those in the last
building. In the same way that there had been lead-lined
cabinets and secured reinforced glass containers with
rods and fissionable materials, this had smaller items
that appeared to fulfill similar tasks. Bolan cast a swift
glance over them while Yuri gestured to the scientists
to back up and away from the equipment.

The soldier frowned. In these cabinets, it looked as
though the nuclear materials were packed into their pro-
tective shells, much like what was done with the war-

heads, but on a smaller scale. The way in which the shells were constructed suggested that there were components that were added that included detonation and timer devices.

There was nothing that he could do about this stage of construction. The material was too dangerous to tamper with. If he could locate the mechanical and digital components of the devices, this would enable him to at least delay production until he could reach safe ground and report.

They were distracted by the shock of an explosion farther back in the buildings. The charge Bolan had laid had gone off, and the shock of the blast made the ground ripple beneath them and the walls of the building they were in creak and groan. Neither man had kept a watch on the time, and if Bolan was momentarily surprised, then so was the Russian.

Suddenly Bolan was aware of a sudden flurry of movement. One of the scientists had broken from the group. He was a young man, and although the fear could be seen on his face as he moved, he was driven by some kind of fanaticism. He threw himself at the Russian. Yuri tapped a burst that should have stopped the man in his tracks. It stitched him across the torso and groin, but instead of bringing him to a halt it was as if the agony spurred him on. With the strength he had left, he tumbled into the Russian. Despite the fact that he had stepped back to try to clear his firing arm, Yuri found himself temporarily entangled with the dying man. He swore as he tried to shake himself free and was inevitably distracted.

There were three others in the room: a woman and two more men. The men were older and slower, but the woman was young and quicker to react. She slipped past the cursing Russian and his deadweight burden, moving toward the section of the lab where the guard's station was situated.

Bolan tried to sight on her, but the cabinets blocked a clear shot. There was no way he was going to fire with anything like that in his sight line. Glancing back to see that the two men were almost on the Russian, who had now managed to shake himself free of the corpse, Bolan ran back the length of the building, diving as he reached the end and almost feeling the shot that he heard crack over his head and smack into the strengthened glass window at his rear. He rolled and came up with the woman clear in his sight.

She was holding an AK-47 awkwardly. The recoil of the first shot had driven the barrel upward, and although she was obviously unused to weaponry, Bolan could not rely on being lucky twice. More than that, if her shooting was that erratic, then there was a chance that she could hit something that would set off a chain reaction or cause a radioactive leak.

He could see the wavering barrel of the assault rifle as she tried to keep it steady on him, as he lay on the floor with his pistol angled up. It was an instant that seemed to stretch forever. He never liked the idea of shooting someone who was defenseless, as this woman was with the lack of skill she showed. But she was fanatical and dangerous; conscience had to come second.

A simple tap on the trigger and he could see the astonishment in her eyes as the AK-47 fell and she crumpled, chest and stomach pierced by the burst of bullets.

Bolan was on his feet and turned back toward the end of the building before she hit the ground. Yuri had two men on him; he might need assistance.

The soldier had no need to back up the Russian. Yuri had dealt with the older men easily. Turning the SMG so that it acted as a club, he had taken them out with one swing. The scientists were not fighters. Any training they might have received years before was long forgotten or rendered useless by age and rust. By the time Bolan reached him, Yuri had the SMG business end around and was standing over the two men, whose skulls had been cracked by his massive swing.

"They have guts—I'll give them that," the Russian said simply.

"And we're going to need them, and luck, to get out of this," Bolan answered. "No explosives here, but take out the rest of the equipment."

The Russian nodded, and as he took a brief look at the cabinets, he heard Bolan begin a methodic and swift destruction of the nonnuclear equipment in the lab. Yuri grunted to himself and joined the operation, ensuring it was quickly completed and they were able to move through the walkway toward the last structure. On the way out, the Russian once again shut the door and killed the electronically operated lock with a burst of fire.

"You realize they'll be closing on us soon and we have no way out?" he said as they reached the door of the last block.

Bolan grimaced. "Two things—first, they're forced

to pursue with caution because they can't just blast their way through without risk. Second, they think we're trapped by the fact that there's no way out. So maybe they're concentrating on following and not surrounding."

"But we are trapped, Cooper," the Russian said blandly.

"Maybe," Bolan replied.

They approached the last building through the covered walkway, the soldier noting through the reinforced apertures in the walls that his supposition seemed to have been correct. There was little if any sign of a military presence. Bolan figured that their tactic might have been to stand back at the barriers presented by the fencing around the compound and wait to see what the party following them into the building would flush out. With such delicate materials, they would be forced to exercise caution. This was what he hoped. It was their only chance, and a slim one at that.

Bolan halted at the door into the last structure, which was unlocked and stood ajar. He could feel the Russian at his shoulder.

"Our last exit door was also open, Cooper. I wonder if our scientific friends were a little lax in security on occasion?"

"I hope so," Bolan murmured, cautiously moving forward so that he could edge open the door. It was possible that it was a trap laid by a desperate guard. It was also possible that the Russian was correct. But it wasn't Yuri who was taking point. Bolan was the man who would be walking into any trap.

Aware that time was tight but unwilling to be a target for the sake of a second, Bolan edged forward. There was too much noise still coming from the camp as a whole, even muffled as it was by the thick concrete and reinforced glass walls, for him to tell if there was anyone in the room. A warning blast or a grenade to clear the room—his usual method of quick clearance—was also off the agenda until he knew what the structure contained.

Taking a deep breath, Bolan kicked the door wide open and launched himself into the opening, rolling and coming up with the Desert Eagle poised to fire, trusting that Yuri would have his back for anyone at his rear.

The room was empty. For a moment, the soldier was puzzled, and that was reflected on the face of the Russian facing him. Then Yuri pointed to a spot over the soldier's left shoulder. Bolan turned and could see that there were stacked boxes of components on a small cart, the top one open. At the side were more stacks, moved from the corner of the large room in preparation for transport.

Whoever had been in here gathering equipment had heard the alarm and panicked; any precautions had been forgotten. It was the piece of luck they needed. Quickly, Bolan reconned the building, which was one large storage facility. Within it were the components that the scientists used for the mechanical parts of the devices they were developing, the guards' ordnance and lab supplies that were used in any other parts of the process. The only things lacking were any finished devices or anything that had a radioactive half-life. This was obvious from the lack of cases with the right construction or carrying the warning symbols.

"This is how we get out," Bolan said, moving to the ordnance section of the building and ripping open cases.

"We're going to blow our way out?" the Russian queried.

"Got a better idea?" Bolan asked.

The Russian's face cracked in a huge grin. "Hell, no, Cooper. But you're sure you're not going to turn us into Spider-Man?"

"No nukes here, Yuri. This is just the electronics and the conventional weapons. And that suits me fine."

Plundering the ordnance to replace what they had used, he set about his task, aided by the Russian. In essence, it was simple: blow the hell out of the ordnance in the room, crack the back wall and take out the stock of necessary mechanical and electronic components for the devices at the same time.

It was a simple plan with two problems: first, they had to hope that the caution of the military on their tails bought them enough time to fulfill the objective; second, they had to hope they could find enough shelter so that the explosion didn't take them out with the wall.

When they had put together the ordnance and explosives, including that which they had left from their own stock, Bolan set the detonator for thirty seconds and pulled Yuri back into the walkway. The blast from the first explosions, which had taken down most of the first building if the blast was any indicator, had slowed their pursuers, but they had no real leeway. This had to work, or they would just be taking as many as possible with them before they were taken down.

There was no real shelter for them, but they huddled against the wall, back to the blast, hunkered down and protecting themselves as much as was possible. Yuri had angled the boxes of components to shield and direct the blast toward the outer wall rather than the rest of the room, but it was at best makeshift. At its worst? They were about to find out.

They could feel the heat of the blast, feel rather than hear its reverberations and the force, dissipated even as it was by the doorway wall, hit them like a hammer in the spine. Bolan shook his head to try to clear the ringing, even though he knew it was pointless, and was on his feet before the choking clouds of dust and smoke that billowed through the shattered doorway had a chance to cover him. He glanced across to Yuri, who stumbled to his feet and indicated he was okay, before moving through the almost-solid wall of smoke before them.

The back wall had disappeared into a mass of rubble and smoke. The interior of the building was scorched, with the inventory shattered into matchwood and twisted metal. At least that part of the aim had been fulfilled.

Bolan and Yuri exited through the gaping hole in the rear wall with one man covering the left, the other the right. They made for the far end of the compound, which led to an airfield where choppers of varying sizes stood idle. Far in the distance, they could see soldiers, but they were too far away to fire on.

As Bolan and Yuri ran, chattering fire rained around them. From behind and to the sides, mobilized men on foot and in jeeps headed toward them. With every passing second, they were closing in. There was no time for thought, just action, each action born and fueled by desperation and the desire to survive.

The fence at the far end had a double gate that had been left unguarded. Maybe this was the result of emergency procedures and measures born of their attack and diversion. It didn't matter; it was unguarded but closed to them.

Yuri did not hesitate. As he ran, he took a grenade plundered from the Iranian ordnance stocks and primed it, lobbing the armed bomb at the gate with an underhand motion. At any other time, Bolan would have admitted that his companion had a good eye. The grenade landed at the base of the fence and detonated. The blast hit them, slowing them only momentarily as they were braced, and took a chunk of gate, fencing and concrete out of the ground.

They raced through and were onto the airfield. In the distance, they could see figures in the tower, but initially no one came out to tackle them. They were halfway across the apron to a Huey chopper when the first men came from the tower to engage them. Bolan and Yuri kept running, hitting the approaching men with spray and pray.

Bullets skidded off the side of the chopper as they scrambled in.

"You can fly one of these things?" Yuri asked as they

made the cockpit and looked out to see enemy closing from all sides.

"Well enough to get us into the air and headed home. See what this bird's carrying. I need you to lay down covering fire as I take off."

The Russian disappeared into the body of the craft while Bolan gunned it into life. He didn't bother with all the checks; they had to go. He took the chopper up, spinning her so that he came back toward the tower. He heard the reassuring chatter of a 30 mm SMG, which shattered the top of the tower.

Making the tightest turn he could risk, Bolan allowed Yuri to spray fire over the oncoming military. Their returns were sporadic as his arc of flight made it hard for them to sight while being fired on.

He kept the chopper low and gunned it across the apron toward the fighter aircraft. If Yuri could disable them, even only temporarily, then it would buy precious time. The Russian realized what the soldier was doing and complied. Even the heavy-duty SMG made little impact on a fighter aircraft designed to withstand much heavier fire.

He whirled the chopper and headed out, putting everything into gaining as much distance as possible between the helicopter and the base. There would be ground-to-air guided missiles on them before too long. They had been lucky so far.

Yuri appeared beside him.

"I assume you have a plan formulated?"

"Fly fast, dump chopper, go deep cover," Bolan replied pithily.

"Sounds good." Yuri nodded. "Of course, the fact that I happen to have a couple of parachutes may just make this plan a little easier. If we happen to land some distance from where this goes down, it will be a help, will it not?"

"Yeah," Bolan said with a grin. "It can only help."

"NOT THE BEST forced march either of us have ever had to take, but it did enough to put the Iranians off our trail. It was just a hard road slog to the rendezvous." Bolan, talking to Hal Brognola via satellite phone, took another sip of coffee and leaned back into the plush velvet and leather sofa in Schevchenko's coastal retreat.

"You did good work there, Striker," Brognola said appreciatively. "Your reports will be passed on, and might go some way to smoothing those ruffled feathers after NYC. The Man will be appreciative. You should see the cover-up on Parchin. They're claiming an accident with hardware after satellites picked up the disturbance. And they're still denying nuclear development, by the way."

"Let's see them argue that with the IAEA and the UN," Bolan said. "I see that there's also a day of mourning for the sudden and unexpected death of a promising council member, too, if CNN is anything to go by. I would have expected some denunciation, given the mess it made."

"What, and have to explain why he was singled out? They're taking their warning and swallowing hard, Striker. That's all we can ask."

"Guess so," Bolan agreed.

"Now, about your flight back. The embassy—"

"Whoa there, Hal. If you remember, I was about to get some leave before this blew up." He looked out the picture window and across the expanse of the Caspian Sea. Despite what lay across the stretch of water, it was peaceful and beautiful in the early morning light. "It's pretty chill here. You might not see me back in Moscow for a few days. I'll let you know."

With a curt goodbye, the soldier disconnected and tossed the phone across the room. It landed on the thick shag carpet, where it vibrated furiously as Brognola tried to call him back.

It continued to vibrate as Bolan got to his feet, stretched and walked out onto the terrace, breathing in the cool morning air.

* * * * *